PRAISE FOR HEATHER FOWLER

"Heather Fowler is a brave writer. She does not blink, she does not falter. There is an integrity in her stories which demonstrates a writer who is committed, confident and sharp, witty and cutting. She cuts deep. She is also very funny, the way Kafka was funny, the way Donald Barthelme was funny. Read her for her pithiness. Read her for how entertaining she is. Let the depth of the stories creep up on you."

— Corey Mesler, author of *Talk: a Novel in Dialogue*

"Fowler's descriptions are exquisite, and her stories absorbing. Her fabulist elements intertwine with reality to create allegorical narratives that expose deeper truths about men and women, about humanity's common fixations. Her heroines are strong, but searching and consistently surprising. Fowler's stories are like spells: Through words alone, beautiful imagery, tremendous substance, and poignant feeling become palpably real."

— Savannah Schroll Guz, author of *American Soma*

"Magical realism at its finest. Great work by Heather Fowler. Recommended."

— Kathy Fish, author of *Wild Life*

"Common emotions that come forth as literal components in the characters' lives are too good to miss. The author's fabulist style, both sarcastic and charitable, is one to be admired."

— Melanie Page, *American Book Review*

"The stories in *Suspended Heart* have made for some of the most twisted, exciting reading I have had in a very long time. They are read with a zealousness and momentum that is like a solid relationship, improving with age and with each re-read. I find these stories to take the idea of love and blast away any cliché notions that love is an ordinary thing. Bitter hearts will be relieved, hardened hearts will soften, and dangerous hearts will finally use caution. Each story is fresh and crisp and offers a new angle on the age-old ideas of romance and sex. The themes of lust and courageous love are never dulled by overly dramatic tales or melodramatic fantasies. The voice Fowler uses is real, and in my opinion, these stories are some of the best tales of love and its consuming ideas that have been written in many years."

— Zach Fishel, *Girls With Insurance*

PEOPLE WITH HOLES

Stories

Heather Fowler

Pink
Narcissus
Press

PEOPLE WITH HOLES: Stories
© 2012 Heather Fowler

Stories in this book have first appeared in the following:

"People With Holes." *A cappella Zoo*. Issue 8. (2012)
"Ex-Boyfriend's Head." *Fix It Broken*. Issue 3. (2011)
"With the Silence of a Deer." *Sententia 4: What She Said*, The All Women Writers Issue. (2012)
"What You Never Thought You Wanted." *Exquisite Corpse*. (2001)
"Bengal Tiger Boy." *Back in 5 Minutes ~ an expression of depression, volume 1*. Little Episodes, London, UK. (2010)
"Anatomy of a Song." *Up the Staircase*. Issue 9. (2010)
"Come, Come Blackbird." *Rapunzel's Daughters and Other Tales*. Pink Narcissus Press. (2011)
"How to Rescue A Drowning Man." *Filling Station*. Issue 45 – The Al Purdy's House issue. (2009)
"You Are One Click Away From Pictures of Nude Girls." *Word Riot* (2008) and Reprint: *Surreal South 2009*. Press 53. (2009)
"If There Is An Airport" *Temenos*. (2007)
"Three Views You Might Have Taken At Pond's Edge – or Quack" *Necessary Fiction* (2010)
"Words Like Love and Cacti." *the stark electric space…an international anthology of indie writers*: Graffiti Kolkata. (2010)

Cover illustration by Siolo Thompson
Cover design by Duncan Eagleson

Published by Pink Narcissus Press
P.O. Box 303
Auburn, MA 01501
pinknarc.com

Library of Congress Control Number: 2012902750
ISBN: 978-0-9829913-8-1
First trade paperback edition: July 2012

Dedication

To the gentle beacon who once guided me back to the greater world of literature, through life's shoals—and made me think that I, too, could have some light to share.

Contents

People with Holes

I found you wearing a hole one day. I didn't think it sexy, didn't even know when it appeared. It was right near where your elbow used to be, so I couldn't imagine how your arm could keep bending. I saw right through it, your hole.

I suppose I could have tried to visualize some little gears there to normalize the thing, some kind of spokes and wheel, but instead there was a nothingness. Your abilities as a partner were not impaired.

I felt the weight and pull of your arms around me afterward, the strength of how it felt when you drew me close. If you had no elbow, you couldn't have done that; I was thorough in consideration. I'd checked, in particular, for the feel of the holey arm's closure. It worked! The thing still worked!

I thought I knew everything before that, everything about you, but the hole made me doubt. You were different. I knew it then, said, "So, this hole came from where?"

"I don't know," you replied.

"But you do know," I insisted.

"I don't," you said. "Give me a break, Alice."

"Can't you give it back?"

You looked at me like I'd asked you to return a child to an orphanage, said, "It's my hole, damn it." You were eating orange chicken with your fingers.

I passed you the chopsticks because your fingers looked nasty and said, "Okay, no need to get testy," but you hated the word "testy." It reminded you of test and test reminded you of failure and failure reminded you of, well, failure. Not that you and I and failure were strangers. We both knew that imposter very well.

"If you had a hole," you said, "I wouldn't harass you about it. I would accept it. Mildly accept it, I might add. Were it somewhere erotic, it's possible I might even use it, kind of, where applicable."

"My whole body is erotic," I said. "You use my holes all the time."

"I know," you agreed. "That's what I meant."

Not long after, we visited the liquor store. No one could see your hole. You had on this faded purple button-up shirt and some Lucky jeans. I wanted to get lucky. I could almost see you as normal, imagined you doing a great unveiling dance for me, showcasing the hole like a sex organ. We watched these two kids in the aisle, stealing candy, both lithe-limbed sixth graders stuffing their pockets with chocolate and sour stuff and laughing. The store owner saw them too, grabbed them by the scruff of their necks and said, "I think you have some things that belong to me."

They were both boys. They weren't laughing then. "Look," one of them started. "Our friends dared us. Here. We'll give it all back. Let us down." But then when the guy released them, one said to the other, "Run for it," and they did. I think they were homeless. The store owner looked from the kids to us, you and me, and then back to the kids. He might have chased them were we not there, but perhaps we looked guilty. We could have stolen liquor.

"Did you feel guilty, too, when those kids were taking candy?" I asked you.

"Oh, yeah. Like we did it, from a baby," you agreed.

"Why did we feel guilty?" I asked.

You shrugged. "Because they aren't old and they don't have holes?"

"Not yet," I said. "Let's try to get rid of your hole."

At my urging, you went to a support group for people with holes. Each night as you prepared to go, you looked at me as if to say: I hate this, but I do it — I do it all for you. You wouldn't reply to my questions about your involvement or how you processed the experience. You did say, "There are holes everywhere, Alice," when asked a really intrusive question. "One guy has his in his thigh. Another girl has one in her neck. A *neck* hole."

"Can she talk?" I asked.

"Can I hold you?" you replied.

"Sure, but does it look weird while she's talking? How big is the hole?"

You didn't reply.

The support group had Family Night one night. We had no children or local parents. We were not married, but you thought I could come. Common law intimates and all. "You're the closest I've got," you said. "You might as well go."

This was the best, most exciting night ever! I was thrilled. "I get to meet all your friends!" I enthused. "I get to see the other holes. The other people's holes!"

"The other holes might be covered," you said. "It's not that big a deal."

But it was; I smiled. I put on a pink and silver dress and extra high fuchsia heels. I spent more time doing my make-up than normal, which meant five and a half minutes. I worried about too much blush. "You look just like family," you said. "Or somebody going to a wedding. Kill the red lips. You look like you might eat me."

"It's not our wedding, so what are you worried about?" I asked.

You kissed me to buy some quiet. We rode to the group in my Honda, keeping a fitting silence for your nerves. You drove, actually. I tried to dampen my excitement, but found I kept tapping my foot, also singing, "Georgia, geo-or-gia, just that old sweet song..." You were from Georgia, which made this extra horrid, but neither did you like my rendition of "New York, New York." Sometimes, I botched the lyrics on purpose.

The event was held in a high-school gym. I don't know what I thought I'd see there. The people looked pretty normal. They were seated in a circle, à la standard therapy group.

The circle had been widened to include family. I sat beside you, and it turns out, the therapist announced, that the people with holes were going to tell us, the attending family and significant others, what they thought we had done wrong in their lives, or what we had done that, in their views, had occasioned the existing holes. Did we know we were to blame? Were we willing to keep an open mind, to help, to listen quietly, without judgment?

Oh fuck, I thought.

Some people with holes had no family, and one lady said, "I hate the idea of this whole night. Where's my therapy? I gotta be the pa-fucking-thetic one who tells about my hole with nobody to help me? We all get a turn, right? Well, if I could get the fucker who gave me this hole to come down here, don't you think I'd already have a smaller-sized hole? All hole-makers and hole-wearers can't repair damage together. I shoulda skipped tonight and watched a show about people who can't sing. Stop looking at me." She had a hole the size of a coffee-cup in her groin. I couldn't see it, but I saw the way the fabric fell in where her pussy would have been.

I couldn't help it, but I kept staring there, like her holey organ might show up if I just glanced hard enough, but people started sharing then. First we heard from a black guy with three brothers present. His hole was on his shoulder. "And this came when you didn't tell me I'd be okay," he said. "When I had cancer and none of you came to see me, because I am gay. Because my lover was there. But I'm still your brother."

Damn, I thought. *This is better than a soap.* Pretty soon the brothers were all crying and hitting each other in the arm. I just kept quiet. I was learning: So the holes weren't random. I looked at your elbow, where your hole was invisible under your clothes. You looked uncomfortable, never liked me to get the full extent of the joke or know too much. "Did I make your hole?" I whispered.

"Would I have asked you here if you hadn't?" you replied.

The bad vibe went on from there. "And you only bother to tell me now?" I hissed again. "We could have done home therapy. Talked about this!"

I was kind of mad, but watched the parade of others, thinking: Who knew people had so many holes? The therapist had her own hole on her left thigh — but it looked patchy. She was in recovery, she'd said. Her hole was opaque, so you couldn't quite see through it, but you could see the colors behind her. *A therapist must evidence progress*, I thought. *She does. That's a good sign.*

As your turn got closer, I could see you watching her. She kept giving you a little nod, like, it's okay, it's okay. You sat very still. The guy next to us had a hole in his wrist. His mother was there, the poor guilty thing. He moaned, "And you kept saying I couldn't do art like Timmy! And you made me feel like a slob. And he didn't do shit with his life. How dare you damage me that way? You didn't help me! You—"

"Keep working with the statements that start with 'I feel' for now, Nathaniel," the therapist admonished.

He looked first to her and then at his mother before he said, "I feel hurt, momma. I feel upset. I feel like I was the child you loved the least. I feel subhuman and never deserving. I'm angry about that."

"I'm sorry," his mother said.

Everybody clapped. The man cried. The mother grabbed his hand. "I'm really sorry," she repeated, caressing his open hole. "Really, really sorry."

Her touch didn't solve his hole. We all knew it was just a drop in the hole-healing bucket, but he smiled. The two hugged. As soon as everybody clapped again and it was your turn, you turned to me. You opened your mouth to speak and then shut it, like you didn't want to talk. You sat up tall.

"Go ahead," your therapist said. "Tell her."

"I—" you began. "I feel—" And then you stood up, slowly, and walked away from the whole group. On the basketball court that reeked of sweat socks and wax, you skulked outside. I kept thinking you'd just gone out for air, that you'd be back.

But I was alone with the holey people for several moments as the circle went on. Your seat stayed empty.

I didn't know whether to stay or go. I went to the parking lot where you'd left our car. It was gone. This high school was in the middle of nowhere. I had no phone because we usually used yours, so I had no way to get home. I came back in and sat in the bleachers outside the circle. The confessions were in high-gear. I figured that after everybody was done, I could possibly make an announcement to publicize that I had been left. I could ask for someone's phone to call a cab, or see if anyone would take me home in the L district — I would pay them gas, I'd say.

After another lady confessed her dead dog had caused her hole with his death, which is why her left foot was holey, because that's where he'd slept at night, the therapist noticed me there in the bleachers, crying.

She told everybody, "Just a second."

She came and grabbed my hand with her soft hand. I didn't want to let it go. "Come on," she said. "Come on."

Soon, I was seated in the circle. People stared, but not unkindly. They kept staring. "What are you looking at?" I wanted to ask. After a while, I got nervous. So many people sneaking glances toward my face, I figured my eyeliner had smeared or that my eyes were puffy and swollen. I also figured I was going to kill you if I saw you again, for causing this embarrassment. I felt confused. Why had you gone? Where? What could you never bring yourself to tell me?

I opened a small silver mirror to look at my eyes. My make-up was fine. My eyes were fine. But there was a big hole in my forehead, so I could see the bleachers behind me — the banners, the posters made with green paint that read, "GO TEAM!" — right through my head.

"Bad hole," my neighbor said to me. "Hard to hide."

"Yeah," I said. "Pretty much."

After the meeting there were refreshments, cookies

and punch. Coffee if you gave fifty cents. I did. The holey people were so kind to me then, talking about hats, wigs, and all. "His was just in his elbow," they whispered to me. "Get a sponsor. Go to meetings. That will help." And "You'll like this group. We meet every Saturday at eight and Wednesdays at noon." They put their fingers in my hole. I let them poke the empty space that was now mine. It didn't hurt. After that, I fingered their holes right back, like in companionship. They were kind about everything. So kind.

Some took off their clothes, here and there, to let me see what they were missing. They all were rather sad about witnessing my sudden arrival to the holed community. They patted my back with affection. "Oh, who cares what you did to him?" they said. They offered to drive me home and help look for my car. They offered all the possible support that holey people can, which is a lot when your holes are in different places. One was a locksmith. They didn't keep secrets, which was, they informed me, a part of recovery. They were flexible, bending where necessary. Really honest.

One lady told me, in hushed admissions, "Your boyfriend, he wasn't really working on his practice, wasn't getting any better. No, we don't think he's coming back. Good riddance, sweetie baby. Tell him and his issues *arrivederci!*"

There was a group hug — spontaneous, not advised by the therapist. I loved these people like I loved a Bob Dylan album! Maybe more. With no big fanfare and no jacked sermon, they pulled on my arms to bring me closer. They swallowed me into their varied folds like I was the hole at their center, the daisy stem of the group, all of them the petals.

Two Angels of the Melancholy Man

Let's say in the big starry sky invisible battles rage constantly. Each person has their own angel or angels in the dark universe, but it's a fight for a man's soul staged up in the sky, an epic feat of lightning bolt hurling and chest heaving — and temporary victories and far less temporary tragic losses — though the scientific data and telescopes cannot see this phenomenon, cannot see our angels at all, but rather reflect the after-effects of these waged wars.

The melancholy man with two hearts, handsome, talented, devilish, had ten such angels, eight of which had already passed. Some had been sucked into black holes of his life's making, some spun into the after-fray with no remaining weapons, dying of starvation and blood loss, and some were simply left gazing down upon him mildly, watching, ever watching, from their newly converted states.

Now why did the Melancholy Man have so many angels? It was his dangerous life. Some might say it was because he was so beautiful and brilliant — and all angels want to die for something worthwhile. Might proclaim it was his novelty, possessing two odd hearts and all. And let's remember his situation wasn't common in any regard. The slug of a woman tending stacks of flat cats on negligible welfare, for example, the one with no love affairs, no college degrees, and no thoughts other than who would win the Midnight Sticky game show — she had only one angel, and he was a dwarf. But one angel could handle it for her, we'd correctly assume. After all, there wasn't much soul in there to save.

The Melancholy Man, on the other hand, listeners, had talents like the angels himself. He could paint and sing and write and pray. Boy, could he pray. He could pray like a motherfucker, I tell you, and all angels like prayers — especially those deep, mournful, and psychologically complex.

And he was attractive. Even angels are sometimes shallow. So he had ten of them, eight gone, as mentioned, the two left up there flinging bolts like mad. Rabidly flinging. One blonde and one brunette. Their battle was valiant.

Regard well, audience, these she-angels of attempted mercy! Whilst he was doing his Melancholy Man thing down in his terrestrial digs, his brilliant, genius, piano playing thing, his I can-never-love-and-my-heart-is-trashed thing — (Look, what a fruitful challenge! Let the bells ring and harps play!) — his angels were fighting for his life, completely under-appreciated, though each good thing that happened to him was actually one of their victories. When he woke up one day and thought, for example, "Let's not sleep today! Let's ride the ferry out to my island abode and watch sunflowers grow! Let's call all our good friends and tell them how great they are," well, one of his angels was definitely upstairs, smeared with char, and bleeding, and likely floating on the black-dark universal sky, recovering but damn proud.

Except there were too many black currents, black holes, meteorites — life dirges — to fling white hope bolts against. They knew this. His melancholy was legend, for he used his melancholy to create the very artwork that made him such a desirable commodity. It was a circle game, angels, the other angels wanted to tell those who wore his badges. Yes, you are valiant, but you are the suicide bombers of the soul-fight world, and while we admire you when you win, there is a certain measure of pity we feel as we regard you suiting up each day in sexy white and ripped garments, with all your skin heaving — note to Melancholy Man's angels: Some celestial beings wear more.

Not that his angels would have been realistic as his angels had they been pristine; in the search for his luminous pain, he had been around the metroplex a billion times, tossing his body around like after-dinner candy, and so it made sense that his angels would have to be of the slightly less angelic variety.

But I digress; there were two left. Just two. These, though I will not name them, were the strongest and most beautiful vixens of the known universe. Their battles could be seen expanding. His soul was large. One patch of sky was not enough. And when it seemed, some days, that they were winning — as the Melancholy Man did more with humor, with happiness, with self-exploration — they knew they were doing a fine job and congratulated them-selves. Except each patch of soul was limited to one area of sky, and his patch was large. Despite this, they kept almost falling out of bounds to fling their contraband at the dark matter, and one day, like two black holes simultaneously converging, though they hadn't previously met, they crossed each other's space.

"Hi angel," one said to the other.

"Hi angel," the other said to the other.

"Nice bolt flinging day, yes?"

"Very much so, comrade-in-bolt."

They fought hard for their beloved in this instant. Oh, Melancholy Man, we shall save you, each thought! We shall win this battle forever, and then you can go on and we can sip angel juice in the sky, suiting up only every so often, if you have a Melancholy relapse — and we will have earned our celestial retirement!

Except each warrior was so busy contemplating her victory and retirement that they didn't really look at each other. They did not team up back to back, as it was two different battles each thought they waged, so when this interstice of space and war occurred, both in the same plot of soul during a moment in their struggles where a second's break in concentration could cause eternal death, instead of looking at the horrors flying toward them in the sky as they fought, via sidelong glances, they each instead abruptly noted the other's badge.

Yes, they had noted this shared badge, but they didn't say to each other — "You're his angel, too?" Instantaneously, shared moments of stupefaction, joy, pride, and jealousy floored them, each regarding the beauty and specialness of the other, admiring the vast battle the other had engaged and the size of the other's soul bolts.

Each thought the other kind of sexy, actually. But while they reflected on this, the dark forces did them in. Friends, this is all to say that the Melancholy Man lost his two angels that day, though there would be more to come, certainly — as attractive and troubled as was his soul.

And when an angel dies, a star is born. Ignore all that malarkey in the science books that talks about dust and combustion. Or don't. But the fact is, angels explode, and stars are created.

If we could see all the stars in the universe, we would know that this corresponds directly to the amount of human lives to have gone down in soul-dark corners, unsaved. We would know that each object that lights our path is the death of another man's dream or an ambition. This is why the sky remains semi-lit at night. This explains too why the melancholy and wild libidinous urges take us over more fully in the darkened sky flecked by light — than in full-scope, redundant, blinding daylight.

In fact, it was the very night that his angels came into contact with one another that some hint of their battle grew known to the Melancholy Man as he felt a burst of kindness and stared up into the gorgeous night sky, star watching in his yard on a first date with a shallow woman he only wanted to lay because she was stupid and uninteresting. Just before his angels bit the sky-dust, for the woman beside him, he looked up and pointed out a constellation. "Watching the sky, this is the meaning of life," he said. "My life. This and playing my piano."

He would have gone on with something deeper, metroplex-museum-art-scene hopper that he was, but he didn't have to. The tacky woman beside him slid her hand up his thigh and grabbed him. Quite few words were enough for his seduction, which was why he could never fall in love — *Was there not a single woman whom seducing would prove a challenge? Oh wait, he had no time for that. His life was artistic, dark, wracked with trials, and convoluted,* he thought.

Upstairs, everybody knew he would soon and again need more angels — not the weak variety either, but ass-kicking Sappho-like barbarian angels. In the meantime, he stared at the sky, pinching date girl's breast, and then the uninteresting woman grabbed his jock and released assorted zippers, pulling him into partial nudity. She needed just one part. She yanked him, by this part, into his house.

Moments later, as she rode his [censored, anatomical], flinging her hair back and moaning something fierce, as he considered calling the other forty girls in his little black book, he noticed a flash in the sky through the picture box window, a light he found terribly sad and terribly beautiful at once. "I'm porking this girl," he thought, "which means nothing, or, realistically, she is porking me, as I am strictly in observational mode, being serviced like a car — and at the same time, something far more beautiful happens miles and miles away. It's like a little death inside a little death. And how wonderful is that? I think I'll write a symphony about it."

He had deeper thoughts about music than he did about women, as was demonstrated by the excitement evidenced by one of his two hearts. Actually, the math of the notes made cleaner, better sense, so he dumped the shallow, nearly invisible girl off his lap and walked to his upright. He did not even say goodbye, which was probably due to his unusual ability to focus only on the necessary. So he tucked his [censored, anatomical] back in, sat down, and poured yet more tunes into his piano, though the dumped girl was not done with him.

He kept his focus through her anger, even ignored her indignant look and cursing and, yes, her vernal screaming, "You are a careless, shallow, self-interested [censored, censored, censored, some anatomical — (Come on folks, this is a story about angels)]!" — because who was she to him?

No one, he surmised. She didn't even listen to his brilliant analysis of the stars, had just started humping on him like a crazed beast, took him inside, was thrown off his lap, and then proceeded in a fury and threw her cheap green shoe at him.

His [censored, anatomical] had known better, more thoughtful women in its lifetime, which it hoped, in a vague but unpromising way, to know someday again. But, "B flat," he thought. "I want to use B flat, in the honor of those two new stars I saw born tonight — or had possibly never noticed. Ah, the light of the heavens is lovely. Lovely. I am moved to grim reflection. And music!"

He sighed, riveted in the tearful strength of his own over-heated malaise. And then, contemplating the jabbing pain in his fingertips that he suffered for repetitive art, which was an occupational hazard, pounding the keys — he called down more and more angels into his fabulously unending melancholic "Sonata, Pas Deux Etoiles," creating heavenly music and weeping for all things ever to come and go in the fine night sky, but mainly for how alone he could be in this dim place where no one loved him quite enough, though he refused to make time for anyone in particular and didn't need real love's confusion in his art space. He pounded the keys some more, his two hearts each beating vigorously.

During a particularly difficult overture, however, there was a cold sensation in his groin. He concurrently recognized his [censored, anatomical] was still kind of itching so looked down, feeling a draft. His last visitor had left him quite revealed, a little stiff.

Can someone send me an angel I am required to do nothing for, he thought hopefully. One there for me and only me? But scoffing, rolling his eyes, staring again at the ebony and ivory to which he affixed his greatest aspirations, he rezipped his fly and went to work.

Ex-Boyfriend's Head

You ever love someone so much that even after they shat on your face and desecrated your every possible value, you had to keep them around awhile? Ronnie was like that. He told me at the end, which was also our new beginning: "I know you loved me more than that green felt hat kept on your bureau by the cuffs, but I'm done. You're stupid and fat and too happy. I don't like happy people."

This pissed me off, so I hacked off his head. He didn't make a fuss, even when the cutting was more of a general sawing. You might say he lay as quietly as possible, smiling whilst strewn across the couch, refusing the slightest hesitation or reaction other than the occasional involuntary shudder. I assumed he was in ecstasy.

"Admit it," he said, after his spine was cut, just before the last bit of sinewy neck-flesh had been clipped, "You like it too. Being a jerk. Feels good!"

"I do not, you sick fucker," I said. "Don't put your damage on me. You're the one who made us get married then divorced the same day and then put all our rent money on the poker tournament."

"You let me do it," he replied. "So you're equally at fault."

"Whatever, Ronnie," I said. "You're so dramatic." It was then I remembered how he had to jack *everything* up times ten, neurotic overblown stakes for his every ridiculous pleasure, but I felt calmer, remembering I was not him, and there was a point where the two of us split as beings, no matter how strung I'd gotten. "Don't forget I can end you with a spike," I told his head, toting it none too gently to the sink. "One of those Susan Komen knives would do."

He whistled. Bugs Bunny or something. "End me. Go ahead: End me," he said, chuckling.

When his head stopped bleeding, I tested the severed part with a towel to be sure it was clean enough to carry and tucked it under my arm before getting on a bus. We were going to my mother's. His body reclined on my couch.

I wore a red jacket and a pair of cords. On the bus, he got all involved in analyzing an old man with brown pants and bladder problems. We spoke of school kids out for a field trip. He smiled benevolently.

When we got to mom's for Lox, she already expected me, said, "Hi Angie, got a job yet?"

I said, "No. No job."

"She doesn't want a job," Ronnie added.

"I do s—"

"Didn't think Ronnie was coming today," my mother interjected. "I see he's not himself."

"We broke up," I said. "He pissed me off. I cut off his head. Don't worry. He doesn't expect to eat."

"I might like to eat," he argued.

"Well, you can't," I said. "You've got no stomach.

A person without—"

"So you took his head?" my mother replied. "Where's the body?"

"On the couch. I'll get rid of it later. He said I was stupid and ugly and too happy," I explained, a little pissy. "I had to have *something!* So I took his head."

"It's true," he remarked. "She took it, even carried it with her here. Now look at us! Reunited and it feels so goooood."

My mother, very understanding, just shook her wet blue kitchen glove at him, fingers slimed with bubbles. She turned and asked, "You want a sack for that?"

We stared at his head. "No," I replied. "I just want to keep looking at it."

"It's not a gazing ball," she said.

"I know."

"Shows similar mistakes, with similar men, and a general lack of progress," she said.

Ronnie sulked. I flicked his ear, whispered, "Yeah, whatever, fucker."

"Pretty eyes, he had," my mother said, sounding a bit morose. "But you won't attract another boy carrying that *thing* around. They'll see you carrying some ex's head, and bam, they'll walk! Just like that."

In response, Ronnie wheedled with his normal petulance, "Don't say that! She's mine. It's a sign of true love she did this head-cutting, her willingness to hurt me and carry me around. Best thing she's ever done!" He paused before saying, in his academician's voice, "Love lies in causing others continuous excruciating pain."

"That is not love, assface," I told his head. "Jesus."

My mother looked at him. She looked at me. She tapped his head with a dripping wooden spoon before saying, "Hey. Is his hairline receding?"

Ronnie blinked, would have tilted his face in his cute I'm-a-dumbass way, but no neck remained. I told him, "You're limited now. Face it."

"He always was a stupid fucker," my mother rejoined, wagging her free hand. "Still, we do what we must." Her voice took a nostalgic turn. "Hey, cookie, what happened to that sweet guy — Julian — you dated? I liked him. He brought flowers."

I fiddled with my purse. "Too much Prozac."

"So you went for Death-Head?"

"Someone for everyone," I replied. "Death-Head was immediately available."

"That's Mr. Death-Head to you," Ronnie insisted. "And I was Live-Boy before."

"I caused a transformation," I agreed.

That night, because I couldn't leave him, I took Ronnie out with the girls. We centerpieced his head on the table while they spoke about shopping and sex with their boyfriends, the conversation rotating endlessly at one point on the definite impossibility of truly reciprocal and simultaneous sixty-nine.

"I had one guy who thought he could," Ariel said. "But he never found my clit, so I was like, okay, your dysfunction makes it easier for me to focus. He was good at other things though."

This is when Ronnie interjected to add, "I never pleased Angie. Maybe if your boyfriends had never pleased you, you'd love them more. You would cut off their heads. There's something about complete rejection that turns women on." He blinked while he awaited their response. Twice.

I slapped his cheek and covered his eyes before whispering, "You're a guest here, baby; don't forget."

"I'm sorry," he said. "I'm crabby. I kind of miss my

body."

"Sure," I agreed. "You were better at running when full-bodied."

Ariel touched his head. "I hate how he's hurt you. Can I kick it?" she asked, tracing his temples and nose with her red acrylic nail, tossing back her ridiculous sweep of platinum blonde curls. His face looked just like an infant's, one who was about to scream. "Just once?" she went on. "I always wanted to kick a head, especially a man's head...I don't have to do it twice."

She twirled the straw in her cocoa and stared at the crowd amassed in front of the Suds and Duds across the street. "Generous," I said. "But he might bruise."

"Come on," she prodded. "I didn't like the asshole before, but now he's just a bigger irritant."

"Technically, he's smaller," I said. "No body."

Miffed, she dug in her purse. Then she said, "If I can't kick him, please leave him in the car next time."

"Right," I said. "I'm on that."

Later that night, Ronnie and I had a good talk. He said, "I thought about what Ariel said, and I'm sorry I wasn't better to you."

"No, you're not," I replied. "You just say shit like that." We watched laundry spin round and round in the Suds and Duds machines because that's what you do when you can't afford dinner and a movie.

"That's true," he said. "But what can I do now? I'm just a head."

"You can tell me why you were ever sweet, if you hated me so much."

"If I were mean from the beginning, you would have never fallen for me," he said.

"Right," I replied. "Which would have been great. But why would you want me to fall for you if you didn't want me?"

He said, "So I could be mean to you later. It's like that. Of course." Staring at his stubborn look, I felt irked again, so I thought about gouging out his ears.

"You do this with everyone?" I asked. "First you get all tender, then, *zipzap*, out comes Mr. Cruel and Evil?"

"Sort of," he said, smiling. "Except Mr. Nice Guy comes back intermittently. And then I leave." He said these things, but he smiled again, in a sad kind of way.

I looked into his eyes. I took his head and opened an empty dryer's door, digging for quarters. "You'd look funny bouncing around in there," I said. "Wonder if it would hurt."

"Don't put my head in there," he said. "My head does not go in there!"

"You should know something, Ronnie," I replied, opening the dryer door wide, scanning the controls, "Before you were mean — I mean, when you said sweet things, you looked kind of humble and conflicted sometimes, like you didn't want to be a jerk. And I know you had girlfriends who hated you before, but you stitched my name onto your arm with purple thread. You did stuff you don't normally. Why?"

"I did love you once," he said. "Right before I didn't. I disassociate."

I had no quarters, so I walked out of the Laundromat holding his head in front of me, looking into his face like it was a divining rod, asking, "Do you really believe all that shit you said about loving someone being about causing the other person pain?"

He blinked, cried a little.

It didn't take me long to figure out that silence was his new tactic, so I walked him to the cliffs above the desert. "Cough up the answer before I get there," I said, "or I'll throw your head over Pike's Peak."

His silence went on.

"It's a long drop," I warned. "What the hell is wrong with you?"

I threw his head in the air, asking, "You ever planning to talk to me again? I could put my fingers in your eyeballs. Pop your eardrums. I deserve an explanation."

He blinked. My temper flared hard. After no further response, I realized this would just go on in the same pathetic way, so I lined up his head near the cliff's edge. I tested its placement with my toe. Like this was erotic, he bit the lip of my sole, his eyes wide as plates, until I pulled my foot away. "I'm going to get rid of your body," I announced. "Maybe rent it out to old ladies."

I drew back my leg to kick him, then said softly, "One day, buddy, you'll wish you spilled your guts — because, after this, you're on your own: No matter how much I love or loved you."

I ran back ten yards. When next I advanced, sprinting like a fool, I gave him a stunning distance-goal kick and almost fell off the ledge. It was wild how his head spun as it cruised up in a half loop, then down from the zenith, dropping to the canyon where it bounced on a saguaro and fell to the sand. Maybe he talked the whole time he was airborne, but I just watched his mouth move frantically, silently each time his face spun my direction, and, because it pleased me, I pretended he kept saying, "I love you," as his head rolled through the sky.

Granted, he could have been saying, "You crazy bitch. You crazy bitch," but I thought about soccer. I'd always been good at soccer. Ex-boyfriend's head. Soccer. Soccer ball.

My foot had connected.

Shrinking

I tell my husband we are shrinking. He does not believe me. Thumbing through the magazines for the Scientific American he will use as distraction as he shits, he says he believes in freeing caged monkeys more than supporting human freaks. Our house shows the signs. When I look around, it's as if everything here shrinks, save the children. All the doorways. All the love.

All love shrinks, except the love I have for the little compatriots, Jack and Jenna. They used my bones to grow their bones when they rested in my belly as parasites — we have bonded! Now they use cows to increase height. Vegetables. Dreams. Children grow. Adults shrink.

I have a new hypothesis: It's not just about our spines, which will compact naturally, which will age — but our whole life, which once included plans for trips to Spain, romantic getaway weekends to San Francisco, fantasies of buying that big house across from my grand-mother's with the drug-dealers and white ceramic lions. The desire for our suburban love life to match, at least once, the romance novels I read at age twelve.

I have long sought my handsome rogue with a tender, almost effeminate side. The husband is all man.

Today: "What will we do this weekend to keep the children busy?" is the new question, not an ounce of joy when issued by anyone, no matter who mutters.

"Park or zoo?" Him.

"Zoo. Hate the park." Me. Or Him.

"Traveling next week. Will leave on Tuesday, be back Friday." Him.

"All right." Me.

Even in bed he is smaller now, a shrinking penis. But I wonder if that's because I think of him less. Do objects or people shrink with less regard? I'm an American. A suburb mommy scientist. He is a fucking prick, a pin in the ass-cushion.

Lately, while he is upon me, in that way that men are upon women, I imagine him a porn star with only one clip available for replay. I am a loop of a video girl below, taking it and maybe calling out expletives in Russian. When I feel rambunctious, I imagine him as part of a rutting horde in the moment just before I pass out, used up and enduring my tenth man, who is him, who was also my third man. I imagine feeling passion; if feigning pleasure is desired, I will fake it. I will ask him to rip clothes. Mine.

To rip is satisfying. I hear something rip, I think: *That must be passion. My clothes had to go. Somewhere. Oh, the destruction!*

But I am practical. I wear ugly things to bed. Not what I'd save for my rogue. The ceiling fan is dirty. The smell of my children's hair is so sweet. The job I need won't go away — and neither the need. Unneeded, unwanted, the husband goes away but keeps on coming back. Boom, boom, boom. That's the door, or his car, or the door to his car, or the headboard, or my head into the headboard.

I am so much water, so much steam. I am a dream diffused into a nightmare. Afterward, when he stands across the room from me, when he strides away, I can pinch his distance between my thumb and index finger. He is that small. I am that small for him too, at similar distances.

I am the tip of the thread that punctures the white space of a needle. He does not notice when I dye my hair. I put a beauty mark on for ten days once; he never re-marked. I got a pimple there. He noticed that.

My children are enormous! Tow-headed marvels. Huger by the moment. They are large when I carry them to bed, gigantic when they cry.

The husband and I do not cry. Who is he?

We sleep. Sleeping increases the pace of shrinking, his shrinking, my shrinking, over which I obsess more and more and more. I am not so dumb as to tell anyone about this obsession, this constant fear that I will fall down the drain eventually where no one will find me, but if I stay here, I will. There was someone I could tell this to once, but he abandoned me, went away. You are here. I can tell you! Anyhow, when I keep shrinking, here's what will happen: You will walk by my window, a wind will blow me out, and I will land in your hair like a small flower from the tree owned by the city. I will have flown from my window. Maybe the husband will have flown from the window too.

If we live on two different sides of your head, we will never meet or see each other again. We may feel sadness. Or a loss. Vaguely. And relief!

Climbing up and down a single follicle will become our life's work. The wind will please and chill us. We will be naked with nothing to warm us but the soft wrap of your hair. Too small for clothes, like lice, we will be grateful.

Our children will keep growing. They will think they are orphans at their grandma's. Will you tell them otherwise, if I ever get down to your ear to ask?

I will know I am living on your head. It is a good head. And you, how big are you? In your own estimation, are you a giant or a dwarf? Careful. Be honest. I can pull your scalp. How big are you?

Not to brag or anything, but children are resilient. I'd bet my children, freaking giants, have outgrown you already. They are ready to take over the world of *every-thing feeling*.

Or maybe you are shrinking too.

With the Silence of a Deer

Artelle found herself outside his cabin in a green wire chair, wearing the head of a deer. It was a stag's head really, a young stag's, atop her shoulders. It was not a mask and was not detachable. She knew this since she'd pulled upward on the head and the thing wouldn't come off. *I am one handsome deer,* she thought, viewing herself reflected in Seth's bedroom window.

Otherwise, shoeless, she wore a thin yellow t-shirt and a pair of denim shorts. She touched her face from chin to forehead, tracing the new contours to gauge the feel of the short fur now covering her from scalp to neck. She scratched and pulled a tick from her neck. He always calls me dear, she thought. Wonder what he'll say now.

Seth had planned to spend the whole weekend with her, but had gone for more bullets, leaving the stag he'd shot yesterday gutted and hung on the porch. Seeing it there still, she remembered her revulsion at watching him slit it open, pull out the steaming organs, separate a few pounds of meat for immediate use, and prepare the rest of the body for the deep freeze, though he hadn't brought it there yet. That must be an afterthought.

That night, they ate deer for dinner. She remembered feeling sickened, even now regurgitating venison from her own gamey mouth. That was how her mother described such meat, she remembered. Like you're eating the digestion of the woods.

The animal on the porch was female. Guess he was too lazy to get a stag. The first time you watch a man not only hunt and kill but *cut up* an animal causes revulsion. His butcher skills were sloppy.

They hadn't talked about his obsessive hunting during their dating months preceding, when they'd eaten out and watched plays, but it came as no surprise to her. In bed, he was brutal, aggressive, so she presumed, in retrospect, that he rather thought himself a hunter there too, this apparent by his clenching jaw and glassed eyes as he entered her and the hard way he laid into her sometimes, cranking her legs up on his shoulders, almost beating at her thighs.

Neanderthal, she thought, but better than a pansy sex-phobe. The guy before Seth kissed too light and couldn't say the dirty words. "I want to eat your flower," he'd say, to intimate oral sex. Artelle had laughed, even sometimes replied, "You mean my *pussy*? You want to go down there and eat the hell out of my *pussy*, Henry?"

"Yes. That's what I mean," he'd replied.

Seth, on the other hand, said the dirty words without hesitation, asked her questions like: "You like this? You want it like this? You like it hard, yeah, baby? You need it like this? Huh? I'm going to take my c—" but thinking about it now, Artelle guessed she and Seth hadn't actually spoken much outside of the bedroom words, meaning the other words that addressed deeper wants or needs. She wasn't sure he knew the *other* words.

Sometimes, what she wanted to say, whilst sitting as a private audience to his ridiculous porn video, was, "No, I don't really like this, Seth. Well, not really. I need more lube when you pay so little attention to my face. But, okay. Yes, it's okay. Just finish," or "Hey, Magellan, can you go for a middle route here — some tenderness *and* some roughness? And how about that oral sex break you use to hold off ejaculation taking me to orgasm instead of just giving you a rest? Baseball. Think of baseball."

Instead, because she knew she could be demanding and had begun to doubt the possibility of a man who could be both tender and rough, Artelle could not bring herself to utter these things, so she imagined their relation-ship progressing in the way many relationships progress, hardly at all for months and then advanced with sudden leaps of unwarranted trust! The sex wasn't terrible, just not much about her. But it was the first time he'd taken her to his private country man place, where the logs on outer cabin walls were ragged with rough-hewn bark, a sharp contrast to his metrosexual condo where they usually met for wine, conversations about sex, and actual sex.

He'd invited her because he wanted her in his Martian cave, she supposed. And the cabin was fine, interesting. Yesterday morning, she'd taken pictures of every room. It was clean, not sloppy like most bachelor pads. The colors were reds and browns. No spiders in the corners. He had killed and mounted many animals. There were some rooms where the animals' stuffed heads were hung, each date of kill on a small brass plaque wherever possible, especially for larger game. His bedroom was for stags' antlers. The living room boasted fox coats and rabbits' fur. The kitchen held mounted trout.

"Strictly venison this weekend," he said. "Deer are quick to shoot and eat. Fresh meat is best. Don't let anyone fool you, Artelle! But you got to have a license to shoot. Don't worry. I'll shoot for two."

Artelle had made a lifetime of not letting anyone fool her. "I don't normally eat much meat," she said, thinking: *Deer all weekend?*

"We can fish later," he said. "Catch trout."

"I want to hike tomorrow," she said, averting that.

"It's good to be vigorously active out here," he replied. "You hike and I'll walk behind."

"I think you just like to watch me move," she said.

"I don't deny that," he replied.

When she first arrived, he'd set her chopping wood. She'd thought he wanted to watch her sweat. Could have been that, but he was lazy too. This was why he used bullets instead of a primal weapon like a spear. "I'd like to see you kill a deer with a spear," she said.

He laughed. Artelle was five foot eight. He topped her by three inches. This morning after he left, she stripped off her sweater and walked outdoors. Today it was warm, morning dew nearly evaporated on the grass, so her feet felt bare and fine. As she regarded herself again, her big deer's eyes looked fluid in the window. She rather liked her long narrow nose. Experimenting, she let her long purple tongue lick her fur. Oh, yeah, that was hot.

Seth returned. She heard his car. He smiled, holding the bullets in a box in his hand until he spied her and dropped them in surprise. He must see her deer face too, she thought, her weird, male deer face. He said, "Morning, Artelle?"

"Do I have a deer head to you?" she asked, but whatever the noise she'd made, it resembled more a squeaky grunt.

On his knees in the grass and dirt, he retrieved bullets. Then he stood, opened his car door, took his gun from the backseat, and walked to the porch where she stood. "Artelle?" he asked again. She nodded.

She walked into the cabin and got a roll of butcher block paper from the galley kitchen. With it, in front of him again, she wrote, "Yes. It's me."

"Okay," he said. "I thought it so." His eyes were on her chest.

"Do you see my head as a deer's head?" she asked on paper.

"Yes. Yes, I do," he said.

"I'm hungry," she wrote. "Please don't shoot me." She dropped to her hands and knees to eat grass, which had assumed a new and ridiculous lure. It was delicious. *Why didn't we eat grass before,* she thought. *It's the new lettuce.* After she'd done so a while, as he stood and watched, she rose and grabbed the paper roll again to write, "What the fuck happened here?"

"I don't know," he said. "But it's happened before."

She made one big exclamation mark six inches tall, then tore off the section and wrote on a clean part: "With whom?"

"My other girlfriend," he said. "At first, we were worried. But she went back to normal when she returned to the city."

Artelle shivered. This happened before? The grass tasted funny, delicious, tangy. Seth held out his arms. She walked into them. First, like a kind papa, he stroked her back — and then his hands strayed to her ass.

"Let's do it," he said. "Let's do it like this. Artelle, I love your body! It's okay if you're quiet this time. She was quiet."

They'd done it plenty the night before, her thighs still sore, but she nodded. It was all she could do. She'd feel silly to write, "No sex," on the paper, or "No..." with several underlines. *Sure, let's fuck,* she thought. *The last girl got home.*

So she touched him back. "Oh, too fucking weird," he announced, as if narrating for someone not present, for posterity: "My super hot girlfriend is a deer, right now, stroking my cock."

When they got to the bedroom, things went the same as before, except they didn't kiss. He kept staring at her head, alternating his view of her young stag's horns with the movement of his hips and the static mounted racks across the room. *He might need a plaque for this event,* she thought, *my deer event,* as his thrusts pummeled her body.

Date of conquest, human deer: __/__/__. Before the rack happened, however, he'd have to gut her and eat her, she decided, maybe like how he gutted her now, pounding away at her cervix; he would take his mid-coital oral sex break as snack any minute. As she thought this, his head dove. Normally, she issued noise, sometimes loud noise, for fun, but not today. Still, fear and confusion made her unusually sensitive.

"The other girl had a doe's head," he said when he came back up to kiss her, wiping his face on the blanket. "Weird that this time you got a stag. Are you some kind of lesbian, Artelle? You got a guy's brain?"

Great, she thought. *He thinks I'm a lesbian because I have horns? Or that I have a guy's brain? Your oral sex makes me want to go lesbian,* she decided.

He shrugged and commenced his final stretch. She looked at her body reflected in the window with her male deer's head — with his body doing its thing. *Damn sexy,* she thought. *Maybe I'm male in these woods because I'm smarter,* she speculated. *I'm your alpha.* Or she could pretend that his window image was her, and he was her weird woman with a deer head. Being unable to make human noise gave her lots of time to think. She wondered whether her horns were sharp enough to gore him and whether her body would go stag.

"This is so much better than the last time this happened," she heard Seth say, out of breath. "Fuck yeah, it's incredible!"

"It's okay," Artelle tried to say, forgetting for a moment that she couldn't talk, deer speech now resembling her tongue lolling out and quietly returning to her mouth.

Moments later, oblivious, he began his usual verbal routine: "You want this baby? You need this? Show me how bad."

"Oh, so bad, baby," she said through her silent stag mouth. "So very very bad. Yeah, yeah, whatever, asshole."

"I can see you're trying to say something," he said as he finished. "Your tongue keeps sticking out. It's so cute! Maybe later I'll get you the paper again. We can talk." But when he went to the living room, he got a beer and put his feet up on the recliner. He took a short nap, didn't even bring her a glass of water.

When she heard him snore, irked, Artelle dressed, took his car keys and drove to the car park where she'd left her Honda. By the time she got home, her head was normal, had already been normal upon arriving at the car park. In the home bathroom mirror, seeing her face, she tested moving her lips and tongue. She was totally human, so called Liza, clearing the new message announcement on her cell. Seth had texted twenty or more times as she drove.

Without reading them en route, hearing only the recurrent beeps arriving, she had already decided not to

see him again, no matter how faux metrosexual he looked.
The man couldn't carry a conversation. The man said the
same things when she didn't talk as when she did. It was
then she realized he had never required a response.

Nonetheless, his follow-up texts to the cabin
experience kept ringing in:

"Artelle?"

"Baby, where'd you go?"

"Fuck, where's the car?"

"Where's my car?"

"You coming back?"

"I know you want more of that, baby, that hot sex
we had."

"Did you stop at the store? Get more beer."

"What a sexy-ass deer head you had."

"It bothered you when I said this happened before,
didn't it?"

"Aw, you're upset, aren't you? Jealous maybe?"

"That was a long time ago."

"She wasn't that pretty."

"Your tits are bigger."

"I miss you."

"Let's go fishing."

"I'll hike with you."

"You can walk behind me."

"Baby, come back."

"All right. I'm getting pissed."

"Bring my car back right now."

"Right now, you fucking bitch."

"I know you're ignoring me."

"You stupid fucking queer bitch."

"I bet you had guy horns because you were going
to stab me in the back!"

"Maybe you wanted to poke me with them. In the

ass!"

"Artelle, did you want to poke me in the ass? Baby?"

"I should have fucked you again and then cut them off."

"I'm sorry. Come back, baby. Please come back."

"I miss you."

"Hey, Artelle, did I do a guy?"

"No way, because you had a pussy."

"Artelle?"

"Artelle, baby, I'm sorry."

"Be a doe. I'll be a doe."

"Bring my car back, will you?"

"Dear?"

After reading them, Artelle texted to say his car was at the car park. He could hike, take a bus, whatever. Not her problem: She was dealing with her deer head issue and staying at the hospital, under much duress, she replied. Please, Seth, don't call or text again.

She obviously didn't go to the hospital. She told Liza, "Dude, that was some creepy shit with Seth in the cabin. He usually wears suits. Out there, the guy kills what he eats and mounts the shit. I felt like my head was a deer's head on his wall, just another bedpost notch. Want to go out for a salad?" She put on a pink dress. She drove to Liza's. "Guess you should be careful when you go to the private-country-man-place with a guy," she said. "Some things are different."

"Nah, nothing's different," Liza said. "You just see men more clearly, outside the niceties."

They drove to a pizza parlor with billiards and a long salad bar. "I'd make a good man," Artelle said, playing "Hit Me With Your Best Shot," on the juke. She pictured her head as a stag's head again, how handsome she was.

Liza nodded, mouth full of lettuce.

Artelle smiled. She ate some lettuce, wanting her antlers back. She walked to the billiards table at the side of the room and used the racking triangle to frame her face. "Can you see it, Liza?" she asked. "The rack he would have made with my deer's head, if I was a deer. With a little bronze plaque and everything."

"Haha," Liza said. "But he never ate you that thoroughly."

"Fire away!" went the gravelly voice from the jukebox. "Fire awa-ay-ay!"

"Good point," Artelle said, looking up through the triangular rack still pressed into her face, tilting her chin up so she stared into the halogens above the pool table, imagining there was a truck or something, coming up fast. She smelled the dewed grass. All was dark except the high-beams. She wanted to get out of the road and dart into the woods, but stood dazed in the headlights, her big eyes blinking, paused. Suddenly, with a deer's intuition, she knew somebody would hit her. Or shoot her. She couldn't speak. Or move. It was that deer silence again. A woman's body with a deer's head. Fuck him — of course she had horns out there!

Now she cleared her throat and touched her human cheek. "Wanna shoot some stick?" she asked. She bent over, giving the guys behind her a prime view of her hindquarters, put three quarters in the slots, dropped the triangle on the table, and racked the balls till they were perfectly aligned. "Go on, Liza," she said.

"Oh, come on, you know I suck at breaking," Liza replied, touching her soft brown hair. "I can't even line the stick up right." A new text came. She didn't look at it. She looked at the balls on the table, thinking: *Break them, Liza.*

Break them.

"You're a guy like that with breaks..." Liza said. "You'll send those round suckers rolling. Take a shot like the bad-ass woman you know yourself to be, Artelle — the one I know you to be. What are you waiting for? Come on!"

Into the sudden silence, Artelle cracked a single white ball into the triangular mass. Three balls were pocketed; the rest scattered.

"That's that," Liza said. "Blood-red seven in first. You're solids. I'll be stripes."

Bengal Tiger Boy

It was right after I told him I'd be fine, though I wasn't fine, that I hung up the phone and pulled the trigger. I'd been at my place, talking to him at his place, two days after he told me he didn't want me. But it wasn't me he didn't want. He didn't want anyone. Anyway, day two after his revelation, we reached the end of the current conversation, and I went angel.

Guess I couldn't take it anymore. Any of it. He'd just gotten a tattoo on his arm of a big Bengal tiger and there was text below the beast that said, "Stronger by the day." His tiger was two weeks old when we last spoke, orange and black, with blue in the stripes, lots of ink, still a little crusty and tender.

After the hole cleared through my head, I remember I thought: I want to see it again, his tattoo. I wanted to see his spare shoulders, his dark furred thighs. Then I was there, at his place. That's the cool thing as a spirit — you just think it, and you're present. I remember, seconds dead, I hung above his bed. He nearly napped, hands tucked under his ears, his pretty blue eyes two-thirds closed. He hadn't gotten the news yet and it would take a good week for him to figure it out because he'd have to miss me answering my phone first, and then try and physically come knock, more than once — and finally get insistent and call my sister.

By the time he found out, my family had arrived to enact much drama (mother screaming "Julia! How could you? Oh, Jesus!"; Katie walking around and around my body, touching the pool of blood, washing her hands; and daddy, oh, daddy, seated at the dinette, holding his head in his palms like a cracked egg) — and they had removed my body, had cleaned things up and took care of funeral planning because I'd left a note and a voicemail that day, and only a good six days later would my lover boy scuffle into my abandoned place, picking up his records and clothes as he came to, both mourning and applying his practical purpose at once.

During this time, this whole week, I'd have been watching him, floating above the 8th and Sycamore St. liquor store where we met, cruising the park where the cops hung in clumps. I'd be flying all over the city, thinking of his Bengal tattoo and how he said he liked me that one day, he really did, but he just didn't have a thing for girls. Boys neither. He had no *thing* for no one. This was his failing. All his life.

He wouldn't have been the first guy I'd heard say that, or variations of that. Oh, no, before I blew that lead, I would have well considered the act of my own attrition, would have wasted years pursuing similarly inaccessible men. Each would have had different reasons for their damage. Marriages. Mental Illness. Abuse. I would have decided this was a pattern. My pattern. To chase the inaccessible and whacked. To want the fucked up. To be the girl with tears like tattoos, like wet facial love letters to distant boys, permanent as those inked onto the eyes of gangbangers who've killed people.

My death was my most splendid and inventive solution. So proactive. Yay, me.

He'd come to the funeral though, Mr. Bengal Tiger boy, my most recent failure. He'd come in a black suit like the ones I always told him were sexy. We would have shopped for this one together, for another funeral, and it would cover his tats, that tiger and the sword below, cover his "Stronger by the day."

For me, I would watch him almost weep. I would have arrived, but I wouldn't stay. My funeral was some sad-ass shit. All my favorite songs playing. My moms crying, wearing her purple floral dress she saved for church. My dad hanging near the back and holding his gut like he thought it would fall off if he let it go. The assortment of pictures of my life pinned to corkboard displays. Tat boy in black shades, solemn in the front row. Almost crying. Yeah, I had to blow that pop-stand.

But I did go to hang from his ceiling some nights, Bengal tiger boy's, when he was naked and sprawled in his aloneness on his bed. Some nights he wore red boxers. When it was hot, he'd turn a fan on and direct it at his chest. He spent a lot of time in bed, staring at the ceiling, if you believe that, scratching his head and pondering the rise and fall of stucco peaks. But I did discover, after a year or so, that he was truthful, at least, about not wanting anyone. He didn't take another lover for four years. Even then, it was almost accidental. Some groupie of his brother's band. And I'm fucked up, okay? Yeah, I wanted to watch him. Nothing changes. I did this five years and then quit.

I don't know why my spirit hung there so long, drawn to his lack of emotion. But that was my problem, continued interest in absences, always had been, and maybe it was about right that I sometimes just hovered rather dazed, post-mortem, where the unavailable desired people were. I'd visit a few. Boys and girls. Tucked myself as vapor into their sides as they rested if I felt like some company. Hey, I was just a ghost then, right? They couldn't feel me. Couldn't know I was claiming them, long after the fact, in a way they could never refuse.

Everyone was happy. They felt alone. I felt together. Kind of worked for both of us, see?

They could not pull me close, but neither could they push me away. I liked that about being dead. I could finger that tiger of his for hours, up and down on the blue-black stripes. Pretending it was purring. Putting my index in its terrible mouth — all the way in to touch his bones. Running my hand over the blade of his tattooed sword. Taking my soul into his body and going in and out at whim.

I could live right next to his heart, all the time, if I wanted to, kissing its hot squeezing mass all night long.

He wouldn't feel me. He would never feel a thing.

Making Love to the Fruit Shooter

I made love to the fruit shooter, one could say, because I liked being his constant target. I used the corner of my mouth as his anchor point. He used the same corner of his own lips, and he shot with his fingers, barebow, sightless. There was risk to this, and danger. While visiting his life as his lover, any number of long afternoons were spent in his company on days when the air was chill, the sun falling slowly like a stringed thing from the sky, and I stood, apple on my head, shivering in the tricky dusk, waiting for the sound of his arrows striking fruit. He liked to talk about the archer's paradox, the way the arrow bent and flexed around a riser upon release, and he had warned me, early on, about the possibility of brain damage from our dating, the possibility of coma, the possibility this relationship could not only maim but kill me. I was dying for a good thrill. "Nock me," I said. "I fly straight."

We had our first lunch at the local café amid the stares of curious gapers. That time, I was wearing a business suit and he a kelly green ensemble that made him resemble Robin Hood. I liked this. People stared in horror when they looked upon him, and then, because they saw us together, treated me as the quivering field mouse of his more pouncing cat. "He is no pussy," I wanted to tell them.

An old lady with a flat face, black spectacles, and green polyester slacks flagged me on the way out of the diner. "Dangerous!" she hissed, clutching my arm and staring pointedly at him, letting out a quick "Bad luck shooter," because he and I were moving quickly from that place like I might be his arm guard, he my very skin.

"But I am a lucky one," I called back to her as he ushered me out. I'll never know whether she heard. That night, in a mysterious absence, he left me for hours and then made a chain of daisies and arrows pointing the way to our bedroom.

"I'm like cupid," he said.

"You very much are," I said. "Where's my chocolate?"

"I feel a growing tenderness for you," he replied, his fingers tracing the rounded curve of my ass as we lay on the tile floor together, forsaking the bed. "You mean a lot to me, and if I cannot shoot things any given day, please know, I'll tell you. Even if I am the slightest bit sick, which could affect my aim. Even if I feel a trembling in my hands. But things could happen that are out of my control, as I explained. A sort of target panic every once in a long while, when I feel an uncontrollable sense of rejection. And you know these are the risks. I'll warn you now, before we begin."

I trusted him completely, trusted the strength and skill of his fingers, noted how they could privately make me cry out, moan and swoon, shriek "Come to Jesus," or come flooding in another way, quickly and easily, with his concentrated rubbing. Often, I stared at his hands, how long and fine they were, how neatly tended. How could hands be so good in one place and not be marvelous in another? His hands were perfect at anything he endeavored. I was his apple girl a long time, slick and wet with the split of pale flesh. For a living, he was paid to shoot similar things off the heads of women on the *Wild Man Marvels* TV series, but at home I was his practice model and he shot what he wanted to shoot. He had done this activity for quite some time, talking often about the various comings and goings of his toxophilite past with tournaments and weekend engagements before the TV gig.

His assistants were all prettier and bustier than me. They kept changing. He'd complain when he got a new one. "All this height flux! Can't they just stick to five-foot-four? Damn actors' unions, fucking agencies, hell's gate producers!"

Before that, he worked in the education industry as a special services librarian who tracked and routed rare books. "When I worked as a slave to the man—" his tirades often began.

"But you are the man," I told him each time. "White. Part of the power dynamic. From a day job, you sat on your ass and that job paid more th—"

"I am not the man!" he replied with vinegar, but this argument never went anywhere good, so I took to nodding and letting it be; I was, at least, good at that, getting better and better, a nodding welter-weight champion.

I worked as a law firm clerk since we met, but when we started dating some two years ago, I had a new job, too. When I got home from work, I'd strip off my gray suits, my stockings, my three-inch heels, and my fine jewelry. This was our ritual. Pulling on the red leotard and green ballet slippers, I let him touch and embrace me: his favorite thing to pinch my nipples through the thin leotard fabric, to see my breasts almost but not quite on display — to dip his hand into the neckline to cup them before we walked out into the air, and to suck them while he cupped them, either through or pulled free from the sheer red fabric. This was foreplay.

We went through a bushel of apples some days. Before he nocked the first arrow in his bow, I pulled my hair back and fastened it low on my neck, my part centered clean-split down the middle like the apple would be. Nothing could disrupt the seat of the apple, he admitted, and I looked like an apple, too, he said, so there was unity in my pairing with the fruit, so much so that he felt to hit the red apple atop my head with his arrowhead, to slice it in half, was akin to separating twins.

"You have no seeds," he said, "but not to worry. I shall put my own inside you." I groaned and then I groaned. Sometimes, he fucked me in the field, not stripping me, solely moving the leotard aside as my back pressed against the grass with his hands on either side of my shoulders. When he touched me after release, his hands were hot, from shooting or otherwise. He drank apple juice every day of the apple phase. He suggested we have a daughter and name her Apple. "You know," he said, "like that famous Paltrow girl?"

"We are not married," I said.

"I thought you were more modern," he replied.

"It's about child support," I said. "You know, should we split." I didn't tell him that I didn't want his baby, which was true. I didn't want any baby. The fucking things screamed. I was sure I wanted nothing to do with them. "I'm just saying," I said.

"That is not positive thinking," he said. "Take care of your green shoes. They're muddy."

Apples were only his newest obsession. Before this, I stood in the field with an eggplant on my head, in a purple leotard, with the same green shoes. He had gone on about eggplants, such deep purple luster, such perfect nutty flavor, such resemblances to the classically painted bodies of women. "Eggplants are actually berries!" he had told me then. "Botanically speaking. Big violet berries. And their seeds have nicotine! Did you know that?" I heard a lot about eggplants those days.

But he was done with eggplants now. "Apples," he told me one night, several months into the newest trend, "were a favorite of ancient Greeks and Romans, were introduced to America by early settlers, who brought seeds. We gave the Native Americans apples, maybe like the way they gave us corn. Apples are magnificent fruit. And it's like I'm your teacher. By splitting the apple on top of your head, I accept your gift." When we walked in from the fields each night, we never ate the apples he split, but left them for the birds. "Nature will take its course," he said. He had straight blond hair that fell over his eyes, which he often blew upward to clear his vision.

Things went on this way. Then one day at the law firm we had a new case. The family of Emma Gold versus Claus Belifrade AKA Fruit Shooter, regarding her sudden lapse into a coma after being lacerated in the head with an arrow. I felt sick and flabbergasted. I looked at all the photos from the shoots, at the blood on the ground the day she was pierced in the forehead, at the pictures of her laid up in her hospital bed, head wrapped in white. I had never watched his show, preferring to think of myself as his best, his real muse, or the true mistress for his art—but in the film clip they had for court, she was dressed as a kiwi, in an electric green leotard, with green shoes, a thin blond girl with Hollywood-ginormous tits standing at attention, her long hair flowing out behind her. And then she was hit. And then she fell. Crumpled, more like. A little round O of a moue on her lips, so surprised! It was good the show had not gone on live that day. I mentioned this lawsuit and footage to Claus at home that day, like one would mention orphans in Somalia, like: Isn't that terribly sad and shocking?

"I know about the lawsuit," he said. "But there are several differences here. Emma did not tie her hair back. This was distracting. She is not the lucky one like you are. Distracting. I work when I'm sick—at work—but never here with you. It was an unhappy accident, really. They'll throw her case right out of court."

"Will they?" I asked. "My firm is fighting it. We could win."

"You should tell your boss to drop the case," he said. "The media owns everything. It's a global tipping point. They call what they can do and waive off the damage. There's no way the family will win. Emma signed many liability waivers before starting with the network. Honey, this is a losing suit. Really. Cases like hers, in this climate, they've been thrown out before. If it weren't so distasteful, they could film agreed-upon, virginal teenage rape scenes and get away with it."

"Agreed-upon rape?"

"Yeah."

I nodded. That's what I did.

He was right about the lawsuit, even after poor Emma Gold began her life as a shut-in with constant care, which the jury was somewhat swayed by, because the terms of the contract were explicit. They even kept a video log where she calmly answered each question about her willingness to take risks in return for her salary and a spot on network TV with bonus potentials.

From me, each day, the apples fell halved from my head. He got heady with his count. "I have now shot close to triple eight hundred fruits from your head!" he said one evening as the stars sparkled around us. "We should film me shooting you! You must have magic hair, hair that deflects any arrows, calls the arrows into the fruit, whispers to the wind, giving directions."

"I believe in you," I said. "This explains my stillness."

"I believe in you, too, and I love that you believe in me," he said. "It steadies my hands." Then he swung me around in his arms, planting kisses on my face, my shoulders, the neckline hem of my red leotard, the hem of it near my thighs, and higher, and lower.

We stood on the same level field when he finally shot an arrow that went over my head without grazing the apple. I heard it whistle as it passed. "Fuck!" he shouted, trying to track where it landed. "Fuck! Fuck! Shit!"

And then he calmed. He caressed me without taking me, rubbing my arms as if to warm them. "Do you believe in me less today?" he asked grimly, and then said, "No more arrows tonight, okay, sweetheart?"

I began to secretly watch his show. I rented old episodes. I watched every bit of the footage I could find. I was so proud. How elegant he looked in the black velvet suit wardrobe picked for him. How debonair he was on those strange fields he shot from, blowing the blond hair from his eyes as he did at home, before shooting various objects, often very small ones, from the heads of some elaborate vixens wearing next to nothing. The videos all seemed quite similar. Except one day, I discovered a stash on his desk that was labeled with the show's title and DRESSING ROOM. They were dark and hard to view. He had some hinky net-cam set up. Maybe the footage was from security cameras. On each tape was what appeared to be motion-activated footage of him and his co-stars standing close together—footage where they spoke quietly. In the first clip, I heard him tell the woman, "I won't hit you. Not to worry. You have arrow-proof hair." To others, he said similar things. He stroked each of those depicted, caressing them like prize produce.

I went to visit Emma at her facility and spent a good while staring at the scar on her face where the arrow had entered her brain, where the hair had just begun to grow again. She could not talk. She slobbered. Every so often, she said something unthinkably close to "Kiwi," but it could have been "Come here," or it could have been "Gimme." I put my face close to her mouth, drawing my ear as close to her lips as possible—but her vocal chords went silent. She just breathed, in and out, as if almost sleeping, and then thrashed her head back and forth for some time. She's a vegetable, I thought, then wondered how close a vegetable was to an apple. Turns out, it didn't matter.

Claus came home that day and announced, with a flourish, "We go next with bananas, my love! Bananas! This will require you to wear a metal headband that holds the fruit upright on your head! But not to worry! I have made this device from a hanger and zip-ties. This way, when the arrow pierces the fruit, it can clearly be seen to do so. I'm not sure if the arrow will get stuck. Did you know banana plants, though very tall, are not trees? Did you know both banana skin and fruit can be eaten? That they have pseudo stems?" He handed me a yellow leotard. This time, he handed me new brown shoes. "The green no longer goes."

I felt the green still went, but later that week, I stood on the field wearing the brown. A cold wind blew. Goose bumps gathered on my bare legs and arms, and I stood erect, with the weird metal headband giving me a headache as the banana stood upright within it like a displaced penis, my own tall banana crown. In the distance, wheat waved in the fields. I looked at Claus in his red sweater and pair of jeans.

I remembered the footage I saw that day of a girl in his dressing room as he wore the same outfit, a new girl, thin, brown, svelte—the footage recent—"I won't do bananas," she'd said.

"Why not?" he asked, moving his hands slowly from her waist to her breasts to her shoulders, with his usual arrogant punning about prowess. "You do my banana quite well."

She slapped him. "You're an ass," she said. I had never seen her on TV. Her refusal could mean everything. But I had not refused him. I gave him everything he wanted; I began to regret that as I stood in my yellow leotard and brown shoes, trying to be a twin banana to the one on my head, trying to see his face clearly in the distance, trying to make a decision about all this that would feel like a huge letdown or a huge relief—and then he did something that helped.

He lowered his bow and wiped the sleeve of his red sweater across his nose. It could have been an itch, but seeing this happen, watching him as he nocked the arrow, seconds later, I instinctively fell to the ground, hugging the earth, and "Get up! Get up!" he shouted. But I would not. "Please, get up," he begged. "Are you okay?"

I kept nodding, but I wasn't moving. He knew I was not listening then, must have known, because he threw down his bow and arrow in disgust, and then, in full view of me, with red nose running clear and yellow, unchecked, onto his lips and chin, began to sneeze.

Sex with Dwarves

People used to die young. This was due to infection and internal bleeding and any variety of persistent uncured illnesses that a poultice or a leeching didn't solve. And they didn't grow that tall; some would say this was genetic or race based, and sometimes it was. But sometimes it was because there were simply not enough nutrients in the daily diet.

So this was why buildings were made with short doorways and children who came improbably to age were married off young. In the time of Romeo and Juliet, thirteen was plenty ripe for a girl to have her virginity tested, taken, and dropped in the marriage well like a coin into a fountain. After her father negotiated the good match and dowered her such that she would be an appealing trade, he would give her away. Literally. Then her husband's home became her home, and his kingdom was her kingdom, whether it be a hovel or a castle, but not really — more like she would be an animated feature of the kingdom. Here are my stables, here is my acreage, here are my heirlooms in the form of silver or paintings or furnishings, and there, oh, yes, there is my wife. Gout was everywhere. Even in fairytale land.

It is possible that all those dragons and magical beasts were strange reactions to indigestive hallucination rather than actualities. Or maybe things like unicorns were the very first versions of carnival trickery.

Take a horn from a ram and glue it on a horse's head. This glue could be made from the mixed medley adhesive you made from the feet of the last horse that you killed since he didn't sire more, too old or ornery to get it up, and didn't pull his weight for the farming, so his old, unshod feet were better used in death than they had been in his later life. His meat was stringy, but perhaps you had jerky or some kind of meal that made it less so. And the ram, you had eaten him too. His hide became clothing and his horn became myth. So you see, things could often work this way when there was no excess to spare.

But this is not what I'm trying to tell you. What I'm trying to tell you is a story about sex — and dwarves — and a fair princess, exiled from her castle, whose name was Snow White, or Schneewittchen, or Snowdrop, or any number of variations. What I can't say, either, during this story, is her age — for she was seven in some tellings of this tale and thirteen or fourteen in others, but in all versions, she had pale white skin and blood red lips. Perhaps this was why the dwarves liked her so much, because all day in the mines, digging and digging and digging, bringing up jewels and other such riches, they did not see the sun or anything that touched it. These dwarves liked a treasure unburied, their names in Dwarven not resembling Happy, Sleepy, Doc, or whatever, but more earthy things like Zircon, Fossil, Hematite, and things of the ground. So when she found their cottage and cleaned it, her skin just as leached of daylight as their own, her lips redder than the rubies they brought up from the earth's core but free from any subterraneous dust or debris, was it any wonder that they, all seven of them, fell in love with her? No. Not really. Not to me. For she was fair. The fairest. And though she had no mother to teach her in the ways of girlhood, only an envious second Queen who concerned herself more with being the apple of Snow White's father's eye, Snow White did not learn how to withhold herself and wait for true love, for no one told her how, or, more importantly, why.

She knew what it was to wait, and what it was to have a wedding arranged, but all of the gentle details like how to adore pianoforte and knitting and do menu planning had been left from her curriculum, almost de-liberately.

And then the stephag tried to kill her, but what's worse, sent a huntsman to do it — as if she were a feral dog or a pig to the spit. And maybe it was that moment, the one, where the huntsman sat atop her with his knife drawn and almost brought it down on her chest, when she glared back at him, did not struggle, and simple laid her hands out flat on either side, a little like Jesus did — that the huntsman recoiled. Her eyes did not tell him not to kill her, her lips did not plead, her body did not tremble. She was due to be married to an old lecherous ass who coveted only two things: her dowry and the prostitutes at the local tavern, and sought to cure himself of the latter's venereal disease by marrying the unwanted daughter of a kingdom that had all but forsaken her. Our little snow girl knew this too, and had heard of the nasty, puss-filled blisters on his member, so this was her wedding night to be, the nightmare of his pale bony fingers and diseased member ripping apart her maidenhead just before he likely beat her for not curing him, since she knew she would not (she was not his first young bride) — and she did not crave it.

Oh, please let me run out to the woods to escape for my life, she thought. The life I don't value — and at least the woodsman, who was about to carve out her heart, the one that sat on top of her, was handsome. Hello, death groom, she wanted to say to him. You have come for me with your knife and I do not resist you. She put one pale hand to his cheek and said, "Yes. Kill me. Have mercy."

The truth was, it was he, then, who resisted her. Could he kill something so beautiful that wanted to die? Could he be the hand to make all warm things turn cold as the winter snow? No! It was his own aching sadness and desire for her, unfulfilled, that made him stand and run, for he could not have her and he could not kill her.

"Live!" he said then. "And take the pleasures you may at being in this exile, for there is no one here to stop you and I will give those in the castle all they need such that you can live a second life, one free as the animals in the forest, where you shall make your reign." He left her his provisions and quickly killed a deer. It was this deer's heart he gave the Queen and, for a while, all was quiet.

Snow White needed lodging. It was dark and it was cold, and there, in the place where exiles went, was a tiny cottage full of dwarves. Now, these creatures were amazed to see her there, but after she cooked and cleaned and lived with them awhile, they discovered that even the beautiful can have accessible souls. And they loved her womanhood near them, having lived, all together, without a hint of heterosexual sex in ages. Yet, it was not as though none of them wanted her, but there was a height differential that made each of these dwarves feel small and unworthy when she stood before them. Additionally, they liked her — and because they liked her, but they also liked each other, they would not decide which one (or ones) was fit to woo her, for they wanted no household strife.

Whether there was a magic mirror, the Queen recognized the scent of deer blood because she was an avid venison eater, or she simply knew the aesthete huntsman had not killed the little snowdrop flower that was her stepdaughter, the queen decided to go have a look at what went on with her tiny beautiful relation. This visit, which actually turned into several visits, was meant to kill the young girl with the snow white skin and blood red lips — the same girl her father already thought dead and thus did not attempt to rescue.

The Queen was a large woman in corsets and skirts. A hermaphrodite. So her movements in the forest were bumbling and easy to spot. First, she would have done Snow White in with colorful bodice laces, pulled too tight, but as Snow White lay gasping for breath on the their floor, one of the dwarves, thinking a bear stumbled drunkenly through the wood, entered and loosed her strings.

Now, like I said, people died young. They married young. Snow White may have already been married by this time if it weren't for the chase out of the castle, so when she almost died and the little dwarf with a black beard and a lovely friendly face took his small digging blade and cut those laces apart, she was grateful. Here began the connection between sex and near-murder. There was a small party that night, and Snow White, full of young hormones and robbed of any dalliance with the huntsman due to his intent on killing her and subsequent guilt, decided to take the small, black haired dwarf out into the woods.

"Obsidian," she said, for this was his name. "I am a princess without a kingdom and I have come to be of the age to marry, but I have no ladies in waiting, no mother to instruct me, and no father who knows I am breathing. I am also having my monthly courses and have heard about sex from the scullery kitchen, above which I once pretended to learn the pianoforte, but had no skill, teacher, or volition. This being the case, I would like to give you my sex in return for your saving my life. Are you game?"

Now it only took this once for Obsidian to discover that he liked such sex. His member, dwarf-like as it was, was too short to pierce her maidenhead and was just small enough to function like a tiny vibrating toy, so as his little penis took its tour of her, she found this pleasurable as well, and they smiled as they walked back from the woods, hand in hand. The dwarves then had a meeting. For all of them wanted so much to likewise possess what Obsidian went on and on about — but it was not fair to the others for only some, but not all, to get this. Snow White presided over the meeting with a little wooden gavel Fossil made her. "Now, now," she said. "I can hear your concerns, but Obsidian did save my life and I only gave him a one-time gift, not continuous free pass for re-entry. The Queen may try to kill me again. Wait your turn! Any man who can save me from my stepmother will get his own little trip to the woods. And that, gentlemen, is my decision."

Sounds fair, all agreed, and indeed, another such occurrence soon happened. The Queen brought a poisoned comb to Snow White on her next death mission and gave a lovely hairdo to Snow White, who, not recognizing the queen due to magic illusions, thought she looked quite pretty so was glad for the visit — until she passed out, the comb still sticking up from her head.

When six dwarves came home that day, for Obsidian was off in the woods, masturbating on the spot where he had once taken her, the remaining six vied for being her savior, though baffled by the comb. Finally, Stalagmite determined that anything jutting from one's head was a problem and yanked out the comb then gave her a drink of his moonshine, which he'd made from fermented pears, and she woke right up.

Since he and the others had been avidly awaiting their chance, no other female dwarves around for miles, their small hands working but not as well as how they imagined her secret place would work, the one Obsidian had not ceased to expound upon the marvels of ("It doesn't chafe. It doesn't sting. It is a warm wet holding place!") — Stalagmite was more than ready to do his part.

In fact, since his member did not pierce her maidenhead either, and he was very kind, she grew rather enamored of taking dwarves out to the woods and very much liked how he laid flowers below her and spent long periods of time rubbing his penis on various areas of her body, kissing her skin, and allowing his small hairy chest to intermingle with the hair on her legs before getting down to business to mount her like a small chess piece atop a white writhing mare, taking his turn.

She grew so delighted with this exchange, for Stalagmite was a far better lover than Obsidian, and enjoyed it so well, she wanted to do this again, day after day, but realized this would cause a fractured unity in the household.

After much reflection, she then decided that she might as well have more dwarves take their turns, provided they were suitably excited, and so, at the next meeting she presided over with her same wood gavel, she announced quite clearly: "Dear Dwarves, I am in the position to make you a unique offer. You have no woman. I am woman enough for all of you. And I will allow you to have me, freely, but you must pleasure me and do all the things women enjoy, including providing goods and jewelry and tokens, and then we will proceed to have sex every night."

This orgiastic coupling of she and the dwarves went on for five gorgeous moons. Often, she was the feast and the bounty of enjoyment they brought her had no threshold. They grew comfortable with her body and their bodies with her body, and, like brothers as they already were, they began to play on her and with her in unison. It was not unusual, for example, for one's hand to play at her clitoris, as the hand of another gently rubbed her anus, while the penis of another penetrated and moved within her, concurrently with the hands of two different dwarves at work on her breasts, pinching her nipples.

Sadly, this lovely interlude of plentiful sex came to an end when the Queen, unaware of her stepdaughter's daily pleasure, tried to kill her once more, with a red, poison apple. When the dwarves arrived home to find their hedonistic princess, for whom each loved so dearly he would have given his life in a thrice, had collapsed again from another ailment, they wept. Though they flipped her torso over and pounded her back, sang to her and brought her jewelry, and played futilely with her hair, she would not awaken.

They created a glass coffin so that they could watch her as she decayed — but she did not decay, so they soon learned that hers was an enchanted death and that she would stay so beautiful and perfect that they could, at will, climb into her coffin and enjoy her as they once had, though with a mournful fervor this time, for they did like when she responded and were saddened that from her warm but slumbering body, they could no longer elicit a response.

Suffice it to say, she was still their princess and

each brought lovely trinkets to her coffin-side, spoke to her, and occasionally considered getting in there with her, all seven at once, and having a commemorative orgy, but they simply waited and watched.

Then one day, a prince appeared. He was tall and handsome. He was a human, just as she was. He begged them to let him take her back to her people, where she belonged, so her people's doctors could save her. She no longer presided over their meetings, but Obsidian hit the remaining gavel on the table and said only, "It must be so," before the others agreed they would let this tall, striking male take her away.

As the prince's servants toted her coffin several leagues from the dwarves, they almost dropped her, or actually did drop her, having carried her like rough cargo, and the glass coffin shattered. Simultaneously, her body jolted, the tiny chunk of poisonous apple in her throat was dislodged, and she awoke.

When the caravan stopped for evening repast, it was explained to her that the prince loved her and planned to marry her, and she was surprised and saddened: Where were her dwarves, her dearest dwarves? And who broke her fucking coffin?

She missed them, she said, but it was later explained to her that the dwarves were inappropriate companions and now she would be taken to the tall prince's castle and act as a regent. She said, "No thanks," and wanted to go back into the woods until it was also explained that her dwarves had wanted her to have this new life, had provided a rich dowry of jewels and gold, and had let the tall prince take her away so that she could be kept by taller, better people, like her. "And you didn't wake up, after all, until you were with us," the careless servants said. "Your dwarves had done nothing for you."

Thinking maybe that this new plan was for her greater good, she acquiesced. She wed that tall prince. She had sex with him on her wedding night and his size made her gasp, made her cry, and made her bleed.

He had not undone her corset or removed her garments. He had not made a bed of wild flowers below her or pleased her nearly so well as the dwarves, instead flinging up her skirts, taking her quickly with the fashion of a poker to a cow, and then dangled the bloody wedding sheet out the window as proof of her virtue to his awaiting countrymen, who cheered from the courtyard below.

Over the course of that summer and the following fall and winter, her new, court-appointed ladies in waiting schooled her as to how to behave like a princess, before she made any terrible faux pas at the court, telling her what, in this land, was or was not at all the thing. And she lived. On and on, she lived.

Her life felt an endless parenthetical omission to the whisper of pleasure. Her prince came to her then, once a month. He was handsome. He was large. He liked men, but did his duty by her, for God and country. She bore him many attractive princes and princesses.

And our little beautiful Snow Drop, Snow White, Schneewittchen girl — what was her future, past, and present? Well, she, between his visits and her birthings and her duties, had pleasurable dreams of fantastic sex with the dwarves she continued to miss — those she once knew to be generous and good, penetrative but not overmuch, named like the deepest bounties of the hidden, granite-shadowed earth.

Anatomy of a Song

Liesl had walked the ceiling all morning. Well, walked, strode, paced, ranted. An unexpected lightness due to recent weight loss allowed this activity, and she liked the way the stucco poked, without penetrating, her bare feet. She was, however, furious and sad. Below her, on the floor, was a plate she'd placed carefully where no furniture could interfere, and on this was a cluster of fifty or so balloons.

As she walked, or sometimes as she stood staring down from a stillness, because walking threw off her aim, she punctuated her morning dialogue with only the best and most awful parts of the song he'd dedicated to her, and then, throwing a dart at the plate, attempted to pop one of the balloons. Because of the law of random success, she started to think the goodness of each awful comment conceived to rebut the song could be gauged by the deflation or safety of the related balloon.

This song he sent, and its lyrics, seemed to scrape her skin off. "You want back your ex-boyfriend and are fucked up," was the paraphrase, though actual lyrics were otherwise. One toss. Pop. A purple balloon. Pop. Pop. Pop.

But between bouts of balloon violence, in the steps that brought her closer to the chucking place above the plate, she also expressed doubt at her own perceptions, while she thought about how absolutely hot he was, which, because it was shallow to think from her groin, irritated her more.

"'You're so light, I could put you in a vacuum-seal bag meant for sweaters,'" she quoted. "Sucking my air out and putting me in storage?" Pop. A green balloon. "But of course he didn't mean this. No," she muttered, *sotto voce*, thinking of his adorable jeans ass. "Weakness!" she shouted. "Stop right now." But the ass thoughts caused an acceleration to the plate. "Yes, he did mean that. Fucker. I'll have him know, I am more than light or heavy! But I am heavy, damn it. Deep." Pop. A red balloon. A furtive sigh. "And let's think of the anatomy of a song. Verse. Bridge. Chorus. Instrument quality. Which to focus on? He might have meant any. I can't imagine he'd hurt me on purpose."

Toss. Bounce. Blue balloon to carpet. Coupled with irritated glance. "But he is hurtful in other things some-times... Fucker." Pop. Orange balloon. Striding toward left corner where a stained glass fixture hung. "But he's so beautiful. Like this light." She took a moment to admire the light, so festive with blue and tan pieces of alternating glass. The blue balloon had not been popped. These two things seemed somewhat connected. But her hands were empty.

Again she descended to the floor to retrieve darts, and this part of the exercise was just the exhausting refrain of the song, she decided, perhaps the guitar solo or musical interlude. Still, she said, "It's not like I was trying hard to lose all this weight, though granted this ceiling walking is a new and unexpected perk." Striding up the wall, she contemplated the room. Couch. Chair. Oak desk.

Television. Big plate. Small balloons. Oh, missed dart on the floor. Oh well. And would he still come to visit this morning? Did she want him to?

From the ceiling, her hair hung like red vines. The radio played, and another man dedicated a beautiful song to a Leslie. "Fuck you, Leslie," Liesl said, completely aware she was irrational. "But Eitan does love you."

Her shirt kept falling, via gravity, which exposed her black satin bra. Her tits were cold. She felt lightheaded and blood kept rushing to her head. "Then the song said, 'she's infuriating mindless, but hallucinogenic precious'?" Liesl's doorbell rang. Him. After ringing, he knocked. She wondered how she looked upside down.

"And this is my song?" she asked, angrier now he was present. Pop. Pop. Pop. Yellow. Red. Black.

She walked to the water-stain room corner. "Is it remotely possible this song is not about me? He knows how hard I've worked to lose this weight. Okay, correct that; I haven't worked hard — but he knows I've felt strange about it. I'm half my size." She stared down at the plate. Six balloons left. "Regardless, that song was not flattering!" Her last tossed dart bounced to the couch.

He entered. Said, "Hey. What are you doing, babe? Did you get my song?"

"I did. Thanks very much." She stepped toward him, still hovering above. "I am walking on the ceiling. What does it look like I'm doing?"

"Well, come here."

"No."

"Shit. That ceiling walking's brilliant," he said. But he looked at her breasts in her bra, which were smaller than before. Or maybe he was watching her neck pulse. "Get over here."

"No," she said, scaling the wall toward the floor till

she stood horizontal to his vertical, almost at the height of his shoulders. From there she regarded the carpet rather than his eyes.

"It's good to see you," he said, kneeling to look up at her. "Good morning." He reached up for her and kissed her, with his palms on her cheeks. "What are you doing up there anyway? What's with the plate?"

"I was thinking about your song," she said, standing her ground, or, actually, her wall. "Now, I want to get down."

"No one's stopping you," he said. But he was in the way, kneeling where her feet would go, so she couldn't clamber to the floor without him moving. He reached up, encircling her back, putting his hands around it, tilting his chin up, kissing her lips with light pressure.

Beautiful ass, beautiful eyes, she thought.

"Come down," he said. "Now." He worked with gravity, pulling her closer. His hands were heavy everywhere, dragging her down towards the earth, or the carpet, or his body, so disorienting that she didn't even remember falling onto him until later.

These things happened naturally, neither one really listening to the radio that aired what seemed an endless commercial break, though other songs had played. Must have been five or six. But she was still above him, rocking him into another series of sounds.

What You Never Thought You Wanted

K's mother said she was a nymphomaniac, and this telling admission released her from guilt. Thinking about the prude, she yanked on a pair of garnet thigh-highs and considered this evening's satisfaction. The idea of sex had wooed her from the day she was twelve when she had creamed her childish panties with masturbatory wet, read romance novels, and touched herself with sticky fingers stained like dime-store lollipops — cherry, grape, apple — incensed with Lady Eva with her manly rogue. Then, a stuttering click from her mother's bedroom door. Then a disapproving frown. But no matter now. She always came with herself even after men entered her body, but there was something dark in consensual sex, something that threatened to consume her unlike the light of masturbation. She enjoyed the confusion.

In truth, it obsessed her. Tonight she would find a man and take him in the street, but if he didn't prove enough to soothe her ache, she'd immediately take another. "Enough" was a word she understood very little.

Who could possibly have enough? At twenty-two, K had slept with eight hundred and twenty-three men — pretty men, ugly men, fat men, old men, girly men — any men for a "fix." She took them with one leg, one arm, or half a heart...size didn't matter.

What mattered was that they came and came again and nothing slowed her search for such continuous orgasms, orgasms swelling on the tides of others, and blissfully subsiding. She adored watching so many writhing in these spectacular endnote throes, spinning in the vortex that would pull them up or down, but change their world irrefutably, if only for a moment. An attractive girl, she had no trouble getting laid. Her skin was clear and resilient, her eyes gray beads in her cat-like face. Men hated her because she left them. Girls hated her too — those tight-faced, pink-lipped prudes, whispering behind their hands, "Slut, psycho, whore. She's mental. You know that."

When this happened, she flew down highways like a migrating sparrow because she did not resent the cobwebs in their crotches, so why did they resent the nectar in hers? "You make men think that casual sex is okay," a plump girl with a sagging paunch jeered. But her response was: "Have they ever not?"

She masturbated into oblivion that night astride the hotel bed, before getting in her rental car and hitting the asphalt. She thought of that girl often afterwards and wondered why other women would stay with one man when she could use so many. Men were just pawns — sucked off, fucked off, and tossed. Garden-variety junk food. Old or young. The same blasting irons looking for a hole. Still, years ago, she had put ads in the paper seeking monogamy: Young woman willing for stable relationship with man of sustainable erection and steady output. Three times a day, or go away. It's a motto. I don't believe in love.

And what was love, if it doomed her to boredom? She got many responses to her messages, and followed these furtive notes from rich houses along the coast to dark apartments on the south side of inner-cities. She went from town to town, taking money from strangers, floating onto unknown highways like a flesh stick on a come river.

Dental dams, rubbers, alternate contraceptives, dildos, vibrators, butt-plugs, and restraints — these were her tools. She had seen more latex than men who made surgical gloves and picked up her condoms by bulk at local Planned Parenthoods; they were free there, if sadly unlubricated, and if the woman at the counters gaped, she said in reply, "I'm serious. Can I please have more? This is only a week's worth." When the container brimmed — red, green, yellow, blue — she emptied it. Sex was a need, but protection a must.

It wasn't exactly the sex she enjoyed — more the expression of the orgasm. The human face was beautiful and funny as it froze, assuming an ironic grace. She had seen many faces in these throes, so many that sometimes a fix became a blinding collage of fixes, one's graying beard blending with another's blond goatee, one's hard chin paired with another's soft nose. Sometimes, with their permission, she recorded these sessions on a video camera the size of a tape player to watch later. Watching her own face on the reels later, she noted how she never came, though she faked it admirably, and laughed at how her bee-stung lips smiled only afterwards. She was 6'2, with breasts the size of honeydews.

Her hair, long and blond, did not lose its luster even if unwashed. When she took a short man, as was her preference, she placed herself on whatever flat surface might be found (once a cold slab in a mortuary), and felt his tiny feet rub at her calves, his knees near her thighs. She loved how little men seemed like ants feasting on her bounty, the thrill of standing to kiss them goodbye, leaning over them, pecking their questioning brows. Goodbye, Bill. Goodbye, James. Goodbye, _____. Sometimes, they kept her panties and wept, sniffing them when she was gone. To gain lovers in prudish cities, she whored.

If the trick got iffy, she had a knife. "Is it so strange," she asked herself, skipping lanes, speeding toward a college town, "for a woman to take sex and money, if that's what she wants?" But the whores sensed her difference — they worked for money or a hit of crack, while she worked for pure bestial joy. On the day she met Max, she was librarian-prim at a University of Redlands, bored with street-tricks, casing the joint for her next brimming boy. Her breasts in a '50s bra, were concealed by pink angora, and her thighs were encased in a long, tweed skirt that skimmed her knees. Max did not look at her as he strode by, which interested her. He would take work.

She strode among the stacks of books, layers of rotten paper scenting the air, and walked behind him then pushed her hips flush with his legs. Her breasts pinioned his wool-sweatered back. "Excuse me," she said, but he did not move, so she grabbed a random book from a shelf above his head, something about theology, rotated her hips harder against his thighs, then stepped back. He was so still, it was as if he did not notice her until he turned, looked directly at her, and said, "K — that was not wise."

Her real name! She gasped as she stared at his face, tan and swarthy, then said, not too nicely, "Who are you, and how do you know my name?"

"I'm Max," he said. "And you've been waiting for me for a long time, like I've been waiting for you."

Her mouth drooped. Was he a goth-boy with a fetish? A freak? Who cared? He could suck her blood if he wanted to; it might be cold and bitter for all he knew. "Okay, Max," she said, toying with him, "what have I been waiting for?"

"A solid fuck," he said, caressing her face with his voice and looking at her body. "A fuck that pleases you." The front of his pants was stiff, and she felt her skin thrum with his comments. They were so true. So to the point.

"But do you know how to fuck, Max?"

"I know how you like it. Best with a man standing in front of you, best when he shakes as he comes, best when you don't come — and best when you walk away first."

"What else do you know?"

"That you've whored, that you're coming with me to the countryside, and that you need sex, so you won't say no. I also know you have no emotional attachments and you like who you are, but the veneer is so thick, you hardly see the sawdust anymore."

She said, "You think you know a lot."

"Let's go," he said. "Take the fuck or leave it, but I'm leaving. Right now. If you want it, you'll follow."

When she got in his car, a gray station wagon, he yawned, tapping his fingers on the steering wheel. "Glad you chose to come. I've been following you for a long time, but never let you see me until today. Interesting, isn't it?"

He was creepy, but she played along. "Why not let me see you?"

"I couldn't," he said simply, "I wasn't ready," and he drove, his thick hands drumming the steering wheel. She liked his steady silence, his sureness, and his thick hair. She liked the sight of him, stiff in his pants, and that he couldn't have been more than 5'3. Already, she pictured the way she might dominate him. It turned her on to think of him on the floor, licking her patent leather boots, though she did not wear them that day. His eyes scanned the road and returned to her.

He said, turning the wheel, "I want to commit suicide and I want to die in the throes of passion, so you have to help me today. I want your face to be the last I see."

K stared out the window as the landscapes grew rural. "How would I do that?" She thought about her knife.

"I won't hurt you," he said. "You'll have to hurt me. It shouldn't be a problem."

"I want to get out."

"No. You want to stay."

"I do not."

He swiped a hand through his hair. "I've followed you all the way up the coast," he said conversationally. "Past Oregon, past Washington, through Nevada, and back again. At first I was furious. I went crazy with the obsession, then I returned. I realized you needed me. So I'm here. I'm here to help you, K." He stared through her, a wild luster in his eyes. "And I could give you sex five times a day, but since this is a suicide mission, that won't be possible. And you want to see my face that way, the way you crave, don't you? Wouldn't that look be so much better in death?" He made a sharp left into a dense spot of trees.

"Maybe."

"Don't lie. Think of my face, stretched in *la petite mort*, the little death, then the larger death, the final orgasm?"

"You don't know me," she said, digging for the mace in her purse. "But this ride has been fun. Remind me to call Freaks Are Us to come get you. Mind if I take your car out when I leave?" He turned down a road smaller than the first, barely large enough for the car to drive though. Branches scraped the sides of the wagon like iron nails on chalkboards. He did not care. The trees seemed closer, less spaced out, and she fingered the hilt of the knife at her hip, reassured by its firm presence.

He laughed, saying, "Don't be so cautious, K. Your life is funny, really. Lighten up. Besides, you like the look of orgasms because you like the idea of a heart stopping, death and rebirth, but you don't like slow suffering, niggling pain, or disease — that's why the condoms. And you don't understand that most men could snap your neck if they chose to. I could, right now. You never understand real danger. You never have."

"You're wrong," she said, envisioning her blade twisting in his gut. "I've hurt people. I know what I'm capable of."

"You don't even know why you need your fix, and I can tell you. Doesn't that give me an edge? Tell me it doesn't."

The foliage gave way to a small cabin and he swerved to park on an embankment, then said quietly, but firmly, "Get out." The cabin was dusty, filmed with a decade of neglect. A twin-size bed sat in the corner beside an unstocked kitchenette. Only the light from the open door illuminated the main room. A twitch of fear stole over her. If things went poorly, she had never made a will — not that she had much to offer. He walked to a cabinet under the sink and pulled out a bottle of scotch and a glass. "Drink?"

"No."

He poured himself one, and sat in the dark at the tiny kitchen table. "By the way, the station wagon is yours

when you leave. I already signed it over." She concentrated on the door, wondering if he was harmless or
serious. If things went badly, she had her knife, but she
didn't want to kill him. Maiming was fine; killing was not.
Still, even if she hated him, she would fuck him. Hate
fucks were often pleasurable. She got wet considering this,
but said, "I don't want your car. I'll leave it on the road
when I get to the city. I don't keep things from my flings."

"You keep money," he said wryly, tossing his long,
black curls back with his scotch. "You always keep
money."

"Who have you talked to?" Her skin felt like
spiders crawled over it, baby widows traipsing on snow
flesh.

"I know you," he said. "Well. And I know the way
you think from the moment you get up in the morning —
brushing your hair, playing with your face, regretting the
tiny acne scar just above your ear — or the crescent-shaped
scar that's hidden by your hair — and I know what makes
you tick. I know you like being scared, but having control.
A false scare. A mind fuck. Fucking the brain! You love it.
The largest sexual organ."

She shifted as he poured himself another scotch.
"Even now your panties are wet for me. I might be a serial
killer, but you'd fuck me just the same. You'll enjoy this,
just like you'll enjoy killing me." He downed the drink.
"So, enough preliminaries. Take off your clothes. All of
them." She considered his cool face, uncertain what to do,
then yanked at her pink sweater, but he stopped her hands
and whispered, "Slowly. Do it slowly." She stared at her
pearl buttons, white as aspirin down her sweater-front,
and watched them shift, as if they had suddenly become
huge and delicate in her fingers, spongy like mushrooms.
She persevered.

"Look at me," he said. "Let me see your eyes."

When she raised her glance, she felt blood creep along her face and neck and was shocked. She had not blushed since she was thirteen, straddling the old pick-up at her uncle's farm, and she could picture the old man's face, everything around him.

"He had a lot of rabbits," Max said. "He killed them on the white wall in that box of a room, his jeans stinking of blood and sawdust. You hated the smear on that wall, the cages outside the door, and the ax right beside it." She closed her eyes, but he kept talking. "You hated the way the rabbits died without screams, the soft, patchwork quilts, and the taste of rabbit stew. There was something unfair in their silence...in how many died before you ever arrived."

"Who are you?" she asked him.

"Keep working on your sweater," he said. "Get it off." It hung open, so she fingered the pink seams. "I want to tell you that I understand you now," he said. "I can read your mind. At first it was cryptic and had to be decoded. But I've learned the code." He suddenly looked joyous, and she trembled, her knees weak, but she tossed her sweater from her body and moved her hand to her skirt. The zipper snagged as she yanked on it, then broke with a mangled *zirrrsp*. The room smelled like tea, scotch, and sugar, which nauseated her. She pulled at her skirt, but did not peel it down.

"Slowly," he reminded her, removing a rusted knife from a kitchen drawer. "Maybe," he said, reconsidering, "you would prefer to use your own." She felt for the hilt of her blade beneath the waistband of her skirt, the warm black leather of the holster, and she pulled it out, unsheathing it and waiting. He said, "Shhh. Finish undressing. Right now." There was something dulcet in his tone.

Her skirt fell off. When she stood before him in her underwear, he smiled with a soft nostalgic look and said, "Those too. Bra and panties must go, but leave the garter on."

She resisted him, looking at the open door. "No."

"I'm not going to kill you," he said again. "So calm down. Your heart beats like a rabbit's. You can run if you want to, but that would be like when you wanted to run from that cabin in Vermont when you were seventeen; do you remember, K? You didn't run then. Why not? Were you afraid of standing in the road in your underwear, cutting your feet on the rough pebbles and the glass from those broken beer bottles? You were afraid of moving away from him, and anyway, he wouldn't let you go. He didn't deserve you. Not a great memory for a summer vacation...but I'll treat you better. I'll show you. Be naked for me."

She peeled her panties down over her tan legs and let them pool on the ground beneath her. Her heart skittered. Vermont. The truck stop man. The memories came racing back like derailed trains. Max stared at her body, appreciated it. She tried to ignore his voice. She would watch him come and he would be weaker. A nothing. She would not kill him; he could live with his sick self.

"I want to please you today," he said and got on his knees, kissing her thighs; he licked her for a long while, bringing her to orgasm three times before he stood. She felt like someone shot up with morphine.

Looking at his face in the semi-dark, she asked, "Aren't you going to undress?"

"No." He sat on the bed and kissed her neck, the bones of her shoulders, her arms and finally her breasts.

He sucked them, slowly, with his lips wet from her juices. "Don't you," he asked, "wish your first lover had been more careful? You hated the taste of tobacco on his lips, and the knowledge of your aunt in the other room — sickening. Age thirteen — too young. Too young, K."

K said nothing as his mouth traveled over her, but she felt sadness and a desire to be free from him, so pushed him away. She said, though not intending to follow through, "How would you like me to kill you, Max?"

"Your knife," he said, "twist it in my heart."

The room spun like a child's ride, illuminated by old memories, but she wanted her fix. Her eyes slid over the dusty cabin, and she stood, placing the tiny video camera in the corner to film them then walking back to the bed. "You don't mind this, do you?"

"Not at all."

"Let's begin," she said, trying to sound business-like. "Then we can go our separate ways. You don't have to please me again."

"Such a shame," he said. "You are so pretty. I like to please you." He unzipped his pants but did not take off his sweater, and his legs were white like carnations against his oak-colored face. His member sprang free, and it was average length, average width, like a pole from his pubic hair. It looked as stiff as she'd seen it in the library, in the car, but he did not let her touch it until he had her gasping on his fingers, then turned his back to her and rolled on a condom.

He clenched the knife in her hand and said, "At the right time, sweetheart, drive it in." She watched him hover as he entered her, fascinated by the fluidity with how he moved his chilled body. He smelled clean, like honey. "You must be cold," she said. "You feel cold." He did not reply but stroked her thighs as he worked on her, standing where she was seated.

On his face, she surprisingly saw love, so closed her eyes and said, "Don't look at me like that."

"Like what?"

"A puppy dog."

He leaned in and kissed her lashes. "I'll tell you a secret. Do you want to hear it?"

"No."

"I'll tell you anyway. The secret is — you already know me." Her eyelids closed. "No, K! Look at me! Don't you remember?" His voice sounded far off and plaintive. He kissed her stomach, talking into it, his words muffled by her skin.

"I don't know you."

"Remember me from Melrose? That tiny bar with the blue lights? You seduced me and gave me a week in your bed. You could have loved me, but you chose not to. Or, maybe, you couldn't love at all."

"You're lying." She looked at his pitted face, his blotchy skin. She didn't recognize him, and his legs felt like frozen ham hocks beating her thighs. K stared at them, amazed by their pale force as he dropped his head to her shoulder. Near her crotch were patches of dusky and cosmetic olive. She touched them and they rubbed off with oily residue. Lifting her fingers, she smelled the cloying scent she'd been so saturated with and asked, "Why do you wear makeup, Max?"

"Don't you like it?" He didn't stop pounding, and it was odd to see him half nude in a wool sweater, the garment covering his chest and arms as he pistoned his hips into hers, so she could not place his face but kept trying. He appeared to near his climax and asked, "Have I pleased you? Tell me."

"Finish," she said, indicating his bucking hips. "Do it to please me."

"Answer me — are you satisfied?"

"What difference does that make?"

"All of it." He kissed her cheeks and slid his tongue over her ear. It rasped like sharkskin. "You never cared for love," he said, pulling her close, thrusting toward her. His organ throbbed inside her.

"So what? Who are you?"

"I was an artist. Stained glass. You asked me to cut you, remember — the purple shard I took to your belly? Here?"

He wrenched his hand between their slick bodies to touch her scar. "Samuel," she said. "Why the new name? You didn't have to deceive me."

"You wouldn't have done repeat business, right? That's your rule."

"Do you know how crazy you are? Following me across the country. What's wrong with you?"

He looked at her as if she were a recalcitrant child. "Have you been satisfied?"

She knew what he wanted to hear. "Yes — yes. Go harder, finish."

He did not listen, but let his voice rise louder and louder to thud in her ears as his hips moved faster and faster. "I am the only one to please you, and what a relief." His voice trembled as he went on. "But I destroyed myself for a woman who felt nothing. I let you consume me. And you never let us make love. You analyzed yourself and tried to be real, but you never could...I had to be harsh. I had to be cold, or you wouldn't let me near you, but you drove me crazy."

He smoothed his expression and cried softly on her shoulder, drenching her cheeks with murky water from his own face as his fingertips sent lingering caresses down her spine. He massaged her breast, then upped his tempo again, saying, "Bring the knife quickly. I'm ready to go."

"No!"

Staring at her, glaring, he said, "I would have eaten glass for you, K. I clawed my way out of the ground. Kill me." His words came out evenly spaced, thick in her ears. He was a glob of sentiment before her. "Now," he demanded. "Now, use the knife."

She stared incredulously as a small white maggot worked free from his socket, and as she watched his still face, the appearance of his approaching release felt false. He could have stopped at any moment. The worm writhed down his jaw. His face contorted, enraged. "If you don't kill me," he warned, "I'll kill you...but you can do it. So do it." The maggot oozed like a tear to drop onto her shoulder.

"Get away from me," she said. "You don't know me!"

"Yes I do!" he said, so firmly, so confidently, that she reached back and buried the knife in his chest. His expression froze, but not in orgasm. She pushed his heavy mass from her body and climbed out, glaring. His hard white penis stood solid under the yellow rubber, which had almost worked free. Angrily, she yanked off the condom, and a faded piece of newsprint fell from inside it, but inside there was no release, no sticky fluid — it was dry as a hole in the desert, dry as her eyes. His erection remained, unstoppable. She pulled up the stiff wool of his sweater and his underlying shirt until his chest was bare, then stared at her knife, lodged deeply. Nothing came from his wound. She tasted her own vomit as she watched oil leak from the wound near the blade, and she grabbed his wrist, inanely checking his pulse, then peeled back his sleeves to see other wounds, dry marks from an old razor, empty but gaping.

"I knew what you were," she said. "I knew it from the start, but I didn't believe it." She whisked the paper from the floor and touched the old newsprint, pliant and soft. It said: Spurned lover takes life in L.A. loft. Samuel Maximillian. Artist. Age 35.

More maggots appeared, writhing from his other socket as she read, and she recognized the scent of honey and chemicals familiar from her father's funeral. Embalmed, he had no heart then, no fluids. His internal organs had been stripped.

She glared at his face. There was nothing like sex about it. She felt dirty with his love, and on her cheeks were the first traces of wetness in many years. She looked at a rip in her scarlet garter, the redness on white in the dark room.

The clipping fell from her fingers, the word lover smeared with a dusty fingerprint: hers. As she dressed, she saw the evidence of her own earlier release, pale and pure on her panties, and her core was dry but her emotions raged. The camera rolled on.

She wanted to rewind the tape. Would it show him? A bird chirped outside the window, beak pointed toward the dead man's car, which seemed to hold a silent vigil. The bird flew closer, and K stared in its black eyes for a long, long while, then strode into the sun. With a dead man's keys in her hand, she drove away, feeling him writhe inside her — fragments of his mangled flesh claiming her womb. She knew they would not wash free.

He would not leave her, and she could not leave him. So this was love? A piece of forever in her loins and no way to remove it? Blinded by the dull back of her eyelids, she floored the gas, careening forward on asphalt in his borrowed wagon, hitting nothing, letting the car decide the road, and spiraling deeper, deeper into herself.

Not a Creature Was Stirring

The four surviving babies lay on the floor, naked and curled, awaiting our return. Their lips twitched. Feverish, they stared at the wall with dull eyes. Their unprotected skin did not keep out the draft, and other squatters hovered, waiting for their death. One crazy drunkard spun in circles on the sawdust. "A plague on them," he kept saying, "a plague!" Through the wall, the house-mates spoke.

"Damn it! We can't get rid of them," the man said, "I'd like to shoot every one."

"We can't kill them," the woman replied. "I don't believe in cruelty. And we've had no luck at making them leave."

"We can kill them. Useless scourge of humanity."

"No. They're starving."

"Not bloody likely when they steal our food."

"I don't know what to tell you."

"Tell me, 'Derrick, we need to do whatever we can to get this filth out of our house. Derrick, it's not okay for them to live across the wall from us. Derrick, I love you more than I love my liberal human rights/animal rights/ vegetarianism and can make this exception for you.' And say it soon. The smell of their shit is making me ill."

"No."

The man sighed and rubbed his forehead and the woman glared. It seemed a habitual argument, never resolved and never quite forgiven. The woman began to cry. I watched her pull her sweater closer. "Hush," the man called Derrick said, "Hush." He put his arm around her and they walked, slumped against each other, from the kitchen. Weeks before, I had been in their bedroom. Her undergarments were boxed in a closet and stank of sweat. I had crawled into their cupboards and waded through their clothes. They were old and unsorted. Beneath their drawers were bottles of soap and medicine. Nothing I wanted. Then we had moved behind the kitchen.

"Hurry up and get out," Xavier ordered. His body shook, his heart beat quickly, and his eyes bulged. We waited, listening for the distant retreat of footsteps. I thought about the babies and wondered what we could take. A crust of garlic bread sat on the table. I scooped up the crumbs, filling my mouth.

"They have so much," I said, "I don't understand why they can't spare any."

"They don't care how much they have...only how to keep it all to themselves. Hurry." We ran across the tile, then went to the cupboards. We stuffed our faces and ran to the hiding place. When we arrived back, a baby had been stolen. "Which one of you took him?" Xavier said. "Which one of you?" He bared his teeth and ran at the closest cluster of squatters, looking fierce. They backed away.

One continued to sniff glue and the other stared at the wood planks. From the passageway came the sound of a small body dragging. It was dark in the passage; there were so many routes that might have been taken. "We didn't," they echoed, "maybe a rat took him!" The smell of flesh was strong in the air.

"What did you bring back?" the glue sniffer asked. "Any bread? Sugar?" I sat beside the remaining babies, feeding them, regurgitating the bread. Doors inside the house slammed. The house-mates argued.

"I am not giving money to the Panda exhibit."

"Ten bucks a month."

"No. Free the pandas. Free the bears. Free the orangutans. What's next? Free the roaches?"

"Derrick," the woman said, voice stern, "I am giving them ten dollars. It's Christmas Eve and I am giving them ten dollars."

"No mail tomorrow. Maybe by then you'll have changed your mind."

Xavier turned from the others and came to me. "Shh. Nothing can be done," he said, "we should have moved to a more private place. Maybe we could find a barn. What do they expect, Linda? They want us out. It's December. We don't stand a chance here in New Hampshire."

"We'll be fine," I said. "We could live behind a restaurant." My nose twitched. "I hate this town. Did I tell you what my name means in Spanish? Beautiful. That's what I heard."

"Your ears are beautiful," he agreed.

"Thank you."

"I'm going back," he said.

"Please don't."

"We couldn't carry enough the first time. I need to go."

He looked so handsome, though he was shaking.

His dark eyes beamed at me. "It's not enough what we brought back, " he said again, then left.

When he returned, he had another mouthful of food. "They came in," he said. "I hid in the cabinet. I found one of the sniffers there. Dead. Neck snapped. Good thing, too. I was about to get some of that food. Linda, if you see the wood traps that have an X on them, stay away. I don't care what's on it. Maybe tomorrow we can search out a new place."

"What about the cats and the owls?"

"I'll go first and you follow."

"How can I follow with the babies in tow? We'll have to stay longer."

"If that's what you want."

"It is. I'm tired. Maybe I'll sleep for a bit."

"You sleep. I'll stay up."

The next day, I found another baby had died. To keep him from the others, Xavier ate him. We huddled close to those remaining and slept. Later, Derrick, in the hallway, shouted to the woman, "Ha! I caught one! I caught one! Ten more and this place will be rid of them. I'll put out the pellets tonight."

The next day, the passageway was littered with blue pellets. I walked past and saw the other squatters rapidly filling their faces. The babies were hungry again. The pellets smelled delicious. I wondered if they would taste like peanut butter or honey. Xavier met me beside the babies. He had already eaten several pellets and had begun to complain of thirst. A blue film was on his lips. "Are they good?" I asked. "Should I feed the babies with them? Maybe this is the house-mates way of sharing. Maybe, they will give us these if we don't steal from their kitchen."

"They're good," he said. "Have some."

I sniffed the pellets. They smelled like wildflowers,

or maybe sex. I ate them and found I could not eat enough. I followed the trail; the more I ate, the better they tasted. A ferric flavor coated my throat. Hours passed. Xavier began to clutch his face and scratch at himself. We ran to exit the house, searching for water. Our stomachs felt ripped open by burrs.

The babies died first, poisoned by the pellets. They could not be carried. Xavier made it outside and looked for water. He twirled in the cold, disoriented. The other squatters were knelt over on the pavement and blood leaked from their eyes and ears — every orifice. The quiet slaughter was deafening. The colony of squatters were nearly all there, whiskers twitching and mouths gaping open.

From inside the house, I heard the woman say, "You kill something because you are afraid it will steal from you. You kill something because it is weaker and lesser than you. You kill and you kill and you kill and you feel nothing."

"I hate them," Xavier said. "Lousy sons of bitches."

"They were only mice, " Derrick said. "Mice don't think. Mice aren't human. They do nothing but eat at the walls and contaminate what's ours. They drop the property value."

The ground on the walkway was icy and slick. We licked it frantically, trying to lap up the wet water where it melted. It tasted of salt. Outside the snow fell in drifts. The heat in our throats increased as our temperatures dropped. He choked. I could do nothing but lay down beside him and keep warm.

Xavier's whiskers brushed my cheek. Blood flowed from his eyes. He stiffened. I couldn't move. I thought about the babies. I wondered how, with so much snow, there could never be enough water to drink.

"I don't like it," the woman said. "I still don't like it." The man sighed and rubbed his forehead and the woman glared. I saw them as I glided past their window — watched their smooth pink faces. I did not care, was glassy-eyed, clean, free of the weight of my body, free to take up space away from them and that quiet house. I stared at the sky until the burning feeling died and I floated up into the hot red clouds.

The sky was twenty and three hundred degrees at once.

"Besides," Derrick said. "You told me I could handle it. This is the way things are done. They don't suffer. Of course they don't suffer. They just run outside and fall asleep."

Come, Come Blackbird

It is ten minutes to midnight in SouthBend, but this is no fairy tale. There's no coach, and there's no prince for miles. It's late, a night with a deceptively light sky, and Fionn tends her hearth in a dark home where only a small fire burns. Her heart is angry and her man is mean. Though this would qualify as understatement, it is no exception.

A baby cries in the distance, this distance more mental than physical, Fionn's sweet girl floundering straight down the cobblestone hall Fionn walks with bare feet. The mommy begins humming even before she even reaches the child's door, soothing then lifting her small girl into her arms and nuzzling the infant's doughy face.

"Now you pretend you didn't hear daddy yelling, all right, angel?" she asks, though the child is so young it is more about her motherly cooed tone than any meaning to the words. Fionn keeps her voice low. "No yelling between us," she mutters. "Promise? Don't forget to swear. Fucksake."

The soothed babe smiles. Fionn puts her down in

the crib for a second, spins, and her dress has altered to the cloth of a princess. No need to wait till midnight, child. It's a blue dress now, blue as the Aegean sea. Long and covered with seed pearls in the shapes of roses and pears.

"If he knew I still did this here, now, all the time," she tells the child, "and if he could, he would take my ability away too, like he takes everything I love. Shoves it into boxes or throws it in the yard bin for the dogs — like the trash, like the bones! But he's gone now, baby. Want to see another dress? Look what your mama can do!"

She spins and wears red velvet embellished with gold rope, low cut, the stuffed head of a lion sewn into the sweep.

The baby laughs.

"Don't worry," she tells the baby. "I didn't really kill a lion for this."

In this day with strange magic, Fionn loves her skill of self-wardrobing. It's a weak magic, as magics go — better to be able to make televisions or gold watches out of thin air — and her dresses each disappear at midnight, but no magic should be discarded. "I should have known I would never keep a love hot as coals, baby," she says then, watching her child watching her back. "Mama started as a whore for her own father, then touch slut for the relatives at family parties who watched as she remained unprotected — but you won't be done that way! Don't tell anyone that old story either. This is our secret! Not that grandmama's love was ever given me — a boy's name she offered! And what did my twin get — Fiona? So I was never the favorite and my twin rips me up, has what I need and what I want — but you, you will be the favorite, Crystal! That's why I called you Crystal, so no-one could speak ill of you." She picks the baby up again, cooing, "You're so shiny. And it's quiet here in the house now that our man's gone. Sometimes I wish every man would just stay gone. This is why I hold you so much," but the child tucks her head into Fionn's neck and sleeps. Fionn, still humming intermittently, says, "You'll sleep all night now; not to worry — all night, Crystal, and no one will bother you. Mommy can never sleep."

Her mean man returns. She can almost taste the hair of his beard. The force of his kiss. "Fionn? Fionn? I left my keys here. Came to get them, but I'm leaving again." The sound of his voice chills her, his shoes and heavy footfalls.

She steps out of the infant's room. "I'm here," she says, confirming his unasked question.

They stare in the hall. She does not worry that he will hit her because he isn't violent, but she wonders where the kindness in his eyes has gone — and where he left it. "You going to try and do something useful while I'm gone?" he asks, staring her up and down, speaking with his deep, measured tone.

"I'm watching the baby," she says. "That's useful. You like my dress?"

"Mind tricks!" he says. "The dress will be gone in a minute and then what? Rags again, Fionn. You'll be wearing rags."

"That's cruel," she says.

"I'm not trying to hurt you," he says. "But you are always wearing rags. Just because people can look at you all day long in a fancy dress doesn't mean it doesn't disappear at midnight. This is why you should go back with the gypsies if you no longer want my protection, because only travelling sales people can make millions overnight with your fancy gowns, but your product is so good that when it disappeared they would hunt you down if you stayed — all those angry people cheated to find only air in exchange for your dresses after midnight. Thief, they'd call you. Deceiver. And I've tried to think of a way we can sell your magic—"

"Kind. Kind of you," Fionn interrupts.

"But it's not coming to me, so you're a useless wife. All you ever want is to walk around the fields, stand in tall grass in the rain, touch yourself here with the door locked, or sit smothering yourself in the bath."

"You never touch me anymore," she argues. "Unless you're angry. I am alive. What am I supposed to do? If you didn't lock me in so much…"

"I protect you," he replies.

"You defeat me."

"Yes, and you leave me cold," he says. "Why would I touch you? I didn't hold your past against you, but now I can hardly look at you."

She touches the hem of her dress, creates the faces of moles all along its trim. She turns to the window. "You used to touch me."

"You hadn't sold me out then," he replies. "You hadn't permitted what you later permitted."

"So, what did I do?" she asks. "Can you be specific? How did I lose you? In and out of this house, you work all the time. I'm not permitted to take lovers, but you won't even give me the slightest comfort?"

The clock tolls twelve.

"This is not a fairy tale, Fionn."

"And what is your fairy tale magic, Jonathan? Your magic used to be your patience and your kindness. That you could make people smile. I think it's a gone magic. I think you lost it somewhere."

"I think we should stop talking," he says. "We'll say yet more we didn't mean."

"Go dream your fantasy, Fionn, you say — but

don't endanger us? We'll I am tired of dreaming in this cold house. Give me something, darling. Anything."

"I gave you a child," he replies.

"Reluctantly, but thank you. Who will I talk to when she grows old enough that she understands my words?"

"You can make friends; you always have."

"Out here in the nowhere?"

"Anywhere, my dear."

"Cold, cold," she says. "I'm about to freeze."

Jonathan turns on his heel. "Your dress has just turned to rags, to tatters," he says. "Look at you now. So. Well. Make another dress. Oh, except you can't do that until the sun comes up, right? Poor Fionn."

Fionn stands before him and says, "Cold. Cold. Cold. Cold." She drops the rags like garments from her body. Luminous pale in moonlight, in starlight, her white full shape and dark hair create a vision by the window. She stands up nude and proud, nipples outthrust, glaring at him. "You can't tell me you don't want me," she says as she watches his desire rise. It's always there when she's nude, simmering. "Should we make another baby, Jonathan? Right now? Here on the floor? Among the rushes and the thyme?"

He's drawn, she knows, but resists. "No," he says, pulling her in hard to kiss her in a way that punishes. "No." And walks out.

She checks back on the baby. Still sleeping. Whispers: "This is what happens, baby, when you don't know what you get before you let a man lock you down. It's terrible."

Still naked, she shivers. "Friends, Jonathan?" she says to his absence. "Who will come get me? We live so far away." She shakes her head. "Here is an abomination. You are all I have, baby!" she whispers fervently. And she walks to the hearth to tend the fire, naked, regardless of sparks. She could put on her rags again, but they make no sense and no difference. A blackbird arrives at her windowsill. The baby sleeps. The blackbird whistles.

She sees a spot of red on his shoulder. "Oh, look at you, redwing," she says. "Look how beautiful! Did you get lost among the cattails and then find your way here?"

He tilts his head, though she doesn't expect a response. She opens the window. He lands on her outstretched fingers, making one bleed. She strokes the blood red patch on his wing. "I wish Crystal could see you," she says.

"Crystal can see me, Fionn," he replies.

While she is still gaping, he turns into a man, similarly naked, but more with muted human shades of flesh and hair. "It's my magic," he says. "I can be a bird. I can be a man. Though no one can touch me when I'm human. This part is the illusion. Like your dresses are mist after midnight."

"Oh," Fionn says.

He settles in. They talk. It turns out that he has been watching her for days. It turns out he has heard each thing she's said. It turns out he has one more magic skill to offer. "Want to fly?" he asks. "I can take one forlorn girl up in the sky with me, but only for a brief while."

"Yes," she says. "Yes. Me."

The window is open. He touches her wrist with his beak and she becomes a streaky brown female blackbird. When he speaks to her now, it is in blackbird, but because she is a blackbird, she can still understand.

"Learning to fly is hard," he trebles. "Careful now. Watch my wings! Good. Follow the air. Feel it! Let the current ride beneath you. Yes! Very good! But we can only be out briefly, as making myself a human and then a human into a bird exhausts me, but I'll be back, Fionn. Soon. We'll talk again. Let's aim for the window."

They fly. She and he fly out above the telephone wires and into the moonlight. He sings a tumbling song. She loves his song. She sings and tumbles.

Soon enough, they return. It's long after midnight now, at least an hour. "I have to stay with my man," she tells the blackbird. "With my baby, too. But thank you for the flight. It was a beautiful thing, flight. You're a beautiful bird."

"You were always capable of flying, Fionn," the blackbird replies. "And me, I'm just a blackbird."

"My heart is so angry and my man is so mean," she confesses. "I love him, but he doesn't seem to love me anymore. He hates my magic and has none of his own."

"Does he envy you your magic?" blackbird asks. "I only have two magics. But they are good, aren't they? I live in that tree right there, lady. You see it? Where the red and green leaves alternate. You can see it from your window. Look for me one day. I will come to see you dressing. And then we can — we can wait and see."

It's like the blackbird might say more, but he does not. He flies out the window and is gone. For a good hour, she says nothing. She checks on Crystal. She licks the rusty blood from her finger and remembers the wind beneath her wings, even when her mean man comes home. Her arms feel like wings. She stands in rags at two in the morning, stretching her arms to either side, and thinks about how tomorrow she will think up gorgeous dresses that have birds embroidered all over them.

No more moles. No more lions. She will wear a dress of flaming herons first, to get blackbird's attention. She will blow a kiss out the window at her little pet and invite him to sit upon her shoulder. She will dance with this bird man, in the air or on the ground. Lots of fun things will happen.

But this is no fairy tale.

At three in the morning, her mean man comes home. He gets into bed beside her, making sure to avoid touching any plane of her. He rolls away, says nothing. He does not need to speak to hurt her. Speech is an old trick; he trades now in silences. Passive aggression post-wooing.

But she closes her eyes then, laying down beside him for just an instant before deciding instead to stand. She keeps standing until the purring rumble of his snores is full enough to believe — running her nails up and down her flesh as if to score herself with talons — thinking clearly now, thinking heartfully, carefully remembering blackbird's red feathers and the body of her flight.

How To Rescue A Drowning Man

These are survival directives:

1. First, stop the boat.

We know you can hardly imagine this is necessary to state here, but it is. How else will you save the drowning man? You cannot idly move forward if the scene that needs remedy is behind you, right? Okay, stop the boat.

I don't know how you do that. Push whatever red button you can find. You should stop soon.

2. Second, enter the water.

Yes, it is factual: You cannot fly through the air to save something submerged in water. This is good to know, isn't it? A little practical tip about saving someone drowning, kind of like, Turn the stove on if you want hot soup. Is that ridiculous to go into? Perhaps so, but survival directives must state and restate the obvious.

3. Third, perform your best Double Armpit Tow.

The trouble is, you must remember exactly how to do this. It involves throwing an arm across the top of a victim's chest and letting the victim's arms hang over your arm as you are sideways in the water, letting that victim's weight hang upon your body as you swim. If the victim is small, you can do this easily. If the victim is large, you must re-evaluate the situation, think things like: How much do you want to save this victim? Was this victim a good person? What if they drown you since you cannot swim that well, or what if you drop them? Do you go back later and pick them up? Does it matter if the victim is already dead?

All things are possible, including drownings and droppings. And remember Step 2 — enter the water. If you are in the water, being pulled down by some asshole, you cannot breathe the water. You will have left the confines of your safe little boat to perform this rescue. On second thought, turn back! Turn back now. Okay — no. Disregard that; it was the voice of panic.

But what if someone fails to do Step 1 correctly as you are busy rescuing the victim? What if they do Step 1, but only momentarily, and then you and the victim are left in that water to die a miserable, shark-bitten death? There is nothing that clearly states in Step 1: Keep that boat stopped until rescue is complete. All things not stated cannot be implied. Do you trust the others on that boat?

Maybe you should consider a few more things before embarking upon actual rescue, like: Is the victim hot — not stove hot, idiot. Beauty hot. Will this be a triumph to save this person (perhaps they are some Nobel laureate), or are you risking your life to rescue an idiot no less idiotic than yourself? How badly do you want this rescue? Will you get sex for it later?

Also, importantly, what will you do if your Double Armpit Tow fails? What if the rescuee starts flailing and falling? What if you drop them and they sink like a rock? Do you re-evaluate your position then, too? After all, if you couldn't hold them once, you may not be able to hold them the next time if you do attempt recovery. Really, should you even get off the boat? The boat is very warm. The boat is very safe. Nice boat. Dry boat. Happy boat.

But, attention — you must do what's right. Stop being so selfish! There is a body in the water, after all — SO rescue, rescue, RESCUE that man, you worm! Now consult Step 4.

4. Fourth, tow the victim to safety.

Using a sidestroke kick or a breast-stroke, provided you have not dropped the victim, swim him or her back to the boat or to the shore. If you do not know what those strokes are, I do not have time to explain them. Actually, I do not know either. Please, I'm a technical writer paid to write tons of this bullshit, only today — well, today I feel a little colorful. Oh, and I hate my boss. But back to the saving. The strokes. Don't know them. Sorry. Improvise.

Are you ready to rescue? Go! Yes! Save! Still, what if you are saving and the victim is wearing on you, struggling with you, wailing or crying and trying to clutch at you? Shouldn't you have been told: "Instruct the victim to shut the fuck up and go along for the ride"? If you weren't told this, how do you deal with it?

Okay, just in case...

5. Fifth, instruct the victim to shut the fuck up and go along for the ride.

This whole saving thing is a little like love, isn't it — similarly (helplessly) underdocumented?

Dangerous!

With negligible rewards. An eternal struggle. And again, what if the victim makes you their victim as you are de-victimizing him or her? Are you that "stunning young person who" — imagine a newscaster's voice here — "died a tragic death today, attempting a rescue and recovery from the _____ Ocean"? Or did such towing make you someone's hero? Again, is the victim hot? Will you get sex for this rescue later? These are the serious questions.

Oh, and this version of How to Rescue a Drowning Man will never be published. I intend to use it, right now, to get me fired. Just consider it the subliminal version of the other overt version.

Then, go. Off that boat. Meet that victim. *Ready...* *Set...* Fuck off, boss! Deep breath...now *Dive!*

The Museum of Solitude

The Museum of Solitude is currently located in New York, starred reckless city of the millions who do not sleep. It is situated on a dark city block where, amid the peal of cab horns, side by side, rest a Museum of Sex with bone corpses fornicating and a shoddy silver dinner cart of multi-ethnic street food, located crossways from a health food restaurant that does not serve skim, soy, rice, almond, or anything but whole cow secretions boiled for sudden lattes.

It boasts no front door, which suggests you must sidle in, entering through the side panels that resemble brick walls. Of course, you have to pay each time you enter. Discovering has costs, costs.

Its price is your sacrifice, your time removed, your time with the attendant. How many times will you enter? Is there a limit? You have an addictive personality, so you aren't sure you won't max out. You sit in a hotel lobby.

"Go down and be with the people," others advise on your tapped out personal computing screen, but the Museum of Solitude beckons. You walk the line. Its attendant, neat and clean, who is possibly yourself, demands her tribute and flings open the impossible entry like you might be late amid your meanderings or infernal rush.

Inside, all the exhibits float on white screens or empty walls. Anything can set them off. You can think that thought again. You could spend hours here. The air is conditioned to suit comfortable browsing.

You are not sure what you are looking for, browsing, perhaps for an artifact from your childhood, one thrown, as if accidentally, to the floor of your childhood room. Anything similar initiates experience. Look! Is it the black sparkly bear whose eyes fell out when you loved him too much? An old backpack with broken zippers upon which you wrote _____ and _____ Forever?

Sure. The garnet garter belt you chucked on the motorway, the misplaced Verlaine library book lost and unread, the diary of a future one could not obtain, twelve falling tears from two ex-boyfriends who said they'd never cry. Oh, great room! Great place of revelation! You visit the Statue of Liberty, and then come back. All has a green cast.

Look around. It's mystifying, fatalistic narcissism replete with replicating memorabilia. Here. You are all here—today, now, always, recovered—in the city that never sleeps, in a borough where a weird pearl horn juts out from the outer wall of a red hotel, though faintly you hear cries of others remonstrating, "Look at me! Look at me!"

You vaguely want to, but are afraid you have grown translucent and if you have grown translucent, what is the point of looking at others who can see the sprawled cityscape behind you? "I cannot!" you will tell them, if you are insolent, "I am observing art here and now, the art of my own hysterical decline!" Hysterical, for laughs, you leave interpretively open—but it is not funny, ha ha. They don't like this. They try harder to get your attention.

(It's a big loud city, after all. Can you truly be so insular?)

"I will bare my attractive skin for you," they say, the vagabonds, total sluts, crime monkeys, but you cannot be reached while concentrating, unless rudely. Someone must poke you, prod, get in deep.

Shifting white scrims become the tips of their nipples. Movies of seismic interjections show on flat panes. Look up. Look down. It's the movies, you on every screen.

"Nice rack," you'll tell your teenage self who gyrates on a stock broker. She looks back and winks, murmurs, "I hate this asshole."

Somebody shouts out from a street corner, "Hey, lady!" Several somebodies.

The attendant, who both is and is not you, hollers from the museum, "Get the fuck out. Can't you see she's trying to be alone?"

Most of the time they listen, retreating behind new scrims that haze and obliterate the shadow horde. Come on, you've seen them. You sigh, relieved, amazed, perplexed you could be here in New York of all places, yet finding the kind of alone you had only imagined! It is like being the last spore on a dandelion before a wish—yet the horde is the same. Will you find a piece of Los Angeles here? Providence? Rome?

In between visits, at the Museum of Sex you learn more about that porn star, what's his name, Jeremy something, he had a big ..., who got AIDS, who self-fellatiated?

"Am I really here?" you ask. The museum warms. In it, there is now a replica of New York. You remember reading a book by a moody guy in Central Park a year ago, how the dark dirt below a tree got all over your bare back and you had to shower before meeting a friend. You remember a trip on a subway to Coney Island. You remember the carneys and nearly forget how you stood on the board walk searching for friends who'd gone swimming in the gray-green sea. There was a man you sought. Somewhere. Possibly on a Sunday, but he's absent. He now won't exist. Can you picture the decal on his t-shirt, some rock band or something? No, you don't know what you picture. He might be a woman. In a gray dress the color of an old woman's tooth.

"You are really here," the attendant says.

"For what?" you ask.

She shrugs, replies, "What do you want?"

"I don't know," you admit.

"That's the problem," she replies. "Idiot. The closer you are to what you want, the more you are aware how not having it stabs your space. The space of ambiguities is worse still, amorphous, hovering between wanting and taking."

You thank her. This soothes and chafes! There is something you concretely want or wanted here in New York, but what—what? You've forgotten. Salami! That must be it. A t-shirt. A postcard. You stroll. On the skyline, you envision blue parachuters sliding down through clouds at the speed of honey—they join the scrims, surviving, dropping far off. The museum gets tiresome, but even when you leave, even when you return to the pulse and the tide of bodies, some of whom stomp and do modern ephemeral Irish dance, nude, evoking the seventies; some of whom point the way to another museum of lab rats; some of whom you saw in the porn place where female Bonobo monkeys pounded inflamed pink genitals on video while others, both male, alternated fellatio—you are still everywhere inside your own personal nowhere.

"Sucks like that, this place," the attendant says.

A city is just a city, you think in reply. A sight, a sight. A person, a person. A history, an alternate mystery in a choose your own adventure. In the game of Life, one pink peg and one blue mean couple. More mean family. Pair bonding means additional complications.

Reflecting back, then forward, you realize the monkeys incapable of procreating captivate your brain until the attendant at the Museum of Solitude raps on your head. "I remind you," she states, quite officious when you grow so briefly fascinated with monkey intercourse that you definitively decide you *are indeed* a rare pink monkey. "You *are not* a monkey. You are a human being, a human girl, and you know what that means?"

"Rejection, monotony, more work with less pay, subjugation, being lied to, falling down," you reply. These are usually the right answers.

"Wrong," she says.

"Then I am a monkey," you say. "Pounding my swollen clit on the wall." To the indignant set of your face, she glares. You say you are sorry. Very, very sorry.

You are not sorry, but you wait and stare dumbly, hoping she will tell you what it means now, what it all means.

She does not. She laughs. When she does so, you tell her that, frankly, you do not know what it means, nor do you have any hope of knowing what it means. You are sick of talking heads and false intellectuals, the morally bankrupt. You tell her you are mildly horny but wildly dismayed she is present because you don't want her to *watch you* masturbate—because masturbation is private, no one can harm you—and this is a *new* museum, the sex one with the monkeys, which is far better than hers, in its *different* location, not where she should curate, so is she following you? You might be wheedling, yet ask: Is she your doppelganger? Have two museums blended?

The "Museum of Solitude does not belong in the Museum of Sex," you state pugnaciously, like saying so will make it so.

"Doesn't it?" she asks. "Lots of solitude in sex." On your screens floats the licentious past of your mind wandering—going somewhere far away, into the shocking moments when your eyes met a lover's eyes to find his unoccupied, or ones where your body had claimed you, shaking, shivering, post-orgasmic, until there was no you, only the painful possibility of a phantom you returning. Apartment doors closing. Pants buttoned. Something cruel said. More than once. The views of your lovers entwined with someone else. The sound of a futile wishing that resembled the tremulous words: "Will you? Can you be true?"

"Is anything true anymore?" you ask her.

After she laughs again for quite some time, she looks you in the eye and says, "The Museum of Solitude is the only true place—but it's everywhere. Everywhere is fair game, including the collaborative art space of city, you redundant hick; visualize my museum migrating, starting in a small closed room where the artifacts expand until the sky's the limit. Transpose, for example, the image of the ones who have hurt you and free-associate. Perhaps now you see them on the back of an NYC cab driver's head. Later you see them in a spoon. Via imagining that they see you, as you see you, reflected, perhaps you can conceive of some strange space from which they might actually look back, from within that spooned reflection — and yet again you pass the ticker tape into my museum, yet again you enter the static of both the fermented past, fluctuations of yesterday, and the newly ostracizing now!"

She's so fucking smart. Along with the cab horns, this bothers you. "Get out of my spoon," you say.

"Spoon?" she replies. "What spoon?"

"I am—"

"Reluctant? Five fathoms deep? Not ready for what you have to tell me?" she finishes your sentence, three different ways.

As you look on, you realize you can see the Empire State Building from 5th Avenue, like a big monkey cock. Phallic. Conical. Made for the biggest female monkey on the planet. Maybe a male monkey.

She walks beside you now, muttering, "Haven't you imagined someone other than a partner while having sex? Used one body to provide sensation while dreaming another?"

"Yes," you admit.

You and she walk the crowd. "See here," she says. "Here, you are alone again. More alone than when alone. That's why you hate those couples, the ones so close."

You agree silently yet completely. "I should have been them," you say. "Life didn't oblige." The walls around you are invisible but inflexible now. Then someone knocks you down. They try to take your purse. You punch them in the eye. There is a mad look in your glare. They run.

"Does it really matter where you are if you can't control when?" she asks, barely registering you have been mugged—or that someone tried to take from you again.

You say nothing, but she is having a grand old time and points to the subway stairs, says, "Let's go down. I'm sorry: You didn't really get mugged or almost mugged. That was a simulation of life's metaphorical intent. All faces that aren't familiar are monstrous as the bumps of the monkey's swollen genitals, are they not? The silver cart gyro sandwich shot with cream, the buildings, tall, looming, the shorter taxi cabs? All are the same filler, but don't fret. The Museum of Solitude welcomes you in at all hours, in all places, endlessly inclusive!"

You picture a nice quite room, all white. It's a place you imagine but hardly find. "Once," you say. "Once I didn't feel alone—for a long time. I was done with discovering me—because I had another museum to study. His museum. I went there on a Sunday, like attending a church. He lived in a mess of ruins. I liked to touch them. It was scary, but I never got lost in myself. Sharing solitude museums advanced my future. I did not live in my past. And then he locked his door. I think it was here. In New York. Was it here?"

"You can never be sure," the attendant says, "that what you thought you saw in his shared museum was actually there, rather than what he chose to represent. Just as he might have been fooled that what he thought he saw in your museum was true—because he could not see it as you or I see it. The experience of the Museum of Solitude is intensely personal. Museums do not combine. And did you know for a fact that his future advanced too? Maybe it didn't. Maybe there are nothing but vipers and snakes in his screens, black currents, fever dreams, but that is the way that it always was. His toxin was the dream."

"New York," you say. "I'm in New York now and dreaming of L.A. So I am not in New York at all. I hover, and the Museum of Solitude follows me."

"Today it's legitimately in New York, the city that never sleeps," the attendant says, bored, "because you came here. But maybe you will sleep. If you don't, it continues. Still, don't wake up if you can't handle where you are."

"Get out of my head," you shout, and she retreats. You call your friends for an intervention, muttering only, "So alone, so alone. Miss you. Please. Save me."

They give comfort. "Oh, wow! In New York! So fabulous! Go to clubs! Have flings! Take lots of pictures!"

She hates them, the attendant, and frowns. When their voices rush in, she vanishes, and you mentally touch their hands, their arms, their feet, their faces, saying, "Welcome! Welcome, friends!" You decide you want sex acts with a flagpole or a rack of beef. Oral. Otherwise.

From far away, voices that are not yours assure you of your reality. "A flagpole? What? Beef? Tall guy. Dark guy. Guy." Perhaps they come from Louisiana, Oregon, Washington State. You are grateful. You have no real, long-term friends in New York, or you would visit them. They would visit you.

You would not be alone. The next time you come to the museum, however, ruminating over the night's two a.m. coffee, it will have been updated with new exhibits. Friends' installations will have grown. It will be a cheerier place.

You can have homemade oatmeal and apples. Whomever you spent the most quality time with will appear prominently. How cheerful the museum is after friends come! You write on your hand with a pen, in case you forget: *Call more friends.*

But soon you walk deeper again to find the same walls of images you've always seen, the ones that scare and sadden you, where the friends are only glimpses. Sometimes, you observe sights that hurt with the delicious pang of forcefully extinguished removal.

"How long has this museum existed?" you ask the attendant.

"As long as you have," she says. "As long as you

will." She has a new look, like a stewardess in royal blue, with a white hat. There is something rancid about her smug demeanor.

You're getting exhausted from too much old news. Projecting a future day, because you haven't slept for two days and travel next to Chicago, you imagine seeing her there. You imagine one million trips from now and her in every city. She'll be lost in the silver of skyscrapers or found in the dark of a muggy Texas night.

Of course, you admit, she's at home too—not just when you leave here, perhaps, but in every homelike reflection. There is comfort in that reliability and a measure of despair. Today, you look again at the Empire State Building, which is a probe. No, wait, an organ grinder! No, wait, a building that looks like a tinsel star crumpled up. There are lots of them, these buildings, with spaces of sky. They all are waiting, but when you see them like this, you realize, like large plots of rising real estate that are not so different from those at home, why even bother to leave one place for another?

They are all the same. Who is here? You look at your hands: *Call your friends.* You would, except your phone—it's dead.

"The Museum of Solitude welcomes you," the attendant says, again at your side. You consult the narrative placard so that you may know where you are in the current exhibit. This is your head, remapping. "New York City, Historical Site of Former Damage," it reads. Bonobo femme monkeys clit-pound with swinging hips. You remember that the shape of a male Bonobo monkey's penis is conical. Where are you today? Liberty. At a statue.

Today, you are still in New York City.

You are nowhere. You are on top of a rickety bunk bed in a hostel room of a nicer hotel, turning in your sheets with one raspy blanket, clutching your black leather purse because you don't want it stolen. The cabs honk all night long, their peals echoing and ricocheting up the sides of buildings like they can't escape. You shiver, tasting lamb and cream.

You visit the Rectitude and Resolution rooms of the Museum of Solitude again, tired of window-shopping Trauma Aisles. The attendant rushes to yank you into the door of your Highest Focal Points, sights you've seen again and again. "Come in," she says. "Come in. Come in. Come in. There is something to see!" She laughs. She keeps laughing and utters, "Don't hesitate. I'll show you things that have most affected you — as far back as birth. Regard me. I'm your docent. Put the headset on if you don't want to lip-read. Wherever you are, be ready. Step forward. We're holding the present in the past for the next twelve hours or years. As long as you'd like! So, welcome. Welcome, Visitor! Regard your life with awe."

You Are One Click Away from Pictures of Nude Girls

Everywhere Larry looks he sees cunt, the dream of it, the salty murmur of satisfaction. It has become overwhelming, with its silver-pink purse unveiled at every glance, traipsing from every corner. Unsated by the pixellated pudendum perused before his work's net moratorium, he views it on billboards, in faces, over garments, and beside coat racks in the employee lounge.

In his eyes, the seething expanse of hairy pearls undulates, and so much unexpected uncunt is enough to drive a sane man mad. Even spied in velvet, it's dangerous, especially in browner shades. Larry is possessed by Aphrodite's pink flower — the bloom peeking from innocuously rose-hued cashmere sweaters, the balding skin of a woman's toy poodle, or the foam-dripping snatch of a cocoa man's mustache. Cunt hides in the fur trim of a commuter's jacket and in sly white clouds over dream-blue labia (or the sopping, gray cumulus with white wispy backgrounds) — it calls to him routinely, "Lar-ry, come out and pl-ay-ay!"

These visions started after he met Susan at the

work shaming-session when she told him to stop surfing porn, and then he told himself, "*You may not plunder sex sites on the job, old boy, so have some control!*" Now, he has this control in the cubicle, but the organs still emerge from the woodwork, glistening like teenage shroom hallucinations from dribbles of the water cooler, or wending free from the pristine surfaces of butcherblock that line the walls. House-pets and the ripped edges of cardboard boxes begin to entice him.

His cunt-quitting becomes a farce of unexpected overexposure — like how a smoker drastically increases intake when imagining no more butts, and then suckles each microcosmic smoke-stack in a seismic rejection of that thought, nursing each butt like the last oxygen mask available on the end-drop of a turbulent plane: Going down? Larry is; he has. He thinks, "*No more cunt? My world is over. I have been trained since birth to pursue this one thing. This will be my devil's dilemma, my heartbreaking loss.*" The physical reaction to perceived withdrawal pounds in his veins like a hammer, surges like a toothache in an open cavity, while faintly, ever so faintly, despite his volition to quit it all, he hears his own primal plea: *No, nonononono! More, and more and more cunt! You will not keep me from the prize.*

Also, age has caused a slowdown in the amount of actual cunt he gets, so he theorizes that this is why this is happening: The more he desires this love blossom, discrete punani, *esprit d'pulchritude*, the more creative his mind grows to obtain it. Can't get it at work, find it everywhere else. Like women in Czechoslovakian death camps who wrote recipes for apple fritters in the absence of flour, sugar, and even apples — he thinks incessantly about his lack, about his desire, onward and upward in hallucinogenic escalation, viewing more and more cunt in unusual places, but left unsatisfied.

And the fantasies are getting worse.

This fixation so consumes him that this morning he saw cunt in the rough black hairs of an old woman's neck on the subway. Those tiny fibers looked like vulgar obscenities, and as he turned away from the woman's smiling face — having been thoroughly shocked, having never had a thing for fat, old cunts — he sighed.

A pity, he decided later. She appeared to have considered him. Perhaps he should have looked deeper. He rethinks the original debacle weeks ago and recalls the exact, unmanning moment in which the cunt began to appear. Though plenty of employees were reprimanded for net-surfing — one girl for writing stories on a free site, one gay boy in chat, and an old lady in a sewing circle — only Larry had been called to the gray-green carpet in Susan's office.

"Why, Larry?" Susan had asked, "Why on earth would you do this at work? Couldn't you check sex sites at home? Explain it to me, Larry. I don't understand..."

She was benevolent and patient, her silver brows knit with worry, her face open and compassionate like Mother Teresa, but Larry would or could not explain it to her because he could hardly explain it to himself. "*Because I'm stupid, with no self-control,*" was the first thing that came to mind as excuse, but he would not say that. Not to tight-assy Susan of the control-top pantyhose — so he stared at her, lowered his dark lashes then said, with a touch of contrition, "I promise to stop. I'm really sorry," but at this exact moment the very first improbable cunt appeared in her eyes.

It sat on her lashes and spasmed, so he sat with his hands folded over his lap, trying not to draw attention to his aching groin. He thought of unzipping his trousers and shouting, "Elvis has left the building," as a euphemism for his rising member (as a child he had always wanted to be Elvis), but looked away from her blinking eyes and off towards the sun-bleached memos pinned to the cork-board above her desk. He stared at her dying cactus and then glanced to the industrial clock on her wall. It was only ten a.m., which meant another six excruciating hours.

"Do you promise to make every effort to stop cruising porn at work?" she pressed, but when she blinked again, he saw another butterfly cunt spasm flying free across her peepers, and thought, looking at the picture of an enormous Rottweiler on her desk, all about the old women he'd read about in magazines who bought large dogs to service them, creating a love for such service via applied peanut butter to their crotches: was she one?

He couldn't stop staring at the picture, thinking: "The Woman and Her Dog. The Woman and Her Pet Dog" — where had he heard that before? "Yes, I promise," he said, noticing the photo was centered, neat, almost too perfect. Did that mean something?

"That's good," she said, following the path of his eyes to her photo. "Do you like my dog?" She picked it up to dust off with her blouse. "Because I love my dog." For a brief moment, she stared with deep affection at the canine face in the frame, before turning a terrible look upon him and saying, "Seriously Larry, let's not have this talk again."

"We won't," he replied.

"Very good." Her cunty eyes blinked. When she glanced right at him, he wanted to tell her that her gaze was daunting, but when she came closer, ready to shake his hand and blinking all the while, he instead wanted to say something crazy — express, for example, that he was sure the sugar-substitute she used became formaldehyde at eighty-some degrees, preserving her stomach like a science class frog, so she should stop using it — say anything strange enough to stop the movement of her dual cunt lids so near, but his throat constricted and he could not. Silently, she offered her hand for a shake, avoiding his eyes, but after he grasped her palm, she pulled it back abruptly and coughed, looking at him like she might be assessing his child-molester potential.

Then she let loose: "I could understand one downloaded page from the net — but two hundred, Larry? Two hundred in the cache? You'd think we'd have harassment suits sky-high. How could you view such smut on your monitor when anyone could walk by?"

The practiced alt-tab stroke was clear in his mind. He shrugged, noticing a run in her nylons, splintering the stretchy sacks all the way up her right thigh.

"You've worked here fifteen years," Susan said, "so I don't want to fire you, but cut out net cruising. One more instance and I'll have to let you go. We have policies to dole out, adjustments to make, people to talk to, and not nearly enough time to waste on internet slacking. This is your first and last warning, Larry: Cut it out."

She went on, but he didn't listen. "Exactly," he wanted to say. "We have work, and work is what we should do, but it bores us, and there's no more insipid business than insurance — so, aren't you going to wake up one day and realize that, Susan? If we worked somewhere more stimulating, even vaguely more interesting — say in a factory or a beauty parlor, even in a morgue — a copy of *Sports Illustrated* swimsuit models might do just fine, but the reward must equal the punishment, dear employer, and so it must be full nude exposure. The Law of Big Numbers causes a parallel proportion for the Law of Stimulating Need." He said none of this, but muttered instead, "Say no more, Susan. I won't need another warning."

"Good." Her cunty eyes blinked severely like an abridged orgasm, so how could he explain anything when she seemed so bereft? Her hair, constricted at her nape in long, coiled twists, reminded him of snakes. In a brown suit, she couldn't be more drab. He thought of birds where the female was duller, and she spoke again, but he blotted out her voice and focused on her lower face where her lips had become an undulating vulva, opening and contracting. The sound of her voice was a drone. He thought: *By zip-code, driving record, age, and multi-car discounts, they beat the soul from us, Susan, the screens for premium are duller than rusted x-actos, and yet, you don't seem to regret the loss of your youth, your joy in this business...* But he sighed, giving up his manifesto as he heard her say with finality, "...so I want you to put the company first, okay?"

She frowned, and he had the sinking feeling she would not understand his musings or rationales — neither that online cunt had saved his sanity while improving his productivity, nor that there was a special lure in emails sent by complete strangers headed up with the ten promising words: You are One Click Away from Pictures of Nude Girls.

"Cunt!" he wanted to scream. "Salvation!" Invariably, he had clicked away from split premiums only to see Hilda and Her Magic Disappearing Cucumber, Sally with Two College Friends, Jill does Two Dogs and Masturbates with a Blender Lid — and returned to work invigorated. But this would be no more. The line had been pissed in the snow, or drizzled in the dry, brown sand. Susan was the joy-killer.

Still, free cunt was nothing to scoff at, he thought, staring at Susan's mouth, still roaming, in his mind, over his veiled manhood, for though he never checked the sites from home, how could he explain to her they were necessary at work? How to explain this desperate need for the mother lode of all pink or petal-soft? Could she find a penis so entrancing?

He doubted this as she said, splish, splash, spasm, "...followed by routine checks. I'll see you in two weeks."

"Penis in two weeks," he replied, thinking of his own.

"What?"

"I said, 'See you in two weeks.'" Well, he couldn't blame her for a lack of excitement. A penis was a tool, he thought, functional, good, but not the bloom of a poppy, not even vaguely reminiscent of seafood. A penis was not beautiful, nor did it have to be. It did not give birth, or have endless orgasms. He said nothing further, but pondered these ideas on his way to his desk and went home five minutes early.

At home, he thought of how his own love life consisted of a blow-up doll named Judy and a few over-viewed pornos. Real girls were confusing. They wouldn't date him, or they would only if he took them nice places and paid for everything then made no advances. When he was younger, he got more sex for less buck, but the bang to buck ratio had deflated just as his stomach had expanded. He'd even gone to dating services, put ads in the paper, done everything possible! He was not picky! He was not adverse to dating women with imperfect figures or less comely ages, but he never seemed to meet the right ones. And little things put him off, like women who micro-managed his driving, or virgins at forty, or girls who asked what he did before asking his astrological sign. He wanted to say, "Virgo, baby," but wasn't allowed anymore. The seventies, he was informed by his mother, were passé, despite the retail industry's recent revival of bell-bottoms, which she'd noted.

He processed premiums. He balanced books. A week later, he called his mother again, always a pride-swallowing mistake. "You need to shoot lower, Larry," she said. "I love you, baby, but you're no spring chicken. Your hair's not too thick either. Unless you strike it rich — Did you buy your lotto ticket today? — you'll never date Angelicas and Shelleys. Go for the Maudes, the Elizas, a girl who might agree to make you dinner and watch a movie on the couch. You're not ugly, but you're no Tom Cruise, Larry. Besides, I have to go. Regis is on, and that's my final answer." She hung up on him.

"Thanks, Mom," he said, considering cold pizza in the fridge. Green mold clung to the crust. Froggy cunt? "You've been a big help, Mom," he said to the dial tone, since he still oddly carried the phone. "Again."

He paused rather than recommencing with an outpour of the self-indulgent monologue he'd enjoyed many times before after conversations that ended badly, the one that started, *Why can't she be supportive like other people's mothers? Why can't she...* " and grazed the lunch meat drawer instead. As he glorified a slice of baloney with a squirt of Dijon mustard, he wondered: Since when had forty-five been the death-knell for easy sex?

He had a blind-date that night, set up by a swinger friend, but when he got there it went poorly. The girl, who had never heard of lip bleach or wax, asked immediately what he did, which actually meant, "What do you make?" He felt more interested in her whiskered mouth than what came out of it. She wasn't happy with him either. "They said you were thirty-two," she said, sucking her soda. "You look older."

"I'm not thirty-two." He laughed, but she glared as

if he had planned to trick her — he and the other bad, bad man — so he almost said, "And I thought you were good to look at without the paper bag," but he hated to watch women cry. He wouldn't do that. Still, all over the restaurant, he saw cunt: cunt in the waitress' tray drinks, on the brocade walls — enough cunt to make her unimpressive lip-cunt pale before him.

Apparently, she noticed his distraction because she left almost immediately when he began to consider the lint on her chair, so he paid the bill and got in his car, cursing his luck. At home, he even got on his treadmill for a furious five-minute run, then fell to the couch exhausted.

Judy, crammed into the closet, had deflated last week and needed a patch. Plus, there was that disconcerting mew her mouth made, like a wind tunnel. He thought about calling an escort service, but had visions of VD or sudden immune deficiency. His computer hovered in his periphery, the screen chanting lowly, "Open the net. Open sesame. Open at home. Buy a subscription and look at me... We're all here, Larry. All the girls you've wanted for years but could never have..." He opened the browser, but was not compelled.

At work, they had functioned as a titillating vehicle away — but at home, he was not nearly as interested. He stood, stretched, and took a walk, noticing how many cunts blossomed in dropped flowers from the dogwood trees, cunt eating up the night. He did not know where he was going, but trudged on until he realized he was two miles from home. His feet ached. His nose was raw from cold air. He sat on a curb as fall draped its melancholy shadows over his shoulders, and he thought, *Oh damn, I'm pitiful.*

He had a sudden urge to never see cunt again.

Maple leaves curled like bent fists on the sidewalks,

yellow, brown, and red — no! More pale — pale red?! — more cunt. He wanted the sky to swallow him like a seasoned whore fellates a finger because it was unfair to see so much of something he wanted yet have so very little.

This was, he thought, *definitely hell.* The next day at work, he put his oomph into his job, tirelessly sifting paper and clicking on the right buttons. Surprisingly, Susan called him in. She said, "Larry, I have to talk to you," and guided him to her office.

When he sat, she said, "You've been exceptionally good about avoiding the net, and I wanted to commend you. Not a single site was cruised this month, and I'm afraid the other employees have relapsed, so I fired them. That's why Helen isn't here. God, Larry, I hate employees unable to follow directions, but that's not you, thank goodness." She patted his shoulder.

Perhaps he imagined it, but she seemed to caress his arm through his suit, her hand stroking briefly up and down, her painted nails swished rhythmically across his poly-fibered sleeve, holding it a second too long, and just as suddenly as she'd called him in, she then said, "Would you like to have a drink after work, Larry?"

Her perfume was spicy-fruity. A pearl-clip ornament for her high heels had fallen off one shoe. "What?" Had he heard correctly?

"Strictly informal. You can say no."

"Susan," he said, "We don't get along. Why me?" She turned to her huge window with its view of the dumpsters and a solitary tree. From her stooped posture, he could tell he'd hurt her feelings. "I like you. I didn't mean it. Okay," he said. "We can have a drink. Sure. Why not? No problem."

Her shy smile made him feel better, but she insisted

on driving when they left, and after they arrived at the bar, she took off her long, gray coat, loosened her hair, and told him about hubbies one, two, and three. Later, when she rubbed her heel against his ankle, he almost ducked under to make sure he hadn't imagined it. *Susan is h-hot for me!* his mental voice stuttered, the revelation so astounding that he proceeded to get drunk.

"I just felt I could talk to you all the sudden," she said. "Like you looked in my eyes and knew what was on my mind..."

Not bloody likely, he almost uttered: It was all cunt to me.

"So, I said to myself, Susan — that man is much nicer than you thought he was. And you did well with what I asked from you, Larry, so I thought I'd ask you here."

"I'm here," he said, grinning stupidly.

After she downed seven Margaritas, she put her antique barrette in her purse and fanned out her hair with her fingers. "Larry," she said, "can I tell you a secret?"

He wished he had a mint to hide his liquor breath. He drank his fifth Daiquiri. She looked prettier and prettier. "Sure."

She sighed. "When I saw all those sex sites you looked at, I thought it was great to see a man who still had a strong sex drive. So many men peter out with age. Like they can't please a woman anymore, so why bother? But you — oh, how should I put this? Well, I shouldn't ask. I imagine you have quite a lot going on." Her finger traced circles in the condensation rings on the table, drawing spirals and odd patterns. "Am I right?"

He said, "Be more specific."

"Oh, all right," she said, leaning in. "I wanted to know if you still want it — I mean regularly. Since Jeff passed away, it's been hard for me to meet men. When I do, they can't keep up."

"I can keep up," he said. Their faces were so close that he watched her lashes flutter, entranced they were so brown when her hair was so gray, and, as he mentally took her clothes off with his eyes, he suddenly thought: *Making love to this woman could put me in crutches. She is my boss. I might get fired.* A jolt of acid entered his stomach, almost bowling him over. "But I've gotta go tonight."

"I'll be in touch then," she said.

"Don't need to take me back," he slurred. "I'll take a taxi. Good luck with everything."

That night he cruised sex sites for three hours, but couldn't get excited. The next morning he walked to the subway, thinking about Susan because she came into his mind's eye and lingered — he remembered her finger, tracing patterns on the table, contemplated her Rottweiler and three dead husbands. "A dangerous attraction," he said aloud.

That afternoon the office air was electric with the spell of women, fully cast. They had the power to draw a man in and make him wait — but Susan did not dally long. She put a note on his desk that afternoon. It read: 1233 Bread St. 7 p.m. Not about work.

He hyperventilated like he had as a child, when he had used his lunch bag to stop the ragged breathing. Inhaling the hammy scent of his noon meal, he calmed and got through the day. At 7 p.m. he stood at her door with daisies, wine, and chocolate. He filled his face with a sappy grin and when she swung open her door, in a frosty white pair of sheer pajamas, having dyed her hair walnut, he saw she was beautiful, though she had been getting more beautiful in his eyes all day. "I'm here," he said.

"I see that," she replied. The wine, chocolate, and

daisies were left in the hall. "My dog's in the yard," she said, "because I thought we might want to be *alone*." Then she shut the front door and just about ripped off his clothes as he fumbled with her flimsy garments, not wanting to rip them since he hadn't bought them, but she tired of this and soon began to strip them herself. The two were soon almost nude, breathing heavily.

"Susan!" he said, a prude for a short moment, trying to extricate himself — but "Larry!" she replied, teasing him, pushing him into the wall, and he called out her name again as if to interject, "Susan, sweet Susan," but she did not cease seducing him.

He then said, "Susan, Susan, Susan," as he writhed on her bed, uttering her name like it was his first baby word, uttering it non-stop for the next several hours, especially when he first plucked the beige shoulder pads from her bra-cups that now sat beside him on the bed — because when she first saw he noticed them, she colored prettily.

"Susan," he said, enjoying all of her afterwards. "Should we do this again?"

"You have my number," she replied. "Use it — or don't."

But he knew he would. When he walked outside, drunk on the air, he felt he had been taken for a carnival ride. Even the unremarkable became amazing. "You tree," he cried. "How beautiful your leafless branches! You cement, how wondrous your flat, even texture! You pole! Hmmm, what to say about a pole?"

But better — there was no cunt in his landscape! He stopped walking and looked down at his shoes as if they or the walking held the answer. Where had the cunt gone? Had he dreamt it? He thought of Susan sleeping in her bed, wondering how he would feel to see her at work. He thought of her dog and her probable stock of peanut butter, but, when he entered his apartment, there was a slight pain in his temples and the dull light of the monitor flashed, so he forgot about Susan. The screen had captured the body of a sixteen year-old girl. She was nude, with long, red hair, and her pubis had been shaved like a tiny heart of curls.

She winked, staring at him from the still-life, and then laughed. "So you finally got some, huh, Larry?" she said. "Click me. Get some more."

He sat before her in his computer chair, wondering if he was dreaming.

"Come on," the girl said, but her desire seemed ominous, her eyes like cold glare. This girl would never care who stroked on the other side of her monitor; she was hard-edged and sharp, Larry decided, taking manly fans as she did with her tight, young body and stealing their money, never offering a single, soft sigh. She was not Susan.

But, as if Monitor Girl could sense his thoughts, she turned to him and said, "You just now realized the sex object always takes you to the cleaners? The sex object does not regret your presence — or absence — because it does not register that you have either. An object is just an object till you make it more, like a toaster. You see yourself in it, and you think you've won something, but you're wrong. You have nothing. I have a boyfriend, see?"

The view on the screen shifted about thirty degrees to depict a young man on the bed beside the girl, grinning. She laughed. "So why would I want someone like you anyway, Larry? Why?" She shook her hair and returned to her original position, dropping her thighs a millimeter wider as if to lure him back.

He thought of an ex-girlfriend who sent nudie pictures to prisoners on death-row. "I just like to think of them, thinking of me," she said. "Masturbating to me. But I never give my real address. That way they can dream all they want, but I'm not there."

He stared venomously at the screen. He thought only: *Susan warned me. She was the one who made cunts everywhere. I saw them first in her eyes.* The girl in the screen seemed less and less present, like a photograph of a painting of a drawing of a cartoon, so he scoffed, bored, and closed her window, but as he did this, his computer shot up five pop-ups of hard, naked girls with immaculate bodies.

He closed their windows too, but they seemed to multiply, kept multiplying, as he shouted, "Stop, already! I have what I want!" Yet still buck-shots proliferated, hacking repeatedly across his screen only to be erased as soon as possible by his clicking finger. As his mouse connected with each tiny X, he felt stronger, but strongest of all as he shut down the last internet search engine with the lingam of his index on the flat gray mouse. The almighty cock-click of a single digit made a giant of his forged resistance.

He didn't need the imagined or artificial. As the screensaver came on, he used the same window closing finger to dial Susan's number, pressing the seventh digit with fervor and listening hard before he was greeted by her soft, "Hello."

"Susan," he breathed, scratching his belly.

"Larry? Is that you?"

"Yes," he said. He pictured the silver-laced cunt he'd known earlier, her face above it swooning, and the hoops of twine curling above his nose when he was face-deep in its heat. He relived the memory of her scent, wanting to be back in her bed, imagining a pet dog he'd never seen, and thinking about how it might moan for affection from her yard. The dog. The damn dog! Did it exist? Shouldn't he have heard a dog that big, a single bark?

He thought about reality and falseness. Nothing was truly real, nothing but the thing in the instant that you choose to see it whatever way and agreed with its own certainty, like he had been consumed with cunts. He grew so obsessed with this idea as he spoke to Susan that he barely recognized his own voice when it crooned, "I have just one question for you, Susan. Are you lonely tonight?" Again, he was channeling Elvis. He felt very smooth.

"Yes," she said, a measure of sleepiness in her tone.

"Good," he replied. "I'll be there soon." But as he said this, the screen degaussed and threw up one last pop-up of the cruel young redhead, laughing at him, so he picked up a stapler and beat her back until he registered only a shatter of splintered glass, an empty hole in the monitor where a woman once was. He went about filling that hole with branches from the birch trees outside, muttering, "Susan, Susan," and then walking to her house, whispering her name like a mantra, a lullaby, a dream, or a saved man's chorus in a soft elegant swan song of which everyone might know the tune, but only he could hear.

Sid, Me, and the Sea

Sid was a man I loved once. He had smooth black hair and tan skin; on his belly was a panel of ocean. He had no bellybutton, which should have been disturbing, but I was too dumb at first to recognize this as a problem. If I lifted his shirts, which were often tacky neon Hawaii numbers, I could watch his waves crash and break. I did that a lot.

When placing my hand on his panel, which was rectangular like a TV screen, I could almost touch the shining water. He said he was born this way because his mother was a mermaid, the sort who gave up her tail for true love and who could not laugh, even after she went human, because laughter was forbidden to mermaids and, in her heart, she had never left the ocean. "She's bitter," he said. I found her story fascinating.

Sid said after her legs split and her tale cracked and fell off, she had moved into the suburbs with his father, who was never a prince among men, more a middle manager, and she now drove a Lexus and did home decorating consultations for money. He said he didn't know what they did professionally before they had him, hardly knew what they did after, because he had enjoyed a lot of nannies. He said this with lascivious intent, detailed how he liked how they'd stroked his hair and kissed his small cheeks, saying again and again what a cute kid he was.

But the nannies were always asking him where he may have hidden things, like their hairbrushes or back-packs. Sometimes, he explained to me, he had a trick he performed where he turned his back to them and made a gone thing reappear. They liked this. It was his panel, which they liked too, said they could watch it for hours and hours. His main problem with nannies was that he wanted to keep them all, never let them go, so was always sad when they had to take other jobs or leave for school.

Sid had other unusual talents. One was coring apples. Also, he was a dynamo in the sack and could sense bad seafood like a master-chef. Many times, he had saved me from food poisoning. "My mother was a mermaid," he said. "Of course I know bad fish."

After much lovemaking, Sid told me all about his love life with the sort of limited disclosure most girlfriends moving into the "significant" realm receive; at first I was flattered. His first lover liked to watch his waves while they fucked. That ruled this out for me after.

He said he was eleven when they first did it and that it had soothed her, put her into a trance. I said, "Who was she? What did she look like?" and he promptly dropped the subject.

We were together three full years before he finally told me that she was a mermaid, too, like his mother, that she had been riveted to the ocean on his belly for a reason, and that their first sex involved not his penetration of her, but her penetration of his panel with her tail.

"Ooh, kinky," I said.

When they lingered in the ocean together, he explained, she could swim into him, often did, until one day she found something deep inside his biosystem, buried within his inner panel that horrified her so thoroughly she swam out of him at once, her blue eyes tearing, fearful, and squinted in speculation, and said, "You are one nasty person, Sid." She never came back.

"I never know what she saw," he said. He said this broke his heart. He wrote piano songs for her, before and after. He sang them. He didn't know anyone could swim away so quickly and never be seen again. He told his mother all about it.

He promised he didn't know what his ex had seen inside him, he told me, but he was glad I didn't see it too. "We're all quite horrifying," he said, "when the real things inside us come out into the open."

I told him I had no idea what he was talking about. "I am perfect the way I am," I said.

"I love your yellow hair," he then enthused. "Your big red heart!"

I told him maybe my heart was blue like his panel, because he didn't love me enough.

"It is not!" he said.

"Yes it is," I replied. "How about more affection?" He couldn't see inside me. Fuck him. Still, he scoffed.

But he introduced me to his mother one day not long after, at a family holiday gathering. I'd been prepared with hours of pre-training and spot testing, like this was a big deal, like I'd meet the whole clan, but we got to her house, it was just me, her, his father, and Sid — and she spoke in some strange tongue with Sid for all of ten minutes at the entrance before she'd even fully open the door. When she did and reluctantly moved aside, she mysteriously cried.

I tried not to take it personally, but I could tell she hated me. I should have worn blue. Or green. I wore red thigh highs and a red velvet dress with little black shoes. I had a black cross on my neck. I probably looked like a shark bite.

We all sat at the table and his dad was really nice, but kind of leery. "You picked a pretty one, Sid," his dad said and winked at me like he thought I was cute. His dad looked just like him, except older and fatter.

"You have a panel, too, Sid's dad?" I replied.

"Nope," he said. "No panel. And it's just Malcolm. You can call me my first name."

"Sid's a hybrid," Sid's mother then explained. "Part sea and part earth. So, did you meet our son at school?" Her subsequent look toward Sid's father was cold yet practiced.

"No," I said. "At the Frosty Freeze."

A silence hung in the air until Sid announced, "Dad, I love Bethany and I plan to marry her." It was after this that his mother took me into the back room.

"I want to show you my tail," she said. "The one I gave up for *all of this...*"

I agreed to look at it. Sid smiled and I flushed as he goosed my rear when I walked past him to follow her. When we got to her room, she opened the closet, but what I saw was not so much a tail as a dried thing with an end fin, kind of like seaweed. "Sid doesn't do well with anyone leaving him," she told me. "Do you really love my son?" She lifted her perfect brown-green eyebrow and met my eyes for once, the only time she ever did so.

"Yes," I lied. "I do. I love him." Now, I had just been pondering this very question in the car. He had a broad jaw and a nice physique. He was moderately interesting and had asked me to marry him — but I had said yes not due to heart-booming love, but because no one else had asked. He seemed a good enough opportunity. He said he loved me.

"Well, I must tell you," she confessed. "He's not a normal boy."

"I've seen his sea panel, mom," I said. "Lots of times."

"I understand," she said. "But have you seen what's inside him?"

I told her I had.

"No, you haven't," she said, smacking me on the back, hard. "Because if you had, you'd be running now! You'd be taking my tail and not saying no about it. Don't you want to be a mermaid for a little while, just until you're sure about things?"

"No," I replied. This was a hard sell.

"Being a mermaid was great," she enthused. "And to think I gave it all up for this shithole. For Sid's dad." She gripped my shoulder with an excess of nails. "What a waste! I could put the tail back on now, but I don't belong anymore. I'd just be an old sea cow." Still, she patted my back kindly as I walked out the front door. She wanted me to like her.

When Sid and I left that day, I said, "Your mom is ominous. She warned me about 'the something inside you.'"

"She did?" he asked, lifting his eyebrow, but he didn't say more, so for a few days I stared into his ocean and hoped for a clue. I wondered if I should go back to his mom's and agree to be a mermaid, just for a brief glimpse, and then go back to being a girl. She had told me it was painful, the transition between mermaid and girl, but if I was going to marry Sid, maybe I should know. "Being a woman is all about pain, honey," she'd told me. "No matter the species. Get used to it."

It turns out, it didn't really matter how painful that transition would be because I never tried. I kept picturing my leg bones melting and breaking as some weird fin thing glommed around them, and then how I'd start gasping for water and have to live in the sea, and I freaked.

Then I freaked on him.

Although I knew I didn't love him enough to endure that switch, I started to demand more aggressively what was wrong inside him, because I didn't want to not know: I was wearing his ring, after all. It sparkled. Sid kept showing me his panel, but he knew I was panicking because he kept saying, every time I asked, "I don't know what it is either! I really don't know."

This exchange went on for a while, but one day after Sid was in a particularly foul mood, I got a call from his mother. "Ask Sid about Nancy," she said, somewhat nervously. "But come get my tail first. I've been soaking it. It won't hurt too bad." This was all she said before the line went dead.

I didn't go. When he got home from work, liking just fine the new tan on my regular human legs, I said to Sid, "Who's Nancy?"

"What?" he asked.

"Nancy. You know, Nancy? Your mom told me to ask you about Nancy."

"She was one of my nannies," he said, wringing his hands. "I really loved her. But I've told you all that."

Sometimes there's something weird between two people and it's not validated or anything, but the distance just starts to feel insurmountable. Sid wasn't touching me so much after that, and then he didn't touch me at all.

When he said he loved me, even though he wouldn't touch me anymore, I told him I was leaving, said I had had enough of his non-touching loving that felt more like ignoring and that it bugged me that he wouldn't tell me anything about Nancy. I said that he had to know what was in his ocean panel because it was inside him, after all — a space both vast and small because an entire mermaid had swum around in there, yet it was a setting localized enough to fit inside him and be entirely situated within his own body. "And what was in there, Sid?" I said. Plus, I didn't think I could marry him anymore. I had to know what was what.

It was in this moment that he said, "Stop. Look into the panel!"

And I did. The waves crashed and broke as I watched, but I felt myself shrink. I was shrinking! And when I got small enough, he picked me up between two fingers, like I was a flea, actually pinching on a bit of my sweater, and then flung me at a diagonal into his waves.

This is when I saw the other women, dead on the shore. Some were dead a long time, with bleached bones. Some had died recently enough to still have flesh clinging in moist clumps. He took his finger, put it inside himself, and edged me further over so I was out of view of his panel. "Stay there," he said, leaning close to his belly. His voice boomed in like a god's: "Don't be visible in the main panel, and I won't crush you. You should have listened to my mom and been a mermaid. Then, when I got in the water, you could have at least swum out. Now, you can't."

"You need to let me go!" I shouted.

But he just replied, "What?" like he really couldn't hear me. It was an interesting thing to be stuck in the off-view section of his waves and sand. There were no people and no buildings. I would have to learn how to fish, for it was a fully developed eco-system, like any other ocean, but I found a stick and did this, spearing them with the sharp end.

I had a lot of alone time there on his shores, looking at the carcasses of his former women. It was funny how their clothes were still around in many of their cases, and these clothes reflected the time when they had passed. Almost all the nannies had on big colorful eighties jewelry and belts or shirts with space age geometrical shapes. The newer girlfriends, the women more fresh, these had on items that more looked like today.

As many memories come back long after they are needed, mine reminded me then of that first night he and I had lain together after sex, how there was a moment I had nearly forgotten about when a woman, tiny, like me now, had walked onto his panel-front and shouted, "Run! Quick! Don't let him love you!" But I couldn't hear her that well, could hardly believe I'd seen her, and his hand had slapped down onto his ocean panel (to quash her I later realized).

"I'm hungry," he'd said then to me, me who admittedly still swooned in the aftermath of our pleasure. "Did you want a bite to eat?"

"Yes," I said then, ignoring the strange vision. But I remembered her now; she'd been so pretty. And now, on this invisible shore where her body lay, I was determined not to be her. Still, there were quite a few women on this invisible beach, so I decided I would do something to warn the new ones due next.

I would throw the early lovers' bones onto the panel proper each time he took a new lover. Maybe, as they'd watch the bones gather, they'd have a clue. While he was sleeping, I decided, I would spell out two messages to them. The first would say, "Be a Mermaid when

Mommy asks." The second would say, "Ask about Nancy."

I thought about this a lot. But, this idea struck me as too complicated before I implemented it. Also, there was the bones thing. Yuck. I didn't really want to touch the other dead women. It was far simpler to spell out one message on his visible sand: "Kill Him" or "He Killed Me." It bothered me not a bit that I wasn't dead when I would write this! I was speaking for the bones of his former women, in their gone voices. I was a saint. A channel!

So I tried this bone spelling in both ways, but Sid's next two girls didn't even notice. It was a good thing he didn't like them much, he being the one who eventually broke it off. But this next girl, Brooke, she made his heart stop with how "amazing and gorgeous" she was. He told her everything he'd told me, repurposing compliments that worked. He took her to his mom's. "Dad, I love Brooke and I want to marry her," he said.

Lazy fucker, I thought. I wondered if he was going through a spate of women with names that started with B to make things easier. I wondered if he'd go next to C names, or let the subsequent letter be random. It's not like there were name cards on the corpses. Now, there were about twelve dead women on the shore where I stood, I could tell he really liked Brooke, and I had begun to grow desperate to warn her.

His mother didn't even show the girl the tail. Maybe she'd been warned. Maybe she needed no more guilt. After all, her intervention had really caused Sid's paranoia and the resultant murderous events in our case. Her plan kind of backfired. But Brooke didn't watch his panel much, couldn't even see the bones, so I experimented with a more drastic step. I actually threw one out.

The one I threw sailed free from his panel and landed right on her chest. It was tiny. "What's this little white thing?" she said.

Sid looked close, smacked his belly, and said he was hungry. A warning smack? I ignored it, threw out a skull next. And then another. When Brooke woke up, there would be eight such skulls I'd tossed, sitting on her breasts, but I left his place while she slept so didn't see her reaction.

When I realized the bones could leave, I tried to jump out a few times and finally succeeded. I landed on her left breast and slid down it's curvature to walk along her soft belly until I could get to the sheet beside her, then to the mattress side, then to the carpeted floor. Of course, I thought: Sid wouldn't tell me I could free myself. Why would he? But, maybe he didn't know this was possible, this dry land escape.

I was still small, but as I walked away from his apartment, after two days of dusty carpet safari to his door, where fleas were a constant terror, when I got under his door and to the other side, I felt myself enlarge. By the time I reached the outer doorway of his building, I was terrier sized, full-sized upon arriving home.

The next time I saw Sid in public, I had already discovered that Brooke had left him. He told all his troubles to the coffee house barista we knew, the same one he chatted up about all of his women, not like this was hard to figure out. He went to the same place every day, she was gay so he couldn't have her, and she was convenient. Anyway, when I saw him, I punched him right in the stomach and left a bunch of red food coloring in his waves.

"Red ocean. Red ocean. Redrum!" I said to him.

"Shhh," he said. "Shhh." He meant, "Don't tell the

police."

I walked away.

He wouldn't bother me again, but at least the waves that broke inside him would tell his story. They'd be crimson. Or maybe his story wouldn't matter anymore. Did I mention I put a bit of cyanide there, in his water?

Well, that is a different story. One best saved for later.

It's so nice to be large again! I don't go for panel men now. Especially ones with pretty things in their panels. Not really. Not ever. Now, I like a flat, smooth bit of abdomen, a little hair there. A mole. A freckle. A normal rumble after food. And a visible belly button.

Sometimes a little belly fat.

Yes, that.

Spontaneous Orgasm Guy, Dick Woods

When a guy saunters into a place and all the hot girls walk up and pay attention, rubbing their hose-slick legs together, inclining their necks and fragrant heads to view him, licking their luscious red or melba lips, well, this might be exciting for this guy, right? You'd think so, sure, the first eight hundred times. But after that cult of womanhood gets tiresome, he's going to get bored. You can only see the same thing so many times in so many ways before it's like a rehashed chicken entrée a chef makes fresh by garnish, only via smorgasbord tray of women. So Dick Woods — yes, that was his ridiculous name — had just started to get bored.

I'd seen him here a few times. Seen the reaction to him. Some people said it was because he was famous, but I had no idea what for. I hadn't seen him on a sitcom. Maybe he was a mogul. Maybe he saved a baby on network TV or grabbed people out of burning buildings for a living.

Anyway, I saw his boredom because I realized, as the women thronged him, how many "Oh baby, I've got a great hotel room and please join me" speeches could he take? He was tired tonight, too, it seemed from my distant table. Exhausted. "Oh, fuck, another woman hot for me," must have been his latest thought this evening. And he had persistent groupies. Good looking ones. I'm just saying, this guy had it going on.

So I watched him stroll in wearing some kickin' Calvin Klein jeans, smelling like Cool Water or Eternity for Men or straight up sex pheromone, standing at the bar in wait to be bought one drink after the next — he wasn't a lightweight; it took a few — and not that he waited long for two booth-tan white girls headed for Bermuda to arrive, but his expression already reeked of irritation. He looked ugly to me with that look, Mr. Dick Woods, yet all the women around him started to pant. They were touching their napes, crossing and uncrossing their legs, leaning up against hard objects.

Now, two in the morning at a bar where everyone's been drinking and you might think this was simply his clean new presence there among drunkards, or perhaps it was their surmising about his perfect abs, or even quite possibly just the look of his chiseled face and tawny slick hair. But it wasn't — even a good looking guy can't get that going on his looks alone. At least, not in public. Good thing I was across the room since he hadn't affected me that way; still, I watched these barflies wearing what appeared to be swimsuits as outer wear or tiny string-bound garments and even though deafened by the *thump thump* bass of beach-scene bar music, I saw their faces O up.

They were literally coming, touching themselves and ejaculating right in the club. Other men swarmed them like bees, taking one or two away who looked easy to pull from his crowd, maybe just looking easy, but spontaneous orgasm man, I just watched him keep drinking, nonchalant — and when a crowd of women had gathered and clung fifteen deep, he just walked around like the troupe who followed were an occupational hazard. To one girl who decided to swoon in front of him, via faux pass out, thinking he would catch her, I saw him mouth, "Get the fuck out of my way," not even reaching out his hands as she fell to the floor. That's apathy for you. That's sheer disgust.

But this is where I come in. She fell, right? At the day job, I'm a paramedic. The ground was concrete. She conked her head hard. I went to have a look. Meanwhile, he and his entourage had moved over a few feet, but as I knelt and started checking this six foot tall green and white minidress girl with the peachy lips and Latina complexion, Dick Woods got interested. He neared. "So, I didn't want to hurt anybody," he said, leaning down to watch me check her.

"Back off," I told him. "I know what you do." Then I made error number one: I looked up at him. Yes, he was cute from afar, but up-close, he was devastating. And he didn't smell like cologne. No, he smelled like newborn baby! I had started my health-related work volunteering at a hospital nursery, so I knew what baby smelled like, not shitty baby, not peepsed baby, but the powdery butter scent that comes from an infant's head and is biologically engineered to make its mama go gaga and daddy too. Baby prehistoric love smell! Nothing better or more en-dearing, so of course the women were hot for him; although the floor where I knelt stank of beer, so it was the disturbing blend of boozy baby I picked up, oxymoronic scents.

As the fallen girl moaned, I returned my attention to her before shouting, "Can somebody get me some ice from the bar?" I glared right at him. "Now!" I demanded, thinking: Men like you make me sick. You might smell like baby, but you seem like asshole to me.

And then a warm feeling suffused my cheeks. My heart-rate sped. I suddenly knew what the women were thinking, what they felt when he came close — like his whole persona hung a silk veil of desire up and visible before them. I began to luridly imagine the room, envisioning group orgy. Everyone was naked, him too, centered in the mix, and he had the most enormous man business I'd ever seen. Still hallucinating as he looked at me, I swear I heard him say, "I will fuck you with my face all night long and only take you with my cock when you absolutely beg, because I know you would beg, Candace, beg well, until I gave you everything you wanted..." Okay, so I wanted to masturbate, too, especially when he leaned in really close to give me the ice, and the things his hallucinations said to me then were so dirty, I can't even relate them.

My grandmother would be shocked and ashamed. And I don't like giving up control, let's admit, but these things would drive me wild. He was going to tie me up and do what with the what? So, of course, in those moments, I hated him more. Fucking prick boy, I thought. "How do you do that?" I asked.

"What?"

"What you do. Get out of my sex head."

"It's a curse," he said. "I'm not trying to."

"Well, I hate it," I said. "Just leave me alone because I don't want you."

Dick smiled, a sweet smile, a smile like you smile at a puppy you have just seen tail-wag for the first time, one that is licking your hand with its little soft tongue and making eyes at you with cocked head. "Is she out?" he asked.

I got wet. More wet. My clothes, a pair of ripped painting jeans and a black Don't Let the Blues Get You Down sweatshirt, seemed excessive. To exercise my medical function, I touched the girl's forehead and gingerly took my time focusing on her face, her eyes, her breathing. She blinked and her gorgeous green eyes fluttered open. Her look was sweet but perplexed. And then she smelled him too. Her neck swiveled. Her back arched; her hips launched up. "Oh," she said. She said this lengthily, *a la* porn movies. I watched her touch her own breasts with her hands then and go through the lap ministration motions until she was done. He didn't watch her. I watched her — because I wanted not to look at him. It was kind of funny, those small sounds she kept making. *Oh, oohoh, weeeah, oh.*

"Will she be okay?" he asked. "I'm not trying to harass you, but I don't want charges against me."

"It's not so bright to stand by and cause a woman to endure a new spontaneous orgasm *while* she's *concussed*," I replied, not too nicely.

"What happened?" she said, a small, drunk chipmunk in his headlights.

"You tried to seduce dick-boy here," I said. "You faked falling. He didn't catch. Tomorrow you'll have a swelled contusion on your head that will remind you not to come back here. And you'll listen to that, right? Because Dick is a dick you don't need. He let you hit the concrete, with your head, for fuck's sake. And then he stepped away."

"Oh," she replied. "That isn't very nice."

"Look, I'm not seducing anyone on purpose," Dick argued. "This is my birth defect, a deformity. It's like how genius people can't always control, maybe never control, where their genius goes."

"Sure, whatever," I said. "So, Dick, can you get some water for this girl? Maybe some acetaminophen? She really cracked her brain. Because of you. Get to it, will you? But don't bring it yourself. Send someone else." He came in closer to me, shocked, interested, his chest pressing my back. "Look, I'm not cute enough to be part of your entourage," I said. "And I'm not an entourage kind of girl. So don't even bother." He touched my shoulders. My breasts sensitized, nipples hardening in my bra below my shirt. "Can you please back off," I said again. I tried to get away fast as the girl sat up. Said to her, "Slowly. But, you're fine. Don't drink anymore," then adding as a repetitive afterthought, "but stay clear of that one, okay? He's poison."

Then I walked up to the bar once more, a bit woozy from his contact, and swigged a quick Guinness before leaving. "He called it a deformity," I said as I reached my car, talking to myself. "Then why do you keep coming back there? I've seen you there before. Admit it, you like it — or you wouldn't go where you know women will flock to you. You'd live in some distant nature cabin. With a fucking compost heap or something. Grow zucchini as large as your second half! Maybe cultivate tomatoes — have a goat, then have determined, celibate relations with that goat!"

I said these things out loud unfortunately — turns out he was behind me. Smiling. Almost laughing. Alone. "But I don't like it," he said. "All that enormous desire from others is exhausting. I only put up with it and seem to accept it because I don't want to hurt people. I'm a sensitive guy."

"But you do hurt people by not refusing them early enough," I said. "Those women, they're tore up coming back to that bar. They ache for you. Fucking bimbos. They stand by. I bet a few of them have little dick shrines. I mean Dick shrines. Dick's wood or Woods shrines. Wait, is that the same thing?"

"I need a night life," he said. "And, no, refusing them is worse. They get pissed. Women are vicious when they're mad."

"I'm gay, you know?" I told him. I then added for good measure, since he hadn't left, "And I've been trained as an assassin."

"Really?" he asked. "That's great. Lady, that's so great because I've been looking for a friend and we could be good friends, the best of friends, because I really like you and it would be an enormous relief to be near a woman who didn't simper at me, who seemed almost to hate me due to her former male-abuse-induced or current proclivities to love other women. Hey, can we be friends? Can we?"

He got closer and closer as he spoke now and, I have to say, he seemed quite geeky cute, almost the type of guy I could be into, self-effacing, lovely. Except I could see his dick in my face again — dick while hallucinating — like a vision that took over the parking lot. Big, hard monster dick! So I turned towards my car to look away and shouted, "Dick Woods, no! We cannot be friends! I have no interest! Go away!" And then I saw the bar women had spotted him, fifteen or twenty or so en route, walking then running, advancing toward him in spiked heels and next to no clothing, what rainbow and seraphim clothing they had on erupting in garment malfunctions as they ran.

"Oh fuck," he said. "Fuck. You have to help me. Lady, help me."

"I don't," I said, "have to help you." But when I got

in my car, he jumped in the passenger seat anyway.

"Yeah," he said. "You do! Out of sheer meanness and jealousy, they might hurt you. Go, lady! You gotta. Just drive! Take me home."

So I drove. But that baby smell got to me. I turned on the air conditioner. I tried breathing through my mouth. I told him, "Can you please stick your sweet-smelling head out the window?" Said, "You know, I really resent that you just got in my car without my permission, Dick. I resent that you followed me out to the parking lot because I don't care for studboys, don't even want you anywhere near me, no matter how important you think you are or for what reason, so when I pull over this car, please get out and leave me alone. Which freeway do I take?"

"12 to the 342 South. Exit Moorelane Avenue. I bet a lot of people want to be friends with you," he said calmly, a moment later, relaxing and leaning back in my car's interior, head not out the window. "Because you're no bullshit. I bet you're a good friend to have. These women say they love me almost instantly. I like that you don't. Who are you, anyway? 15345 Camino Noutillo is my address. Please take me there. And what's your name? I do think you're pretty. We're going to be friends."

"Candace," I said. "Stop talking." But I kept hallucinating dick anyway, him in my car, and I started to come just as I pulled into his cul-de-sac driveway. Now I used to have this thing about masturbating in public places, so I knew how to do it stealth, coming that was, and I couldn't let him know that he had gotten to me.

"Look at me, Candace," he said when I put the car in park. "How about you glare at me again? I like that."

"Look, I'm not really gay," I told him. "Not today anyway. But I don't want you. Not for your head or your heart or for anything, spontaneous orgasm guy. In fact, Dick, you make me sick. All dicks make me sick, but you make me want to vomit because you feel sorry for yourself about these women chasing you, but you're the one who keeps showing up at the bar. You're used to the attention. Yes. You like it. You're even so jaded and callous that you didn't really care what happened to that girl who conked her head until she seemed to have serious medical needs — and let me tell you, Dick, that is fucked up."

"I don't mean to be fucked up," he said.

I kept staring straight ahead. "Get out."

"Look at me, Candace," he entreated, touching my shoulder.

"No. I don't want to."

He started touching me then. His hand shook, the one rubbing my thigh closest to him then walking his fingers up to my waist and breasts, and then putting his other hand up my skirt, angling until he looped his fingers over the top of my panties and had his fingers inside them. "OhmyGod this is hot," he said. "I love that you don't want me."

Seemed to me, he was so excited to pursue the one girl who didn't appear to sweat him, me, so it was like spontaneous orgasm Dick guy's Easter! Or Christmas! "Please just let me do this to you with my hands," he said. "And then let me do you, here or in my bed." His real touch was as good as the hallucinations. I wanted to flow with them, let this playboy have his way with me right there in my car, but there was one problem. If I got into it at all, he'd be instantly turned off, go running for the hills. I'd be just like the others who wanted him then. It would all end as abruptly and idiotically as it had begun. And I didn't want to get involved.

But, sometimes, the problem was co-dependently

related to the solution. Dick was in my car. His hands were in my panties, both of them now. He put his fingers to my lips, smelling of me, for me to suck. He liked my dropped lashes. I had to end things. "All right, Dick," I said. "Give it to me. Oh, Dick, I want you to fuck me something hard and fantastic right now! I've been hiding it all along, but I'm just as chick-slut as those other bar hangers on. Do me. Please do me. Feel how wet I am? Soaking fucking wet for you."

He retreated into his skin. A look of revulsion stole over him. His hands stopped shaking. He got out quick. "Candace," he said sadly, wiping me off on his jeans. "Candace! You turned into something horrible!" And then he ran.

The baby-scalp, love-me smell still hung in my car. For days. And I knew where he lived. That was the real crux of the situation. I could go back for another bite of that obsessive crowd-apple of desire, the one that smelled like babies and made strange women come. I could compete with the hordes. Or not. This was my neighborhood bar. I could come here just to drink. No point pretending you don't desire someone just to make them want you, right? For what — a lifetime of pretending disinterest? No. I liked my men like shots. Straight up. Without the pretense or dilution of ice.

So, "Bartender," I said when I returned there that next week. "Another Guinness. Oh, and let me know if you happen to see Dick Woods, pheromone bar-stud boy coming. Because then I'd have to bolt. He nauseates me!"

The bartender was new, had been cool to me all night — and when I say cool here, I mean cool as cool should always be used, not as random slang, but as an actuality or a personification to indicate a chillness. But at these remarks, the ones disparaging Dick, cool bartender looked up, interested all the sudden. Abnormally in-terested? *Oh, no,* I thought.

And: *Don't look at me like you suddenly want to lick me, too.*

And: *I'd say that I was gay except I fear that this may turn you on.*

And: *Yes, you see my soon to be drained beer right? That's all I really want from this situation. Can you accept that? You're going to have to.*

And: *Sure, and thank you sir; may I please now have another?*

The Moth Girl

Mick captured the Moth Girl on June twelfth of 1993, three months after Randy left the Big Billy Circus, when they were in the process of touring Cincinnati. Circus buses trailed each other single-file like ants on the road; the tiger cages followed gaudily on ribbon-strewn flatbeds, and Mick brooded in his trailer, thinking about Randy and picking acne from his chin.

He adjusted the tilt of his wheelchair and said, "You shouldn't have hightailed it out, Randy. I have our millions right here, right now." With his hand atop of the bell-jar, Mick wished Randy could see him now, with this little, white slip of a girl in the glass entrapment, screaming at the top of her lungs that she was Memory and he should let her go. She was hairy; that's what she was!

Mick put his hand tightly over the jar's opening as she dive-bombed his palm. Her teeth sank into skin like tiny needles, and, "Oh no," Mick thought, "it's another hallucination to be gone in the morning." His last hallucination had left him struggling on the lap of the Most

Beautiful Fat Girl in the World, Yolanda Berro Fellini, but she was real (he knew her), and the fantasy wasn't. Anyway, he preferred to call it a dream, and in this dream, he had climbed Yolanda's body, kissing her every inch, and inserting his fingers into her fat-folds like placing metal hooks in the crevices on hillsides, straddling the mass of her flesh as if he climbed a great, benevolent, *montagne de peau* — and in his dream, he'd said, "Why do you want me, anyway? I was born with stumps. I'm not much of a man."

She'd replied, "I'm enough woman for both of us, enough man too." Her eyes were enormous and bovine, her lips the fellating lips of supermodels. She wore red lipstick and pulled his body toward her when he faltered, sustaining his armpits with her strong hands. She hefted him upwards, her dark Latin curls falling over his face as he navigated her blooming chest.

When he grabbed the bulk of her shoulder, the fantasy almost ended. His ear — that small, soft shell — had pressed so firmly into her chest that when he lifted his head, an unsticking noise occurred, whose sound so heightened his eroticism that he found himself unmanned, loosing his love juice in hot streams down her thighs.

He sweated rivers. His palms slicked, and he slid down her torso in that moment, staring sadly up, like a noodle bolstered between her calves. Yolanda. The hallucination, the dream, the Most Beautiful Fat Girl in the World. She stood on the fifth stage most afternoons, this one too, gathering admirers, but she was out of his reach, both literally and metaphorically.

"Drugs," Randy would've said about Mick's current vision, but Randy was gone, and Randy had talked burnout before the Eye-Ball miniature golf course, where a thousand blue-eyed balls ordered from a Taiwanese firm rolled over green astroturf to fall into holes shaped like sockets made its debut five years ago. It was amazing Randy had stayed as long as he had.

Mick looked at the shrieking jar-creature, wondering when she'd disappear. Would Randy see her? He kept his hand on the opening, writhing with both excitement and self-pity. But, what did that matter? Randy was gone — Randy, who had been the father Mick never had, making him at home in the circus when Mick had been bounced out of too many foster homes.

They'd met at the Motel 6, where Clyde and Emma, the crackheads, had left him, where Mick's pudgy glance locked looks with Randy's smiling eyes. But Mick hadn't expected Randy to take him in and give him half his stuff — or half his job. Mick hadn't expected anything, but when Randy came out, trailed narrowly by a hooker with red stockings, Randy picked up Mick's duffle and said, "Wanna join the circus, kid?"

Mick agreed, and that was that for the next ten years, but lately when he missed Randy, Mick remembered cruising the parks in Randy's beat-up van, almost feeling the slick tilt of his wheelchair as he slid down the wooden ramp Randy had built, hearing the slow crunch of his wheels over that frosty grass as they maneuvered out past the park's deserted areas.

Randy had told Mick that girls were all secretly interested in cripples. Randy was a sport. "Hey Mickey," he'd say, "Would you look at her! She's a beaut — how much money have you got?" Every week, rain or shine, Randy handed Mick his hard earned cash in crumpled bills, and Mick kept them in his pocket to give back when convenient. Then, each time Randy chose a girl, Mick peeled three twenties off the wad, then waited to be dropped at the circus before Randy headed for a motel.

Three days later, Randy would still be talking about the girl like he wanted to marry her, so as far as Mick could tell, Randy knew the good girls from the bad.

But Mick had never been with a hooker. He was twenty and had never been laid, but he remembered being propositioned by an older man in a burgundy suit one day when he was fifteen, in a store called Ero-Bon. "You could make a quick couple thousand if you'd be in a porn-movie with a girl I know," the man said. "You look kind of like Christopher Reeves, and she's a good little piece. You do have a — well, you know? It makes no difference if it's small."

Randy looked at Mick, whose cheeks reddened with embarrassment, so Randy balled his fist. The red-suit man went on to say it would be the first porn movie he'd make with a man with no legs. "You have any experience with the ladies, son?" he asked. "It's okay if you don't."

As Mick shifted uncomfortably in his chair, Randy took the man's wrist in his palm and squeezed it, then glared, holding the hand on Mick's stumps, saying, "Can't you see this boy's got legs? You must be blind not to see them—"

"I'm talking to the boy here, mister," the filmmaker squeaked, "so butt out," but Randy just cracked the man's wrist in his hand, breaking the bones, then turned the spikes of his tin ring out, having already depressed the ejection button. He whispered something malicious in the filmmaker's ear as he made the man bleed before planting his foot in the burgundy ass. The man ran out and Randy told Mick, "You don't want any girl of his, Mickey. There's good, hard-working girls like I get, and then there's girls like his. Sluts."

If only Randy could see this little spitfire in the jar, Mick thought, maybe he would come back. On closer inspection, Mick noticed the jar-thing's breasts, tiny and perky beneath a fine layer of hair, but — "Stop looking at my chest!" she shouted, then, "Go away!"

Mick stared at her whimsically, not caring, thinking of the last spit-beer croquet game he'd played with Randy in July. "What I wouldn't give," Randy had sighed, "for a few hysterical tantrums and a big 'wow' like we used to have. There's nothin' Mickey. I tell you, there's nothin' like it." The red ball clicked into blue as he threw Mick into the loser corner.

"The time will come, Randy," Mick had said, rolling to the ball, "You just got to be patient for the big-time, the freak that'll make this place rich. You've done a good job."

Randy looked pensive, scratching his thigh, and swung his mallet with tender precision. "Waiting? What is waiting, Mick? Another day of working like a slug." He took aim and smacked the ball, which hit the pole, and the game was over. "Okay Mickey," Randy said, "gimme your beer," but Randy hadn't even taken pleasure in hocking up his loogie like normal, just made a little *pptteu*, and Mick took his beer back and drank it.

In the early days, Mick knew, Randy was a man on fire. The circus had dancers and monkeys and tigers and clowns; the circus had game booths, electric rides, and a freak show. Now there were just dancers, a monkey, a tiger and the freak show. Everything else was too expensive, the costumes had frayed, and the dancers now doubled as clowns.

Since Randy left, his freaks had left too. The "mermaid," though she had no legs, was tired of wearing the smelly fish tails they purchased for her, the man with half a face went into soaps, and Mick's current menagerie was both tired and tiring.

A new gimmick was exactly what he needed — something to make them proud again, to get the love back. It had been ages since they'd caught a pair of kissers behind the tents and scared them with a freakish prank. In fact, capturing the whitey girl was the first real piece of luck Mick had had since that blond Vegas dancer sat in his lap for free.

The fantasy with Yolanda was one thing, but the whitey girl, she felt real. "Ouch," he yelled out, painfully cleaved from his daydream of finding Randy by another clamp of her piranha teeth. "You could bite the skin right off me!"

"Let me go, Mick, or I'll bite again," she said. "Let me go!"

His hand smarted from the first bite, and even more from the next, so he looked for the wire-mesh piece to place over the hole. "Ease up," he said. "Just another minute, please, Girly."

"I'm Memory!" she screamed. "And I demand to be let go!"

He laughed. Memory wasn't a white mothy thing — it was a collective, an undefinable phenomenon! He had no way of knowing whether it was real and factual, or came to be after a while, growing stranger like a changing imprint that deviated with time — but he was sure that memory was not her. And where was that bit of screen, anyway?

This was a perfect example of his memory theory: He remembered leaving the screen in the dancers' tent, but just then saw it on the table, so he had been wrong. His memory had tricked him. She hadn't. He grabbed the screen and prepared to move his hand away from the opening, thinking: One thing was for sure — this creature was nuts, and she would draw a crowd.

He switched hands so his other palm covered the hole, staring at his bitten skin where blood poked up. He removed his other hand quickly to tape on the screen, then stared at her again. She was just the tiny angel he'd searched for while looking over the help-wanted ads that morning. Actually, she was a miracle, because with his few skills, Mick was certain no one would hire him so he'd have nowhere to go.

Randy had believed in Mick's tongue and a half, but no one but a circus manager would pay him for it. Besides, it was a tiny flap anyway, noticeable only over a projector screen, but hard to discern otherwise. Still, perhaps if he practiced, Mick had thought, played music, and attempted mirrored routines with samba beats... Except no, Mick reasoned, he wasn't worth a dime — a cripple in a wheelchair with a tongue and a half — no big shakes, but they would pay to see her.

He'd known she was a hot ticket the minute he'd spotted her hovering over a photograph of him and Randy on the wall. She was six inches tall and six inches wide with her gossamer wings spread open. Her face looked starved, and "The flesh of photographs is filthy," she'd said. "Filthy dirty. Blech, blech, blech. The tent, the dog, the car, the thanks, the grudges, it's too much! Why these things were ever invented, I don't know. Old portraits painters had the right idea. One person. One setting. Artificial pose. The old days!"

She had, of course, been talking to herself, and her voice was a high, gargley sound, but she was beautiful. Her white wings glistened with black circles on their upper halves, like a death moth, so The Moth Girl, Mick decided then — that's what he'd call her.

He'd build her an exhibit complete with a mag-nifying screen and a series of night blooming flowers. "The

Moth Girl," he said again. "In her twilight garden."

"I am Memory, you idiot," she asserted. "Moths have insect faces."

"And her twilight garden," Mick adjusted. "No — near her twilight garden..."

"Memory!" she shouted. "I'm Mem-or-y."

"You are a figment of my imagination," he said, "but if not, you will be called 'The Moth Girl in Her Twilight Garden.' Hey, Gloria! Come in here for a sec, will ya?"

Gloria, the chimp trainer, entered with Charles, the masturbating spider monkey. Charles wore a dirty pink uniform. "Yeah, boss?" she asked.

"Do you see a hairy thing that looks like a woman in this jar?"

"Yeah, boss."

"Good, then go get Davey."

"Davey's feeding the tiger because the mice act is out."

"So what? Get him," Mick said, looking closer at Memory, who then exclaimed, "You pointless twit! Let me out. At the very least, give me my feather!"

"What feather?"

"The one stuck on your sleeve, wasting my time by eliminating memories of lint and dryer sheets. I have work to do, Mickey, work, and your little relationship with Randy is the least of my worries." She glared and said, "There's a man down in Brooklyn who, if I don't get there, will never eat his favorite sandwich again because of yesterday's heartburn. There's a girl in Cleveland, who, if I don't get there, will never get over the sight of the house she almost rented with a fiancé. There's a boy in Des Moines, who, if I don't get there, will never forget the kids at school teased him about wetting his nap foam this morning, and who, for that reason, will fear naps for the rest of his life. Do you want more examples? Let me go! This continent is just a small part of my worries."

Mick pulled the feather from his sleeve and swept it through the air, saying, "Abracadabra!" but, "Stop that!" she shouted. "If you control the feather, you must know how to use it! Watch and learn: I'm concentrating now and I'll ask you a question: What did you eat for lunch today, Mickey?"

Mick could not recall.

"Okay, let's try another," she said, "When you woke up, what did you do first?"

Mick had no clue.

"You see!" she exclaimed. "I took those things! Out of your head! I cleaned those details away. Now give me back the feather or bad, bad things are bound to happen. Even good things might happen, which will, in turn, be terrible, because nothing will measure up. I mean everything and nothing, Mickey. I know everything about you, but you are only one man. No more. No less. Give me the feather."

How crappy, Mick thought, even his delusions told him he needed to be lorded over. At least Yolanda and he had been about to make mad, passionate love! This little woman thing wasn't going to give him anything but a headache.

Mick ran his fingers over the feather and couldn't remember what he'd just been thinking, so looked at her again as she reached for it, but kept it distant and then slid her feather into the kind of plastic sack a pair of prize earrings come in. "Memory," he said. "Hmmm."

That night he asked the others, and they voted to call her exhibit "Memory and the Pain Reducing Feather, $5.00".

He went back to his tent. "So I can't give it back because you can't go. But I will hold the feather and you'll will people into forgetting things," he told the girl. "But just so's you know I'm a good guy, we'll split the profit, fifty-fifty."

She sighed, looked resigned, and said, "I don't need money, Mick. You'll get it before long."

"Are you hungry?" he asked her. "Want a ham sandwich?"

"I eat thoughts," she shouted, spinning in her jar. "And yes, I am starving, so bring in the crowds! But I only do the top layer. No more. No less."

The first three days went rather slowly. He sat beside her, restless, and each afternoon, Gloria ushered in slightly larger groups. He waved the feather as Memory concentrated.

By the fifth day there were a hundred people waiting outside, and by the seventh, a thousand or more. Mick grew amazed. He made tons of money even though the Moth Girl listened to what the customers said they wanted and laughed in their faces. Instead of being angry, after a light demonstration of one forgotten thing, they cowered as if she were a God, so Mick, too, began to fear her.

He remembered how, to one man's request, she looked at him sadly and cautioned: "George, you don't really think I could take away fifty-three years of Charlotte, do you?" When he smiled apologetically, she said, "Forty seven years, fifteen minutes and 3 seconds is how long it would take — considering the tertiary and quaternary elements. I'm sorry. You may not live that long."

"Is that all?" he asked, waved happily, and left the tent, crying as if purified. After that, she'd simply wipe the surface of their thoughts and tell exactly how long it would take to forget whatever trials they most wanted to evade. Teen love was the quickest, unlucky accidents the worst, and "You can't forget just what you want," she admonished. "I don't work that way."

Then the money rolled in, in earnest, but a strange phenomenon happened all over the circus; not a single trivial detail was missed by anyone. Mick's brain felt crowded. Thoughts lapped up on each other like dogs. Yolanda wore a new dress of red and gold brocade, and Mick thought about it fifty-eight times one day and a hundred and three the next — but actually, perhaps the first fifty eight were repeats and the next forty five were new.

Still, every day the Moth Girl asked, "Can you feel it yet, Mickey? Does it bother you?" and one day, in the beginning of the next week, she asked to watch the news. An old television was brought in and the broadcast did a special about lawyers: *Tests conducted yesterday at the National Law Institute showed a record retention rate of 93% for first year law students.* She turned in her jar and said, "Welcome to long term trivial memory, Mick! The lost seven-percent was what they just hadn't read. Can you feel it yet? Your head will explode. Let me go."

People streamed in from all over. Mick wrote Randy a telegram: Come back STOP The circus is making money hand over foot STOP Come immediately STOP I'm making $5 a head, and lines are flooding through towns STOP We're in Dayton now STOP Follow the masses STOP I'm in the big tent STOP Your sometimes son STOP Mickey.

The Moth Girl grew more and more incensed, and Mick thought about Yolanda all the time. He also thought about money. He was rich. It had been nine days since the tent had opened, and the Moth Girl now insisted on watching the news, every minute, while at the same time wiping away thousands of thoughts — no longer asking what anyone wanted to forget, just looking them over and shouting out a count.

Mick stayed up all night for the crowds, giving himself only three half-hour naps, but, meanwhile, the news got worse and worse. Wives killed husbands, parents left squalling toddlers on strangers' doorsteps, and delis lost business. Mick thought thoughts in tandem: Yolanda's bare abdomen and my little ear, Randy may come back, Yolanda's huge nipples like belly dancing dills, Randy and the midget, no more ham sandwiches, I'm tired, I'm tired, I'm tired.

Even politicians committed suicide from the sheer unforgettable nature of the Poe hearts beating in floor boards, but in the tent, Memory's feather waved and waved. The next day, instead of sleeping, Mick went to Yolanda's tent and sat before her.

"I have to ask you something," he said. Her green eyes blinked with seeming interest. "Did we ever," he asked, "that is, do you ever remember me coming to you and my ear making a soft sucking noise as it slid down your abdomen? Do you remember telling me you were man enough for both of us? Do you remember being close to making mad-passionate-love — with me?"

She asked, "Was this when we were traveling through Cincinnati?"

"Yes," he said, "Just then. Do you remember?"

"Yes," she said, "I wondered why you never mentioned it. I thought you changed your mind. I felt so sad about it, Mickey, so very sad."

"I didn't change my mind," he said. "I thought I was dreaming, but I have to go back to the tent now."

"All I can think about is a pair of silver shoes I had once," she said. "I remember every swift turn of my ankle and how I ate dark chocolate gelato while wearing them. Do you know why, Mick? Those shoes recur in my thoughts almost daily. Faces are unforgettable now. I'm thinking of leaving the circus and going into real estate networking. Is this a good idea?"

"Come to the tent," he said, "to the front of the line. I'll help you."

When he returned, Memory tapped her nails on the glass, sucking her cheeks to mimic a starved woman, so Mick walked to the entryway, loosed the rope, and let in the crowds. Some had waited upwards of two days, living on lemonade, pretzels, and blooming onions.

"I'm hungry, Mickey," the Moth Girl said. "I am ravenous for thoughts. Can you feel it? The world caves in on itself. Humanity needs cleansing. You are only one man, one man."

"Yeah, yeah, diminish me some more," Mick said, sliding money into the safe, but at this exact moment, a special bulletin came over the airwaves: *The President of the United States has been shot. Sources say it was an old schoolmate who was once a victim of his boyish pranks. Investigator, Tim Banks on the scene –*

Memory clutched her abdomen and staggered. "I was afraid old business would occur to someone," she said, but Mick continued to usher in the crowds as five-dollar bills slipped from his sweaty palms to litter the floor. Memory yelled out numbers and twirled in the jar.

Suddenly, Yolanda appeared at the tent with both Randy and the midget who strangled mice. "Mickey," Randy boomed. "I've been thinking about your telegram for days, for days and days and days. In fact, it's all I think about."

"Make him stop," the midget said. "He won't eat Rueben sandwiches. All he talks about is you and the days when you guys cruised the parks. I fall from his head altogether. He almost forgot to bring me here. He's going insane, or in love with you — I don't know which."

Memory called out, "Thirty years, hahaha." Bills thickened all around the tent floor, landing at their feet, accruing like dandruff on shoulders. The feather in its plastic casing vibrated and pulsed.

Yolanda said, "I have to admit, I love him, too. I love your ears, Mickey, more than you'll ever know."

The crowd jostled and pushed. Memory called out, "Seventy two days," and the crowd pushed harder, some scratching their heads fiendishly as if thoughts had become head lice. Mickey rolled to the rope and latched it to block the steady stream of newcomers. "I am only one man," he said, spinning dizzily, trapped.

Memory laughed and laughed. "You know what to do!" she said. "You know!" The midget wore her mice-strangling outfit, a green pinafore with orange buttons, which pulsed in Mickey's eyes. He couldn't breathe. When it was only Memory and his friends, he zipped down the front view flap and looked around.

The crowd shifted from the front of the tent to the exit flap and stared in. Many sets of eyes crowded the small opening, with thousands more waited behind the first group. There was going to be a frenzy.

"Can you feel it yet, Mickey?" Memory shouted. "The flesh of photographs is filthy, but the world's mind is worse. Let me out. Let me go! I can help them."

Yolanda stared at Mick, Randy repeated how much he missed him, and Mick moved purposefully to the jar, ripping the net away. He yanked the feather from the plastic bag and dropped it on the table. "Take it," he whispered. "Go."

She smiled. The crowd ripped the flap and threw their money in, hoping to be the last of the unafflicted, while Memory, The Moth Girl, flew free. She twirled and giggled then laughed at the five-dollar bills floating in the air like drifts of green snow. Mick rolled over to Yolanda and put his ear to her stomach, ignoring the bustle, and then, like in his dream, he climbed her body as Randy dispersed the crowd and closed the tent down.

Three hours later the circus lot was vacant, and they were finally alone, Mick, Randy, the midget, and Yolanda — so Mick kissed Yolanda, letting her red lipstick smear on his face and pressing his head to her chest until the calm, round beat of her heart blocked out his thoughts. The beating was now steady, but not unforgettable.

He pressed his ears from one breast to the other so that a soft sucking sound might continue. As the news played from the TV, he settled in closer to her body, letting Yolanda hold him as he imagined the Moth Girl's feather caressing his scalp, her hideous laughter growing further away. "Hey, Mick," Yolanda asked suddenly. "What were you thinking just now?"

"I don't know," he said, scratching his head. "Finally, I don't know. I really don't know. Can you just imagine that?"

"I can," she said. "It's hard to remember the little things that swim up all the time, don't you think?"

"Sometimes, but maybe it's better we don't," he replied tiredly, nudging her breasts with his chin. "I like to remember only what I have to. Life is better that way."

Then like a comforted infant who suckled deep from the mother's milk teat of his absent recall, he pressed himself deeper to her folds, and slept.

If There Is an Airport

If there is an airport, it is one of dreams. If there is a dream, it is one of shadows. If there are shadows, there is not much more but the thoughts of a short man meeting a short woman on a runway of forbidden desires, in a foreign city belonging to neither, where there is no time to sate the urges of years spent talking yet never meeting.

Does this man bring with him, after a five-hour drive, a board game they may play in this airport where her plane arrives? Does he himself arrive or not? These things are mysteries. If he drives and arrives, with this gesture, does he do so to show her she does, after all, mean more to him than an idle fantasy he uses only when necessary to stimulate years of unfulfilled loins — or does he simply not come, not drive, not arrive, not anything — mainly not doing a damn thing except sit in his house with his wife he cannot make love to, abandoning his literary mistress in the sacred name of cowardice or possibly virtue?

Are cowardice and virtue interchangeable at times? If he does not arrive and she lands only to

disembark to his non-arrival, non-romance, non-justifi-
cation, does this mean, then, that she was right in the
perceived unbalance and can view him as a taker who
does not ever give back and is cancerous to her soul? If she
is beautiful enough, is there no way he cannot arrive? If
she truly moves his heart, will this force his hand onto his
keys? If he does not come, will she want to take a razor-
blade to the finest, whitest part of her neck?

If she does not want to cut herself, will she crave to
disappear nonetheless?

If there is an airport, it is one of dreams. It is one of
shadows and possible culminations. It is one of strangers,
who are actually online lovers, possibly meeting, and it is
the answer to a number of irritating questions, like: Is any
of it real, this talking we do?

Or, if (dolled up, beautiful, waiting) she finds he
does not come and adds all up to the idea that he has truly
never gone out of his way to entertain or pursue her,
should she, as she thinks, simply let him go? Can she hate
him enough? Is she too beautiful for such self-destructive
behavior—too talented and loving to not be so well-loved?

And, in the end, does she? Let him go, that is? Of
course. She is married, too.

This story, this airport, was always a tragedy. His
wife will continue to sit on his couch in his home where his
dog barks and his cat meows and his children fight and
kiss. There will be no double break-ups and then new
wedding at the end. Leave that to Shakespeare who knew
how to make a dark thing light. Still: The man loves her, he
says, so what if a dark thing is light but patchy, like stars
in a black blanket of sky?

What if it sparkles and dims—or is like white
horses, bright figures sparkling on the greenest hills, in
front of the bluest skies, riding free on the spirit's darkest

days?

The sound of the plane is a whir. Still, she almost knows too well he will not come for her, for he never has. Inaction is his action. No, she thinks. He will not come for her or with her. For he never has.

Most days his hands engineer his own comings (and goings). But on this day, are those keys to his single-family dwelling and his single-family car in his hands and possession for a ride towards a need that is wearing her name?

Is there a need? Perhaps she is only a want, like another slice of pie after dinner. Like a massage given by a whore, like a twenty percent tip...but the plane will land soon. "Please buckle your seatbelts," the pilot announces as she fixes her trashed make-up. More tears happen, more and more, added to the sum of those that came before. She cannot wipe them away quickly enough. The engines or her thoughts buzz. Yet, there is hope. Since she hasn't arrived yet; there is still possibility, plausibility...

He knows she is coming. What if he is standing there, waiting for her?

But if there is an airport, it is one of dreams. If there is a dream, it is one of a woman crying for any number of reasons but mainly because the lobby is full of people that don't include him, if she suspects correctly. Can she picture her own unraveling? Yes. Or maybe she will stop crying and smile as the well finally runs dry, for she will have cried every single tear she can imagine already over preceding months. Or perhaps, if he is not there, she will simply fall into that carpet like mist to linger below the other travelers' feet.

Or maybe she will re-center, stand tall, walk proudly out and phoenix above the thoughts that are sweet poison in order to reclaim her inner warrior. For she will remember, when he doesn't show, that she doesn't need him. She never did. She is better off without him. And she will recall that she has always made this self-reclamation, in the end, no matter how dumb her acts — or how she may feel like a crushed petal left to the undersides of other people's shoes.

The plane drops its landing gear. If there is an airport, it is one of dreams. She checks her seatbelt twice. If there are dreams, there will be an awakening. She applies mauve lipstick. If there is such an awakening, she will feel the earth again, having been so sick of air below stances that she could write a manual about how to avoid such frippery as building thought castles on such shifty mediums as sky. She puts her hand to her heart like she pledges her allegiance, but to what? To what does she owe allegiance? *My country tis of thee...* Does she long for this awakening or fear it? Both.

Both.

Either way, in this airport, which is made of dreams (or which is real) — *Your seat cushion can be used as a flotation device; it will swell and protect you, really* — or in this place where two people who purport to be enmeshed in an impossible love don't normally interface, will there be an opportunity for something predestined, or something unbearably laced with despair? Will the beautiful woman disembark soon to find something she never knew? Will it be him?

She stands. She follows others down the aisle. In moments, she will have entered the space she wonders about. Does she hope this will be a dreamlike place where the air will wear a person like a coat, where the very tables speak, and where her fantasy of this man, dreamt a thousand times on the plane (the one where he arrives with a game with wood tiles under his arm and a smile on his face), be enacted? Will there be a moment where their hands will palm the air after stirring coffees with no cream or sugar, stirring just to stir and then palming each other's hands after so many words, endless words, love letters, poetry, stories, and long absences? Two palms, connecting.

And even if they cannot have each other after this day, not then, not ever, is this act that he might arrive, that he might let her touch him and look at him, enough that she could bear the rest of her life without him, asking him to change nothing of his home, but possibly then, figuring out a way where their friendship could be built, if not on undeniable love, then on something else (or the very same thing it had always been based on: dreams) such that it might begin differently and anew?

And if they sat across from each other then, what would happen when this happened, this fragile palming of air and then the other's palm, an act they had so oft discussed? Would it be electric? Would they sigh? Would they die right there and solve all problems by having two sudden, yet freeing, heart attacks? Or would they simply recognize the care they feel and felt, which is and was real, then complete the game of words and tiles for the day — the woman having won with her placement of seven tiles, an often lucky number, spelling the simple word "refrain," and then, in two opposite directions, walk?

And would the word "refrain" mean to her the part of a song that most moves a soul, or "Please, do not enter into that labyrinth that is my heart again"? Would each, in such an airport, during such an exit, after such a culmi-nation, move away fondly, never to be seen together (again) or in the same place twice, but writing to each other as friends, always and again, long time friends who write their pain in stories and poems and sometimes to each other, checking on the weather where the other lives, on the idea of dreams and airports with no solutions due to earlier marriages and circumstances, and check in, every once and a long while, on the dangerous inquiry topic they cannot, all the time, avoid—which is the relative status of the happiness of the other's life, which was never one of dreams but of real-world hard edges, quiet beauty, frequent boredom mirroring contentment, and the firmest, most wakeful ground?

If this is an airport it is one of dreams. Seven years of them, ferried back and forth in email and letters, heated exchanges that could, quite possibly, have a zero sum as she steps off the plane.

The woman disembarks. She is beautiful. She looks up and around and down. If there is an airport, she cannot see it. She sees only people, for this is how fully she seeks him in that waiting room; walls do not exist, only flesh and sunlight. Her scope of that room is dreamlike. And yet, he is not there.

If there is an airport, it is one of dreams. Dreams (dying, dying). Amazing, she thinks, how quiet the sound of one heart breaking can be, as quiet as the wet that begins to slide down her face, carrying several shades of shadow to her collar in hot streams as she strides to claim her baggage.

Does the world whisper crisply then like fall leaves rustling on trees and then fall all around her as she steps outside to rent a car in the outer lot to drive off onto a road she has never traveled before? Certainly. This story was always a tragedy.

You knew that. You knew that. I swear.

Room Full of Scars

Earlier that summer, Shella wanted to demolish this room, but it had grown from the time she purchased the house on Belgrade eight years previous, into a place that emitted a sickly pallid energy. Squinting, the early contractors could not be convinced to enter, touch the walls, or remain. It had the feel of something intimate or personal, like worn stockings. They had no idea how to remove the wall coverings that, pink and pearly and thick as sound-proofer's foam, gleamed annually more luminous with her increasing experience.

"What's beneath this fabric?" they asked. "And is it radioactive?"

"It's only scars," she replied, as though personally affronted.

"Well, those are load-bearing walls, lady," one guy said, scratching his belly to reveal a tattoo of a Japanese symbol. "Aside from the light, that's another problem."

She'd only called two businesses since more seemed like unnecessary humiliation. Besides, they were right. Something otherworldly gleamed from the shadows to emerge from that doorway. Even when she entered by herself, with great hope, enjoying the light's full spectrum as she did and unlocking the door with an ever-present key on a 14 karat gold chain around her neck, the room glistened so brightly that not even morning sunlight could compete.

After scar after scar had been flung upon the walls, she admitted the inside was nearly blinding, the memory of four dead children as inventory, two divorces, one botched bankruptcy, a dangerous illness, a substantial loss of income, a punishing loss of friends, social anxiety, vanished faith...her list went on and on. Regardless she considered herself an optimist.

This was how it could exist. Shella was smart and pretty: Shella, with her long black hair, gamine legs, and huge dwelling eyes. No one could take these from her. Hair up in a Psyche's knot most days, mildly weathering her late forties in the flowing skirts and loose garments of a lifetime bohemian, she found no shortage in the men she attracted. Women either. Like visitors to a foreign country known as Glorious Visitation Despair, they wanted to touch her hidden sadness and thought to find it in the false temple of her body. But beauty existed independently of happiness, as it always had.

Of course, later, when she told them how she maintained her composure, how she kept the sorrow down, they wanted to see the room. She dreamt of refusing their curiosity, but could never tell them enough without physically revealing the blinding éclat of the place that beckoned, the room that enticed all voyeurs like an under-bed diary, as if to say: "Come in. Come in. Although this might destroy you. Do you really want to see?"

Their answer was invariably yes, but, once there, some hesitated at the open door and then fled. Some entered for a moment and later, clutching abdomens as if sucker-punched, exited slowly, apologetically, backing out of her home as a small animal might whimper and retreat from a predator's lair. Though the room held thick emotions, the most frequent complaint she personally received from her lovers was that she herself remained unable to be moved, stoic, possessing the glory of a statue with a similar lack of sentiment.

"She comes in the bedroom okay enough," she imagined them whispering to friends. "No problem there. But what comes afterward is pure stone."

Well, of course I am stony, she thought to herself. *I give all my luster to the room. All my feelings. The room protects me, lets me function. Don't you have any flaws? I bet you haven't even a thought closet!*

And yet, when another young curly-headed man arrived, one with whom she wanted to have meaningful verbal intercourse, one to have survived both his first and second viewings of the room only to return and kiss her gently, tucking her softly into her suede blankets, when he emerged the third time, shaken and visibly trembling, she decided anew that either her lovers or the room had to go.

"I've got to get rid of it! What are walls if not shelter?" she asked him one morning. "I must be a person fully united. But if the room goes, if I cannot use it to calm me, will you stay? I ask now, but I will not beg."

"I wouldn't ask you to beg," he said. "You're above that." He was the age her oldest son would have been, so she often regarded him like a sometimes son, one who was also her lover, a smart strange boy who molested his lover-mother and took her to the limits of carnal and tender passions, sleeping afterwards with his hand near his mouth like a child, as if about to suck a thumb. "I want us to be together all the time," he said, while wakeful, spurred by his desire for her, which seemed to grow with more contact.

"But one day," she said, "you'll look at me and I won't be the pretty older woman, Lucian. I'll be a hag who has tricked you. You'll watch the girls your age and feel I have trapped you in a web inside a cave. By then, I will need you far too much to let you go. I don't want to live to see that day. So you're free to go now, if it's kinder to us both."

"I don't want to leave," he replied with vehemence. "I won't get tired of you."

"All right," she replied, partially believing.

The contractors came again, their quotes astronomical. After she and her boy-child made love that night, Shella took a razor into her scars with faith and hope, remembering the gentle smile he gave her for even her smallest effort, trying to scrape the pink-white tissue off the walls both with the blade and her own nails.

The cutting hurt pleasurably — like when she was nine and sliced her thighs to relieve anxiety — a mixture of bravery and foolishness. To cause new pain to end current pain seemed unlikely in theory, but, in practice, the chemicals concurred.

Lucian was so proud. "You're mine, scars and all," he said.

Later, "I'll cut more free," she told him, and then she addressed the walls again to liberate more scars, speaking with a firm, almost parental persuasion, saying, "Come off now. Do as I wish."

Whether they took notice of her edict was unclear. Initially she thought, if their liberation went well and she destroyed the room, the energy it housed and grew, the light and sensations, might return to her in some sort of radiant re-birth, recovering her ambitions like the parents of a retrieved orphan might regain the cast-off fragment of an earlier, once mutilated future. But to pry a chunk of scar from the walls, ripped and torn, and then apply it to her skin only proved painful, a blistering of flesh where the history met its maker.

"Shella, keep trying," Lucian coaxed. "Can't you do more?"

"I'll try," she replied, but the more scars she cut, the more pain she felt. In the walls, gashes remained in the places where she'd removed bits of tissue, though it was only when her scars again met with skin that she seemed lifted from the placating emotional slumber of the last eight years into the mixed and florid spectrum of the present.

She grew more sensitive, but unpleasantly moody. Her young swain tried, yet couldn't handle the burden of her emotion.

He simply could not cope with her life's revival. A few days later, he took his leave, saying, "I'm sorry. I thought I could handle you, but I can't. It's too much." He kissed her face to reinforce his inadequate apology.

The break-up sex, for both, was a toxic pleasure, each limb tasted slowly, each body part held or fondled as if to wish it and their former bond goodbye, hours spent to end their liaison — her newly replaced scars kissed, touched, and tasted. Though she could not feel his kiss through her wrecked tissue, to know that he put his mouth there on purpose soothed her.

She continued to attempt her change, but there was new fall-out at work. Unlike during the years when she had ripped scars free and flung them to the wall as they accrued, able to respond to any visitor with calm, she was now damaged anew, with nowhere to release the present's trials. *I cannot fling them into this house and call it progress,* she thought. *Not to the very same walls I'm trying to purge.*

She considered anti-depressants. She drank. She called Lucian, but he had a new lover five years her senior. Resultantly, she felt cheapened that his former desire for her had not been unique. She'd been a type, so returned old scars once more to smooth the walls, but their energy had partially reclaimed her, even after leaving her body.

She reopened the phonebook to find more contractors to tell her how, without entering the light room, they could create new load-bearing walls for the house such that the ones that flanked the room were made redundant.

Since again contemplating the room's destruction, she visited her scars more often, but the more she entered, the more she experienced a lulling complacency — *here I am, all of me,* she thought. *Smooth. Pink. It's okay if only me likes all of me. I don't need anyone. I can't trust anyone else and that's for certain.*

Still, dismantling the room may be productive, she maintained, because only when she forgot the room could she deal with life's mundane details. It would cost forty thousand dollars to build the extra load-bearing walls, she was told, possibly more for city-sanctioned blue-prints and special architects — all this necessary before the wrecking ball could come to wreak its havoc.

The room's destruction was a constant topic of her conversation, yet to hover there between estimates and meetings made her doings almost traitorous. If betrayed emotion had a color, she decided, it was the color of a light bulb sparking in a dark basement when a single cord is pulled, the aftershock found in the eyes. "I don't want to believe that I must have a secret place for my sadness in order to be fully immersed in my own life story," she told her therapist Mel, "but I'm drawn there again and again.

The room is so bright and beautiful. Nothing compares. Who else has such a room?"

"Fully involved in your own life story?" Mel asked, staring at his clock. "Is everything a story for you, Shella?"

"People let you down," Shella replied. "I see that now. All people."

"And romantic commitments are now out of the question?"

"Yes. I hate those," Shella replied. "They're bait and switch."

"I am worried about you," he warned. "You missed two appointments last month. Where were you?"

"You haven't helped me," she replied. "I wasn't motivated to come."

"Where were you?"

"Out to lunch?" she said.

"At five in the afternoon?"

She missed the next four appointments in a row and didn't return his calls. Listening to his insistent messages without reply gave her pleasure. She took no calls from work either. Soon enough, she was fired but hardly cared.

All night and all day, the room lured her despite its cluttered interior, despite an extra half-closeted vacuum, travel luggage on the floor, board games unused for decades strewn on shelves, and the letters, so many letters from her past, tucked in an open promise trunk. It seemed to effuse the quality of a probable explanation that would never come. "To kill this place," she told a friend, "would be like eliminating one's sole remaining bad habit and then letting boredom evoke a newer torture."

She took to cleaning this room. Though the door hung open like a slack mouth as she worked, not even her cats would visit. She kept the contractor quotes handy but never booked the service. Two years passed, funded lightly by unemployment, and the room's luminosity dimmed not a stroke. It neither gained nor lost luster.

Not that this appealed, but she lost her sense of time and fantasized sometimes, late at night in bed, when the sounds of the streets entered as brief cacophonies, that if she were to be robbed and a criminal entered through the wrong window, he or she might be trapped in her light, and by the time she found this criminal, he or she might be dead. If, however, the individual survived the room and grew to enjoy it, Shella could marry them.

"I am hoping for a prisoner of war?" she asked herself. It was bad will to hope that someone would enter her house and get trapped in her scars. *Just my luck, they'll come through another window,* she thought, *take all my valuables, and leave.*

To repent for her awesome self-pity, she forced herself out from her house. She got a new job, now more powerful and lucrative. She craved another partner. Anything that might be done to normalize the appearance of her life, to force it forward, she considered.

An older man would be good this time, she decided, still singed by the last one's lack of endurance, one who had weathered many storms, one for whom she would be the one expected to leave first. She wanted someone calm and dear, a partner with a level of suffering to match or exceed her own. Nonetheless, she acknowledged it was strange to appear so outwardly cool, knowing she sought a lover who both housed and could handle a tornado of emotion.

The problem of misrepresenting herself worried her. Was this duplicitous, her placid new hunt for a man while she outwardly remained so calm? Should she first seek a friendship and share her problems honestly, and then, later, possibly after intimacy, attempt to unveil her enormous untapped reservoir of needs?

So many times in courtships, she'd offered her body first, or her body only, but the room seemed to want her to pursue something more now, and if a room had a personality, she explained to a pushy, new, knowledgeable therapist named Lilith, this room was Genghis Khan. She wanted it gone, and yet at once she wanted to be owned by it, stifled by it, safe, along with acknowledging that she knew it was unhealthy to repress her flickering future by living in her shining past.

Unclear that the room of scars was not an elaborate metaphor at first, Lilith wanted to delve deeper. "Shella, if the light is so bright as to be blinding, what do you see when inside the scars?"

"I don't see inside the scars," Shella said. "You're not listening. The scars are on the walls. It's the room that's blinding."

"Okay, what do you see inside the room?"

"I see the scars," Shella said. "Like the memories connected to each other. I see the things I never want seen by others and I own them. I don't disregard or deny them because they are my history. The scars shame me only when I share them, and because they scare people who prefer that I remain peaceful, I habitually diminish their connection to the whole. But I am so bored and unhappy, so confined. The room is in the back of my house. It—"

"So this room actually exists?" Lilith raised one thin sculpted eyebrow.

"Oh yes."

"As a real room?"

"Didn't I say so? Would you like to come visit?"

"All right," Lilith said. "One day." But she approached Shella and knelt before her, touching Shella's hair and face. As often happened, Shella observed, an attraction was created. Like others, her therapist had been unable to resist the slow measured patterns of Shella's speech, her tragic beauty, her calm aplomb. "I'll come to your house," Lilith said. "But if you demolish the room, if the room no longer exists, what do you imagine will happen then?"

"I've considered this question for many years," Shella replied. "Either my light and scars will return to me where I can again feel at the level where I truly emote, or I will be debilitated by the force of the pain returned to me, battered, if you will. To keep the room intact could save my life, has saved it in the past — or this reclamation could kill me. But I believe the situation needs a remedy sooner rather than later."

"I think you should let the scars return," Lilith said, poking her desk with the tip of a sharpened pencil. "You should call them back. Because no one can withstand the room by itself, but if you learned to control the light, it could become a beacon. If it were harnessed, possibly, you would have the possibility of love. Your protection is important to you, but what's more important: learning to share your full self with others or self-indulgent protection of an embarrassing history?"

"Others can't handle my history," Shella replied.

"Really? How often have you tried?"

The faces of at least twenty lovers scrolled before Shella's eyes. "Lilith, if I had a nickel for every time I tried to love, we could meet every day for a year, and I could pay your bill in full."

"So you want people to like a fake version of your real self you don't reveal?"

"I like making money and working, without struggle," Shella answered. "I like people to like me for who they think I am, who they want me to be. Why be myself? It adds complications."

"Yes, and I like leaving splinters in as opposed to pulling them out," Lilith said, exhibiting her first instance of savvy, "but I think we both know what happens when a splinter is left to fester."

At this, Shella leapt up and hugged her. "You're such a bitch," she said. "I like you ."

"Oh, really?" Lilith muttered, surprised, reddening at the cheeks. "Congratulations, we've survived our first argument."

"I thought therapists discussed rather than arguing."

"And I thought patients weren't supposed to lie to the one who tries to help them."

"I never lie. That's part of my problem. I live in a state of confusion."

"We will begin with that next week."

That day, when Shella returned home, the room glowed brighter. Despite the new window coverings and draperies, now, even from the street, the difference was noticeable. Hoping to dim the room further, though reluctant, Shella again entered and removed scars from the walls. These, she applied one by one to her hips, striding in and out to monitor her home's appearance from the road, checking for normalcy from the exterior until the room was again indistinguishable.

"I have to get rid of that room," she told Lilith at their next meeting. "But what then? I invite the world to see my pain, like an exhibition? If I keep adding scars to my walls, the house could be condemned. Or, perhaps I build a gate, to hide the light? But I haven't enough room at the property line."

"Can you call more contractors and mean it this

time?" Lilith asked.

Shella called three different contractors. "I want," she said, "to demolish that last room with a wrecking ball, smack down the two outer walls and privately demo the one closest to the house. Since I hear those are load-bearing walls, I will need new load-bearing walls built to support the house beforehand, inside adjacent rooms, to bolster the structure.

"Can we see inside the room you want demoed?"

"No," she said. "No one goes in there."

"So you want to build new load bearing walls in existing rooms?" they asked. "Seriously, lady? Makes rooms smaller, makes your house worth less. Why not just make that last room into a nursery? Oh, but you said you don't have kids."

Four children in a plane crash. Gone. "The room has to go," Shella said. "It has bad memories." She smiled the smile she reserved for escaping traffic tickets and said, "Money is no object if you can design a plan that will allow that room to be eliminated without additional damage to the home." Though she heard them speak desultorily as they left, chatting amongst themselves about a woman crazy enough to pay thousands to make her house smaller, she did not care.

As the new walls were finally commissioned, the dates finally set, a sense of progress pervaded her life. She found an old man who'd lived through the loss of his wife and two children in a car crash. He responded to an ad Shella put out for a Survivor's Support Group. A few women also joined. In this group, Shella felt comfortable, but it met only twice a week.

One day, she invited the man home. His name was Hugo. He was shy and handsome.

"I haven't been with anyone since the accident," he

admitted as she removed his jacket the first time, kissing his neck after taking him inside. "I've been rather isolated. I'm not sure I'll be able to please you," he continued as she stripped off his clothes in her bedroom. "I am sorry I am crying," he admitted when her head dipped down to capture him in her mouth. "I just never thought I'd have such — experiences — again."

She found his gasps beautiful. Partially sentient, two tears fell down her cheeks as he dressed afterward. He clung to her fully clothed then, like he mightn't let go, yet remarked, as if she were the benevolent force of kindness itself and not a person with her own needs, "I don't know why you did that for me."

"I've had my losses too," she confessed. "Maybe our recoveries could be a match."

As the contractors planned their work, she told the old man her sorrows. He was unafraid, which she appreciated, bragging to Lilith, "I want no more cowards in my life, so he's perfect! Hugo listens. It doesn't matter what I say. He doesn't judge me. Still, I think he'll be stolen somehow. Something will happen."

"You doubt the reality of your happiness because you don't remember it," Lilith said. "But it's okay to feel good, you know?"

"Right. Nothing bad will happen," Shella said. "We'll be okay. Everyone will be okay."

Still, lately as she met with Hugo, their every conversation felt furtive, like they met in a secret clubhouse of adulthood, confessing things about grieving that normal people could not absorb, delighted in the other's understanding, lack of shock, lack of fear, lack of shrinking away. Finally, trusting Hugo, though she'd sworn she'd stop showing the room, she told him of her scars and her plans. He followed her in. "If I wear them all again," she admitted. "I don't know what will happen. I'll be an emotional wreck. So when the ball comes to demo the room, I already plan to take vacation, in case I'm hysterical or can't speak. It could happen. It's happened before."

Hugo touched the walls of the room with his fingertips.

"I'm telling you this because the destruction of this room could kill me," she said. "Sometimes I picture that the walls will crumple, with the tissue attached like adhesive gum. The room will not become rubble, but a mass of slumped light and cracked vulnerability. And will the scars fly off the walls and come to me when they are unprotected? Will the light shine out to all the neighbors? I don't know..."

"I don't know either," he said, feeling the scarred surfaces with his long fingers and crying like a man who could read Braille in exiled tissue. He stroked her walls further, not to read them, but rather to soothe. "I'm not afraid of this room," he told her. "But you knew I wouldn't be. There's nothing here to be ashamed of."

She kissed him fondly, throwing her arms around his neck like a daughter might embrace her father. "Will you promise me one thing?" she asked, her eyes wet. "I don't need you to love me, but now that I've found you, it would break my heart to lose such a confidant. I know one day you will die — myself as well — but for now, you are the most important person in my whole life because I tell you what I can't tell anyone else, so I'm grateful that we met, for the bond we've made...but will you check on me after the wrecking ball comes, no matter what I say? Just promise me, that for a few weeks you'll remain my friend, no matter what happens next, no matter how I act, no matter if I scare you or push you away. Will you?"

His hand stroked her back like it had stroked her walls. "Shella," he said. "There's nothing you could do or say that would keep me from being your friend."

"So that means yes?" she asked.

"Yes," he said. "Forgiven in advance."

"You sure I can believe?"

He gave her a blank look she took for assent, but later that night, in the rational light of the pendulum fixtures above her kitchen island, she nearly scrapped the demo plans yet again. The room drew her as it always had when the house's hollowed quiet gave amplification to the echoes of her solitude. Where was Hugo now, she wondered? Could he be believed?

She'd noticed a hard round object in his pocket the other day and decided more and more that it must be his stripped wedding band. He must carry it with him everywhere. In the time they'd been together, he had not once invited her to his house. The wrecking ball was poised to come one Tuesday from this day, and the sudden risk of him seemed abundant. Her wants from Hugo could be a problem. Was his silence his own wall? Who was he really, if not a complicit silent partner in her every unnamed grief?

Though he'd spoken of his children in the group, she revisited her memory now for his revelations about his dead wife, which were sparse, yet sometimes he'd ordered food for Shella that she had not chosen. He'd indicated preferences for her dress and hair, like re-creations of someone else's habits. The more placidly she bent to his whims, the more he smoothly, silently sculpted the reality of her into his wanted perceptions.

Does he know me at all? she thought. *Two solipsisms conjoined, is that what we are? And if I collapse under the weight of returning emotions, will he even come near? Will he support me?* She dreamt that night of her past rushing toward her like a tide of water brushing the glass wall of a beachfront property, one memory pounding soundlessly into the next as if part of a set of incoming waves, their volume muted only by dividing glass.

She unproductively obsessed about Hugo's ex-wife. At their next meeting, she suggested Hugo focus on his grief about his spouse, from which he retreated. "What did she look like?" Shella asked. "Was she pretty?" This she ventured after the official group, when the others had gone.

"We don't need to talk about her," Hugo replied.

"I think we do," Shella pressed.

"I don't want to talk about her then," he repeated.

"Can you answer the fucking question?"

Hugo seemed older, shaken. He touched his sleeves at the wrists as if they lacked a button. "She was tall, dark, with slender legs. My children had her eyes."

"Which were what color?"

"Moss green. When will the wrecking ball come?"

"Don't distract me, Hugo. Did she please you, in bed?"

"Yes, very much. Can we return to what will happen to your house?"

"I think I need some alone time before the wrecking ball," Shella observed, brushing her long hair with measured strokes, pulling roughly.

"My wife is gone. It's my children I miss most," he said in her hall. "You might remind me of her a little bit."

My mouth is not my mouth, she thought. *My hands are not my hands. Who do you think of as I touch you?* That day she did not seduce him as had become their pattern.

She walked him out ten minutes later and let herself into the personal room, peeling a new scar from her psyche and flinging it to the wall.

This time, it fell, without sticking, to the floor.

"But what I'm telling you," she told her therapist, "is that he was hiding something. I can't trust him. Once I've lost trust for people — it's — well, it's irredeemable. They become horrible versions of themselves — like a haunting, villainized, like people I never knew."

"Of course you can't trust him," her therapist said. "I think he uses you. He was clear that you look like his ex-wife."

A tear that would not fall stabbed Shella's eye. Again arriving home, she noted the room hue no longer matched the house. She called Hugo and said, "I have reason to believe you will not weather my upcoming changes, and I should not have asked. I'm calling to say I can't see you anymore."

"You can depend on me," he said. "Forgiven in advance, like I said."

"No," she replied. "I bear you no ill will, but the room brightens further and I can only think you'll give me more scars, above and beyond those I have and find unmanageable — on or off walls. I may be paranoid, but I'm fragile, so I'm sorry."

He said nothing.

"Besides, I might not need a wrecking ball after all," Shella mused. "Lilith thinks I can call the scars back by myself. I'm going to do that now, Hugo, before construction starts. Please hope I'll be okay."

She hung up without waiting for his reply and walked to the room, thinking of the directives she'd been provided by Lilith, sitting in the center of the carpet, closing her eyes, and calling her scars to her gently, as if they were children, feeling them detach from the drywall to float and arrive for absorption, each pain evoked and recalled, each argument, each loss, slight, and misgiving. *Four children, gone in one blow. Two marriages violated. The sickness. The blood from her lungs. The nurses. So many nurses.*

In lotus position she absorbed them one after the next, pairing her awareness of events like skeletons with the flesh of them, her returning feelings.

Four hours later, she woke on the floor of the room, and the walls were bare. Her scars were again on top of her and inside her, roiling about hungrily on her flesh and psyche like predator fish in a sea of chum, like the force of human-wrought turbulence.

If returned light eked from her eyes and ears and mouth then, she could not tell, but she walked into the garden and stroked the petals of a nearby lavender plant with great satisfaction. She ripped the buds from that bush stalk by stalk, pulling upward from the bottom of the stems. She canceled her meetings with planners and the work of the contractors, despite the loss of her deposits.

Carrying the scars caused a few outbursts that week, but the weight to be borne was so enormous that the surplus of emotion, to Shella's surprise, caused not an irrational storm of disconnected actions, but an even stranger calm than before. At the same time, she felt more about immediate things. Hugo had not called her back. He had not come by. A fierce hatred claimed her for two days and was gone after four, replaced by sadness.

He returned six days later, asking, "Are you okay? Is it done?"

Shella nodded. "A lot's been done."

"I came to offer my support," he replied.

"You're a bit late, aren't you?" she asked. Had he found her stooped in her room, weak, reeling — had he carried her to the living room and fed her soup and water immediately, had he come to check on her within days of her ordeal, she might have believed him, but he was a liar to her now, one who could drift apart with little impact. "You mean nothing to me anymore," she said. "Though I remember there was a time…"

"I want to thank you for desiring me," he rebutted. "I'm sorry I didn't come sooner. I was afr—"

"Hugo, stop, that's done now," she muttered.

"It can't be. I've decided I lo—" he began, trying to stroke her hand with his own, his voice breaking.

"No," she said, her own voice lost in vibrations. "Don't speak the words…I have nowhere to put your love, or whatever you want to give me! Not now, or when you let me down again, which you will, Hugo — nowhere to put it when you walk away after the least frightening exchange. You see, I am self-sufficient. There is no longer a vacancy. The light is on, but my house is full, of me!"

"I'll build you another house," Hugo argued, "we'll build a house together," but from her eyes the éclat of the former room then shown so brightly that he witnessed light tendrils leaking from her eyes, her ears, her nose, her mouth, and he knew he could not touch her.

In her presence, there were no more soft pink walls, only a woman so illuminated it appeared she might light her own skin on fire, needing nothing external to make her whole. And she no longer resembled his ex-wife, it seemed, so he pulled her closer with heavy hands, kissing her sunlit mouth.

"I want no man," she announced, shoving him away. "If you were ever worth wanting, you'd run to see a past like mine. My feelings have returned and it's a beautiful energy a body full of memory can carry, Hugo, one an uncommitted man can't handle."

"But I need you," he said.

"Yet you weren't here when I needed you," she replied. "Forgive me, but I remember you told me I would be forgiven in advance. I suppose you did not lie, because you didn't plan to be there when I'd need yours. But it's too late today. You see, I have no walls for these scars anymore. I am the room and the light and the walls and the scars at once. I have become the very walls!"

She quieted and sat glowing on her couch until he left, leaking energy through her pores, yet cognizant only of the color and sensation of her skin, which felt rubbery and looked pink as the insides of the conch shells that evoked her name. She was, as she considered herself, an ever-failing organism made up of nothing but the experience that marked her body, an organism surviving that experience and transforming it into the private electric company of her own pellucid life.

A multicolored light spilled in continuous floods into the room from her still face, a blue cold light blending and dancing with a white warm light, these two, in motion, falling everywhere. For a long time, this radiance was the only indication of signs of visible light in the entire house, the illuminated non-expression Shella's open face provided to the scarcity of prying neighbors or nighttime drivers who might wonder, in passing, why the lights were left on night and day, though didn't inquire — her open face that regarded nothing nearby in her living room, not even Lilith when Lilith finally arrived; Shella's face that gave light without receiving it; a face that was, most days, imperviously, determinedly, blank as a board, both dull as a ghost's sheet, hauntingly empty as a mirror with no person's reflections, and silver as frozen scars.

When Happiness Comes, Answer the Fucking Door

Happiness came for him in a black fishnet body stocking with kitten heels. She came in a white dress over her suit, wearing decadent cheetah jewelry with multiple straps and closures. She knocked quietly, as was her way, and he opened the door, glancing at her long blond hair and disreputable getup for a long time before saying, "What the hell are you doing here?" He did recognize her, vaguely. He had seen her before.

"You called," she said, "so I came running." She made this sound half singsong, like a pop tune played in a common register, but she smirked, tucking one pointed toe behind her other ankle.

He looked at her like he regarded a magazine salesman — a balding, fat, and irritating one. She was none of those things, so he sighed. "Well, I'm sorry you wasted your time, Happiness; I don't need you." But he turned his body to glance out his back window with gray drapes.

"Bullshit," she said, pushing past him to sit on his couch. The seat was black velvet. The Flaming Lips played in the background and the light coming in was amber from the dawn and flimsy like a negligee. It was five a.m. She touched his face and hands and elbows and knees. He seemed almost a man too molested. She brought her lips close to his before saying in a whisper, "Then why, Alex, did you call? I know you need me." She thrust her tongue in his mouth.

"Must have been a wrong number," he said later, heart still racing. He thought he'd have a heart attack, wondered fleetingly if he should email the police for an ambulance. "I don't call anyone. Don't even use the phone. I lie about using the phone, to cover myself. But I live alone and that's what I like. I've tried this whole happiness routine before. I know I don't like it."

She thought about this and as she did, her hair, follicle by follicle, retracted into her scalp until her cut was a pageboy. Instantly, it turned black. "You never knew real Happiness," she argued. "But maybe I wore the wrong outfit." Her clothes changed to prim librarian with harlot make-up. "Lots of people want me, you know?" she said. "I could have been confused about you, I suppose. Look at me again."

He did. "The black eyeliner is better," he said. "You looked too pristine before. Your face. And your body was too revealed. Definitely not my cup of tea."

"Well, alright," she said. "But I'm better now."

They sat, eyeing each other. "I suppose I might have called you," he said. "Accidentally. But I didn't really want you."

"Shut the fuck up," she told him and kissed him again with plenty of tongue. She was not moderate. Then she rubbed herself all over him, like he were a green hotel lighting fixture she'd rub with her every centimeter till he shone. She visited for three days. She burned his bills. She fed his cat. She took his unfortunate wanderings into self-doubt and turned them into molehills. "Mountains," she said, "are for better things." Sometimes, when he forgot himself, they smiled.

But he was a doubter, excelling at unfounded doubt. "I have trouble at work," he said. "I fear I can't do it anymore."

"That's what I'm here for," she said. "You got too sad and dulled yourself like a knife spent peeling potatoes."

"I must correct you. I'm at the top of my game," he said, indignant. "But I'm afraid people don't like what I do."

"You're a leader," she said. "Though your current passion is lacking."

"Fuck you," he said.

"Okay," she replied. "Right away." She brought an hourglass with her that day, flipped it over. "Watch this," she said. "For one hour, I want you to be like you were before you acknowledged your invisible defeat, before boredom took you upstream. Take me like a lord with a shivering virgin. Take me like you fucking mean it, Alex. Stop demurring."

He lasted only half an hour. "That's disappointing," she said. "I know you have more in you."

"I have to work," he replied. "This isn't helping."

"Yes," she said. "It is helping. It is your work. Come back to life, please, Alex."

He went and stroked his gray curtains, his black sofa, pulled a pair of Tristesse's underwear from between the cushions, and set it on his coffee table like a conversation piece. "I had her here," he said.

Happiness rolled her eyes, said, "Like I care about that troll. She's not like me." She torched them right in front of him before saying, as she pushed him down below her, "But this is why you've had problems with people like me before. You sabotage. Yet, look! The universe has dropped me into your lap like a mint cream dappled bonbon and you should smile. I am smile-worthy, good to have in one's lap, an excess of joy profit," and then she rode him until he whimpered and squirmed, their bodies linked together, until he lost himself in his animal being, until he secreted the end of his joy spasm from his mouth and cock, sound and semen. "I am your good luck charm," she said, kissing his moist cheek. "And I'll stay until you want me to leave, so when you can say you do, definitively, I will go. But don't give me that fake wanting me to leave stuff because you want to hurt me and push me away. When you cut me then kiss me, I know which thing is true by how deeply you tongue my throat."

She ruffled his short black hair. She regarded his sparkling blue eyes. She turned into a black cat in his lap and sat and purred, nipping him.

"Let's go to the park for a pretzel," she said, returning to herself. "Happiness is better unconfined."

"I like your hair more blond," he said as she left that day. "Long and blond."

"Okay. I'll be back," she replied. "When I return, you'll have what you want. Happiness is better not instantly fulfilled."

"I'm just some guy," he told her. "I may have called for you, but I didn't really want or deserve you, and you don't have to change for me. Ever."

"Pffft," she said. "That's what happiness does. Sees a need — fills it. I love you strangely, in all the jejune, dangerous ways. I love you without mercy or reprieve. That's how you need me." She slapped him then for good measure, because he wanted that. He had to admit, later, that it pleased him for his cheek to redden and warm so fully, to experience in that instant the curious sensation he had then of missing her terribly as she left.

But he had long-term habits of deep shame. Tristesse kept coming over, pulling on his hair, waving her blue hair extensions in his face, pricking him and encouraging doubt. Still, Happiness was never far from his mind, even as Tristesse fucked him royally with all her standard tricks, with all her pain and memories, and in the absence of Happiness, he could think of the most amazing and kind things to tell his Happiness, but he never did. The more he wanted her, the more he wanted to refuse her, so when she got there next, as a token of resistance, he refused to answer the door.

This happened for a month. Finally, she knocked hard. "Hello, Alex. Hello! Happiness here. Open that fucking door and talk to me!"

He did, but he pulled her in and shoved her into the wall. He hated her reminder and reminded her that he hated her. He punched her full in the face then strangled her, found himself saying the most awful things. When her cheeks were bruised and swollen, he threw her on the floor and raped her. He then took her by the arms and cranked them behind her back. "I'll break your bones and trash your heart," he said as he pushed her, facedown, into his pillows like a ragdoll. She relented to his whims.

"You're hurting yourself," she kept saying, whenever she had breath. "All the while, you're only hurting you."

"You ignorant cunt," he said. "I told you I didn't want happiness. It doesn't belong here. Not with me. How can I be any clearer?"

She looked like shit when she rose. Tears streamed down her face. Her make-up was smeared, her clothes disarrayed. "I won't turn into Apathy down at the Battered

Women's Center," she said, weeping. "I won't do it. That's not my way."

His phone rang. Both knew neither would answer, but the ring was relentless.

"Bet it's someone else to make you unhappy. I wish your phone rang like a cheetah's chuffle. I came because you called," she said then. "Who's calling now?"

"I don't know. I don't call anyone," he reiterated. "Hardly anyone calls me. And I swear, I never called you, unless while I was dreaming – sleeping perhaps."

She looked at him sadly as the bruises disappeared from her face and the rats left her hair, which turned all red and curly then. She was an object in repair; leaving her visage, too, was the blood from the cuts where he'd shoved her into many sharp objects on his walls and floors. "Next time you call for me," she said. "I won't believe in you. I won't come. You'll be begging and I won't come."

"That's fine," Alex said. "I never wanted you."

"All right," she said. "Well, I have to go. I'm needed a lot. Wanted. Have lots of appointments."

"So, go," he said.

"I'm going," she replied.

It was only later, in the mirror, that he saw the bruises on his own cheeks as he shaved, noted the gashes and sores on his arms, felt the pain in his ass – all that pain he had given her returning to him, tenfold. "You have done this to yourself," he could almost hear her say. "Tsk, Tsk, Alex. You called me."

The mirror where he shaved was still fogged at the bottom and top from his shower. "I'm a fool. A reckless and ridiculous fool," he told himself. "I could have kept her! I needed her so much." He had to stop shaving a moment because his hands shook. He then wanted her back so fully that he wished for all the world that he could take her into his arms and hold her kindly, as he should have done the last time. "I do this with everything," he admitted into his solitude. "Drive it away. Look! I even drove away Happiness, and she was ready to be each thing I wanted, however I wanted her. She was an angel. A beautiful fucked up angel in fishnets and heels. Oh, shit." And he looked at his bruises and his own forlorn face, then the lamp above the bathroom mirror with its frosty glassy shells.

But in the mirror fog a message appeared as if traced by an invisible finger: "Call me," it said. "I love you; I will always love you. I want to stay with you forever. Can you accept me? Love, Happiness."

But he knew he wouldn't call. He detested calling, though he would think about calling many times, not actually doing this calling but avidly longing for it, knowing she would come running back if he simply beckoned, if he simply mustered the courage for one half-assed apology coupled with a resolute willingness to enjoy his life again — or for the first time. But such calling was hard for him who didn't use the phone (except perhaps while dreaming), impossible, he acknowledged, well beyond his abilities or affinities, though her house calls, he now knew, were regrettably done.

Three Views You Might Have Taken at Pond's Edge, or Quack

You found out one day that the man you loved was a duck. This bothered you at first; how did you not equate his words with quacking? How could you have inspired such a transition? Were you a quackologist, a web-footed-animal whisperer? When he came to you, waking up beside you where your lover had been the night before, he seemed to imprint. He could not be without you a single second, quacked bloody murder when you worked, and was not recognizable when you first saw him in bed with you because you saw only a duck. You had no idea your lover had vanished or become this duck. Granted, now, you can see certain stunning characteristic similarities between him and a duck, but then you saw only man or duck, as mutually exclusive categories.

You thought Steven had left. This bummed you out. He had chiseled lips. He had green hair. You gave credit to Clairol, not Mallard. Even as a man, he could swim in the most masterful circles and arcs. He seemed nurturing. "You are the best swim partner I've ever had," he said. "You work me out hard." He even took care of you when a neighbor's child gave you head lice. His hands were so soft, like feathers, like wings, smearing the mayonnaise on your head, tying up the plastic bag. "The lice will be dead," he said. "And then I'll comb out your hair." He was unflappable. Dulcet. Gorgeous.

Before you met him, you used to go sit by the pond and watch the ducks, fed them stale bread, stared out at the water. You hadn't done it recently. You were happy enough with Steven to avoid such lonely romantic activities as those embraced by the solitary, educated, wistful, or geriatric.

You were coupled and bright! Finding Steven was a dream come true! Happily! And then one day you woke up, remember, and there he was, as a duck? Then, all that duck would do was to follow you around, first silently, then quacking. He was into preening. He could not whisper things to you as you watched your shows, but he nestled on your lap. When you kicked him off, he began shitting on the carpet. He was a small wet bird, dousing himself whenever he could by turning on the kitchen sink. The house grew to smell of small wet bird, which seemed completely foreign. You told him, "Fly away."

It was not like you wanted to live with a duck forever. He didn't even let you go to the bathroom alone. He quacked more and more as days passed, but said no words. You lived on words and abhorred noise. "You are not my lover," you said. "My lover left this duck here for me to care for, as what? A parting gift? A dinner? I should take you to the park." There was something right about feeding ducks at the park and then eating them at the restaurant. A balance. I nurture and I'm nurtured. You had no stale bread, so you opened the package on the counter and let it go dry. This took two days before you could decide it was bad enough for pond-food. Waste of good bread, while it was good, went against your nature.

Your duck quacked, which was all he could do, but he didn't leave. You weren't his lover anymore; you were his mother. He only had eyes for you. Imprinted eyes. But he arrived fully grown. He was no duckling. You threatened him with the knife, chasing him around with it, but when he lay on the table, flinging his wings out like sacrifice, as if to say, "Carve me!" you took pity and got used to him. You could eat the slaughtered birds, but found you could not kill.

So, I found out one day that the man I loved was actually a duck. I was irked at first since I ate duck often, *canard au basil,* and had no use for a live specimen. I wondered if I had entered into some bizarre fairy tale where this was my hero's quest: Figure out how to get back your man, who has suddenly and impossibly become a Mallard duck. My man's name was Steven. The duck I called Quack. I sat on the floor with him and tried to talk to him. "Put one foot forward if you are Steven, Quack."

He did.

"Now put the same foot forward again if this is permanent."

He wavered.

"Can you write with a utensil, maybe hold it in your beak?"

He put his other foot forward. That could have been, "No," or "I don't know."

I gave him a pen. He bit it with his beak but couldn't lift it. I tried to kiss his beak, thinking: frogfrogPrince, frogfrogPrince! — but that did nothing. I opened the window and said, "Please fly away. I'm not really a pet owner. You see, I kind of hate pet-stench. I like birds *au natural.* In the wild. All animals, that is. Wild.

Please fly away."

He looked sorrowful. I couldn't be sure if I was putting human feelings onto a duck who had none, but I felt for him. "All right, come here," I said. We sat on the couch and watched a fat bald man trash starving starlets. I fed my duck sardines. He rubbed his green head on my belly. I stroked his feathers casually in a downward motion, like petting a blanket.

I do think he was Steven and that he was sad. When I took another lover, he dive-bombed the other man's head. "This fucking duck is crazy for you," the other man said. "I've gotta bolt." The other man deserves no name and so I do not give him one.

Later, I talked to Steven. "You've got to stop ruining my love life," I told him. "What has gotten into you?"

"Quack," he said. "Quack, quack, quack."

"Yes. I know, quack," I said. "That was very insensitive of me. But you aren't my lover anymore and I need things, you understand?"

"Quack!" He stomped his webbed foot. "Quack?"

"When we tried using that thing before, it felt like a gynecological speculum, Steven. And your duck bits — they're just too small; I am af— "

"Quack!"

"Right. We'll not go there."

I bought a small dog's sweater and cut it so his wings could fit through the rents. It was cold, I reasoned. We went for walks. Because he only quacked, I could not imagine what he then said, except I realized I embraced my tendency to replace this new quacking with the things he used to say. "Isadora, you are so beautiful. I love your hair. I love the long curve of your neck and the exotic slant of your eyes. The trees are in bloom in the park. Observe!

There's an old man with his wife; isn't that beautiful?"

"Maybe if you go do a girl duck here, you can turn back into a man," I said. "Maybe that's what it will take."

He looked away. There were Mallards at the pond. "Quack," he said.

"So go," I said. "Try! It would be so great if you could come dripping wet and naked out of that pond, all manly as you used to be. And then I would loan you my sweater and you and me could run to the car like you were a flasher! Go! Go try!"

"Quack," he said.

"Quack, quack," I said, and he seemed perturbed, shaking out his feathers as if to aerate them. He waddled to the pond's edge. He quacked loudly, angrily at the water. It was almost like he said, "Come over here, you fucking female ducks, so that I can do one of you to please my girlfriend! She thinks this will fix me!" Of course, I had no idea what he said, and he had no takers. All the birds just flew away. And then resettled on the pond.

The girl stood by the side of the pond, the young woman in an elderberry sweater, standing beside her small Mallard duck with a pink, self-modified Yorkie sweater, and she was talking to the duck. It was imperceptible, what she was saying, but the conversation was quite earnest. The romantic intellectuals seated pondside could see this, even from far, far away. At first, the duck waddled off to the pond's edge and quacked. The other ducks scattered. And then flew back.

Lilies bloomed in the pond water. Families fed the swimming ducks dry bread, but did not feed her wigged-out duck. When the other ducks had landed back on the water, after the obnoxious quacking stilled, things were pretty serene. Then her duck got in the pond. She watched him and gave him a thumbs up. He was strangely unsocialized, her duck, or remote, and the sweater he wore wasn't helping. He could hardly swim.

He came back to her, quacking to request she remove it. She did. She knelt by the side of the pond and pulled it free of his wings and head. It was tender how she did this. "Quack," he said.

"Quack," she said. And then she lost her footing and fell into the pond, slipping on the muddy ledge.

There were many perspectives to this event. You could have sworn she fell into the water and disappeared, if you were watching close. Or, you could have thought that she became the new female duck in the water, briefly. You hadn't seen that duck before. But you could have only accepted this idea for a few moments, if you thought about it at all, because by then the girl had reappeared.

I wasn't thinking about any of this. I wondered what happened such that the beautiful skinny girl with the long black hair could sink completely below the shallow water. I observed how the golden haze of afternoon sun made me blind in spots through the dappled posy park. Perhaps she'd been blinded, too, I speculated, which had made her slip. Things were yellow and mottled. Things were bizarre and mundane, dead and regretfully alive.

But five minutes later, dripping with pond stench, the girl came out of the duck pond, strangely naked, shivering, muttering obscenities. "The duck king, duckling! Fuck with him and stay?" she asked no one. "Watching me before this, ate my bread, became human, couldn't stay forever — but please live with me now? No, no, Steven! Why would I want that?"

She went silent, climbing back up the ledge, then, "No!" she shouted at pond's edge. "I eat ducks! Don't forget! I don't swing that way! And another thing, what's

up with that mallard rape flight impulse? Fucking per-
verts!" Wherever her clothes had gone, which many might
note were floating at the center of the pond, she did not
have them. She held her breasts with her arms crossed
over her chest and shivered. She picked up her keys she
had left on the bank. She seemed coated with lily leaves,
too, like they stuck to her. She was a bit muddy. Her neck
really was quite something. Pale and white. Swannish near
her long pretty hair.

Somebody gave her a blanket as she walked
toward her car. One of the watchers. At the last minute
before she drove away, a single duck, maybe hers, flew to
her car and sat on her windshield. He quacked until she let
him in. They could be seen kissing there for quite a while,
her lush lips puckered on his hard bill.

She was saying something about sacrifices as she
opened her car door to let him out. Something about fairy-
tales being cautionary tales. Something about happily ever
after as mythical, illusory, and categorically false — something about how a person can't change into something
they never wanted to be and still be happy. Ever. Or after.
She then remarked upon how his initial deception did not
create a follow-up need for her later transition. "I thought
you were a man!" she said, finally. "You wanted me to
change the whole time! You never were a man! You never
even walked like a man, though you talked like one!"

Her duck looked at her like she was his mother.
Her duck hung his head. "Quack," he said nasally.

"Yes, I know, Quack," she told him, leaving him
there at the park. "But — quack."

White, Lab-Rat Shaped Penis

For many evenings, Etgar wouldn't show her his rat. At first, he was rather private. Too private, Sheila decided in another mild bout of post-date couch groping, her green butterfly underwear sliding up the crack of her ass. Six dates in and the most she had done was to grab his tight runner's back-end, stroke his chest, then clutch his shoulders closely at the end of each outing, seated on his couch or standing at his front door in her low-cut wool sweaters and faded jeans, staring up into his eyes and tilting her head back far, but not so far as to look like she were passing out or epileptic, humming and breathing her desire into the air around them as if to say, "Kiss me, Etgar. Do it. Do it!"

His house smelled like oranges, she thought, like oranges and his vegetarian best friend's German beer bottles. "Kiss me," she said again, just before she thought, *And then take me to your bedroom, the only room in your home I have not yet seen.* She even dipped her false lashes down, going for demure, hoping he might find this falling posture irresistible and about to tell him about her well-noted, formerly at least, talents with fellatio.

He appreciated the gesture — the first one at least, as he hadn't yet been told about the second. "Look, Sheila, there's something I have to say," he said, this murmured as she stroked his brown curls when they sat on his stinking couch, a rose chintz gift from his dead grandmother, just before he finally took Sheila's small hands into his, stared into her amber eyes, and let his gaze survey his rooms.

This was, she decided, the talk. The one you never want to have.

"My penis," he announced, with no small measure of hesitation, "is really a rat."

She sighed, having thought the gay speech was to come, or the married or psychotic speeches. "Of course, Etgar," she said, expressing reply in a way she felt was very soft and understanding. "All men's penises are metaphorically rats. I expect that, and yet it doesn't diminish how I would like you to give me your rat. All of that little rat." He paled, so she was about to expound, go in at length on the topic, but he palmed her mouth then replied, dopey and morose, "No, Sheila, my penis is really a white lab rat, pink feet and all, and you should know this." His hand smelled like grain.

Then he put his other fist in his pants, opening his palm there, stroking something as if to comfort himself, and then reacting like he'd been bitten before rapidly pulling out.

She tossed her short red hair over her shoulder. "My mother always says I find the weirdest men. I mean, truly, how do I do this again and again? Men like abstract paintings. Is there a sign on my forehead, Etgar? One that reads: Only approach me if you've got major problems? Like you think your penis is a rat? Okay, fine. So your penis is rat. A dirty fetid rat. Can I have it? I love your dirty fetid rat."

"He's not dirty," Etgar asserted. "He's clean and white — though temperamental."

"So what's his name? Your rat?" By this point, Sheila eyed her keys on his kitchen counter and stood to go.

"He doesn't have a name."

She launched another long sigh. "Okay, Etgar, dear and special nameless-rat-penised Etgar, if you didn't want to date me anymore, why didn't you just go for the normal explanations? I'm not pretty enough. Too scarred. I don't make enough. Or I'm too smart. Maybe I'm too fat for you, though you certainly could have mentioned this by date four when you saw my... I—"

He stopped her with his lips, kissing her, pulling her onto him, then unbuttoning his own pants, and unzipping them. "Here, Sheila" he said, through the slur of their combined lips, holding her tight as if to prevent escape. "Touch him. It's true."

She reached for him to feel a nosing on her palm. And a soft furry texture. "Oh my God," she said. And then his penis rat bit her. "Ow!" she shouted. "That little fucker! I think I'm bleeding! My finger is bleeding."

"He's not nice to strangers," Etgar said.

"I'm not a stranger." She stood, eyes flashing. "And if that little fucker weren't your penis, Etgar, I swear I'd smash him right now. Like a bug!"

"You're glaring rather venomously at my groin," Etgar remarked. "It's making me uncomfortable."

"It's to be expected," she returned.

"Well, all right. Let's talk more about this, over dinner."

They elected to go for Chinese food. When the

Sesame Chicken came, she inquired about his rat's feeding rituals. "Just rat food," Etgar said. "Run of the mill rat food."

"And does he grow?"

"Not so much," Etgar said. "Not in a while." Turns out this rat penis had been around since Etgar was about twenty. He just "grew into it one day."

"So you've done it with this rat?" she asked.

"It?"

"Don't be coy. Yes, it."

"We've had a few girlfriends," he said, poking some chicken with his chopstick. "Been intimate that way." He turned pink as the bow on the Chinese hostess's hair. "Yes we've done it, me and former girlfriends, with the rat."

Sheila asked more questions, sat silently as the waitress appeared, and finally inquired after getting her fortune — *Something unusual is coming your way* — "So what you're saying, Etgar, is that the rat kind of stretches out and tucks his arms and legs into his body and then you use him till he pukes?"

He paid the bill. "Yes, that."

"And the puking is like coming — biologically?"

Etgar nodded.

"So, it's pleasurable?"

"Sheila, please—"

"I want to see him," she said. "Up close. Maybe feed him."

The relationship progressed. A month passed. The rat did a good impression of rigor mortis during more intimate moments. Sheila looked at him a lot, often as he did the disappearing rat trick into her body. "He's got red eyes," she observed in a day's aftermath. "You think that means he's blind."

Etgar laid on the bed, stroking the rat's head to soothe him. "Don't know. I need to wash him now. I like his fur clean." It was then that both noticed he was looking a little tired, quivering like normal, but seeming to slump. "I think he's sleeping," Etgar said.

"I wonder why we can never see his tail," Sheila replied, stroking him with her finger. "I mean, rats have tails right?"

"Oh, I can see his tail," Etgar said. "I've seen it before. He can come off you know." He took Sheila to a silent movie festival that night. They talked more about the rat. He took her to an art exhibit the next day with hanging bits of foil. He liked her more and more he said, twirling her around in the concrete walkway leading out to the parking lot. "I love that you appreciate all of me," he enthused. "Even my rat. Is that hard for you? That I'm this way?"

"Never liked penis that much anyway," she said. "I mean, regular man penis."

"So, everything is fine?"

"It's fine, Etgar, fine," she said. "The size is good." But, Sheila, for her part, had begun to fear for the rat. That day, he didn't seem to hold straight for long. Afterwards, she confessed, "Well, I'm feeling kind of sorry for your rat. I don't know if he likes this. Remember when you told me about how he just balled up for weeks at a time with Geena? How he just refused to perform for Jennifer? I know he likes me, Etgar, because I feed him and I stroke him, and he's doing his duty by you, but sometimes, and I could be imagining this, I think I see a faraway look in his eyes. A wanderlust. I mean, he doesn't run. And when you spin that globe around on your bookshelf, I swear he follows the spinning as if mesmerized. I mean, maybe all this fucking is like rat dousing to him. Like a terrifying nightmare that never ends! Do you ever wonder if he'll drown? Do you ever wonder if he wants to be free? I know if he got free, you'd have no penis, but maybe it would be kinder to the creature — and frankly, Etgar, I worry he doesn't like to be in my mouth. That, and his puking thing. It's starting to get to me."

"I've explained all that," Etgar said. "It's when I come. It feels like coming. You douche later. You said it doesn't taste bad."

"I know, but… the rat." She insisted on having a conversation with the rat that night.

Etgar sat patiently, pants down, in the living room. She stroked the tiny creature's head. She said, quite dulcetly, "Dear little rat, you haven't bitten me in a while, but do you ever long to be free?" From her sack, she pulled out a silver wheel for him to run on, placed it on the floor. "You have four legs, does this tempt you?"

She began to spin the wheel, again and again. The rat, for his part, perked up. He did his stiff rat pose that they used during sex. She stroked him with her fingertip again and stopped the wheel. He slumped back down. "Sometimes a rat just wants a little run, Etgar," she said. "Can you let him out to try this?"

"It hurts to take him off," he said. "I'm very sensitive."

This conversation echoed through several weeks. Finally, Etgar gave in. He took off his rat. It was then that Sheila saw his tail, the rat's tail, had a deep fleshy groove between Etgar's hips, into which it fit when the rat was mounted, red like the inside of her vagina. "Etgar," she said. "Without him, you almost have a pussy."

"I don't want to have a pussy," Etgar said. "I want my rat back on."

"Can I touch your pussy?"

"No."

"I'm just asking for a few days of liberation," Sheila said. "Let him run. Let's see how he feels. Sometimes I think he wants to be free of you."

This was fine for Etgar until he came home one day and found them in the bedroom together, Sheila's hand wrapped around the back of the rat's rump. He felt she was cheating on him with his own penis. He dropped his bag of lettuce and lunchmeat. "How could you, Sheila?" he asked.

She looked up at him. "Your rat begged me. He said he needed me so much."

"My rat doesn't talk," Etgar replied.

"Yes, he does," Sheila said. "He's a very suave talker." They got in a terrible argument. She left his place. For days, Etgar sat in his own slump, watching the rat run in the wheel and considering forcing him back onto his own body. He didn't call Sheila. His rat got more muscular, almost before his eyes.

One day, right in the middle of a talk show about love, his rat approached him, sniffing at Etgar's crotch. "Does my penis want back on?" Etgar asked.

"Why yes, Etgar," his rat said. "And I need you to call Sheila back."

"What do you want Sheila for?" Etgar asked, pulling his boxers low.

"I want to fuck her of course," his rat said.

"Hmmm," Etgar said.

He opened his legs, trying not to look at the indentation, which seemed to have deepened. His rat settled back in. Etgar felt stronger. But he was conflicted. "If you talk, then you have a consciousness," he told his rat. "If you have a consciousness, your consciousness is not connected to my brain. If your consciousness is not connected to my brain, then isn't it like Sheila has two boyfriends if we go to her together?"

"I knew I shouldn't have talked to you," his rat said. "Call Sheila. She misses us. A penis should never talk to his man. There are risks. A man can get jealous of his penis. Would you go get our woman back already?"

"Sheila might not want us now," Etgar said.

"No. She does. I called her today," his rat replied. "She wants all three of us to go to the horticultural gardens."

"She was very mad when last we spoke."

"I've smoothed things over."

Etgar stared down at his little clean rat. His little clean rat's red, possibly blind eyes. He wanted to bash it to bits.

"Did you have a name?" he asked it, still feeling polyamorous about the Sheila issue.

"I have whatever name you give me. Isn't that how a penis works?"

"Yes, but do you have your own and separate name?"

The rat chose not to reply.

"But how can I know that Sheila loves me for me?" Etgar asked. "I am the brains of this operation."

His rat closed his beady eyes. He said only, "If all she wanted was a friend, I wouldn't have been involved. But I shouldn't have told you anything, Etgar. No point opening things up. Call Sheila. No, I shouldn't have talked to you, Etgar. It confuses you too much when we don't always have the same agendas. I'll be quiet now, a good little, quiet, puking penis. Call Sheila. No, really, I shouldn't have talked..." The words spun around Etgar as if in a wheel. His rat looked up at him with a beseeching glance and tilted his head toward the table where the phone was, twice, with a pointed expression, before stiffening once more into the pose they both knew. "She needs us both. We work together," his rat said. "You do the outings. I do the plunging. It's natural. And you should always acknowledge the significance of your penis, Etgar, your dirty little rat and silenced romance partner. No, no, no, really, Etgar. I'm sorry. I should NOT have talked. She loves you! You and only you. You were happier with me quiet. But ring a ding ding. Ring a ding ding! There she is. By the phone. Just waiting! Looking hot! Looking like that sexy art freak mama you can talk Kandinsky with, with A cup, nearly bare pizzazz! Maybe she's wearing one of those sexy black berets you have a thing for. I should never have said a word, so I'm remorseful. Me, your rat. Your penis. Or perhaps, you just shouldn't have listened."

Madagascar Hissing-Dress

"You need something," the sales guy said, eyes surveying the dark interior of his long narrow shop, "to protect you, I think." Nina touched below her left eye where a profusion of sage and eggplant bruising remained.

"Something not to hurt me, for sure," she replied. With her heart-shaped face, large blue eyes, and long straight hair, she had kind of features that got her noticed with or without injury. Even the shape of her bones seemed prominent beneath egg-shell skin. "But I got rid of him," she told the man. "I just want a gun. In case he comes back. Your place was closest, and I see you advertise guns in the window. I don't want it traceable."

She walked away from the counter and turned back to say, "Don't think this is normal for me, the bruising," extending her hands as if in a plea only to realize her wrists were coated with bruises, too, and her knuckles scraped. She wanted to kill Davey Sinclair then, if not for being a low-life with a penchant for talking romance then for getting violent, for causing her this embarrassment with a stranger.

She'd used a breakfast tray over Davey's head, but not until after a struggle, him so drunk and stupid it was a comedy of evasion and mercy. "Fucking asshole," she said in the soft voice she'd use to relate a mystery, remembering.

"What's that?" the salesman said.

"Oh, nothing," she replied, fleeing her recent memory and observing him now again as if he and the shop had just begun to exist. The shopkeeper had a Jew's nose on a fine long face framed by black hair that fell over his left eye. His look seemed gentle, his olive skin pale and clear, but most she registered his eyes — kind, almond-shaped eyes, green — the kind of eyes you could drown in, like a limpid pool. He was young, too. Handsome. Mid-twenties.

What was he looking at her for? She felt an old woman at thirty-five, but this was something many had told her she was not, though what did it matter what they thought? If in her mind, she felt a hundred years old, every mirror lied. She looked appreciatively at the way he wore his jeans. Said, "Mmm, mmm, mmm," like he evoked the memory of a successful business lunch or a nice man, attractive and harmless, rare.

"I don't sell modern guns," he said, turning his slim back toward the distant display. "Only unusual weapons and sundries. This is more like an antique store, lady. Were you hoping for a LeMat Civil War revolver? I got one. All the chambers work."

"No. I don't want something ancient."

She repressed the urge to ask him not to look at her, abhorred his pity, abhorred more that he saw her weakness so clearly, and she wondered if she looked like a starved rat. She had lost weight with the boyfriend before Davey, but could never be thin enough for Charles

Millwood II, of the Maine Millwoods, who was like to have engraved cutlery even at his summer house. She should have known his penchant for middle class girls was just that — fantasy fodder that bordered on complete objectification, with no intent for further interest than a prolonged roll in the sheets until the newness wore off. *God*, she told herself. *Will you ever be less stupid?*

"My last girlfriend Beth could wear catwalk clothes," he seemed fond of saying. "She could wear my shirts like a dress." Well, fuck her, Nina thought. Did she displease you, too, for some other, equally shallow, reason? And fuck all rich guys. Not a one had a shred of decency. How many times and in how many ways had she learned that in her past? *She should have known better*, she told herself silently, for the five hundredth time.

"I was hoping," she told the clerk, enunciating clearly, "for anything you might have that would make me feel okay about what I've been through…this means men."

It could mean a few specific men, she decided, surveying his friendly appearance, but it more than likely meant men as a whole. She licked her full bare lips, stroking her tribal arm band tattoos and watching the young sweet thing before her, who seemed a shy boy in his watching her so intently from below his long lashes.

She brushed her thick blonde hair away from her face where it fell long and heavy. She was about to dye it brown, turn it to dreadlocks — anything to decrease her appeal. "I just want something that will devastate any motherfucker who tries to treat me poorly," she stated. "I don't care if it kills him."

"You're pretty," the sales guy said. "My name's Noah."

"Nice. Biblical name," she replied. "You got an ark?" She realized she was flirting and almost kicked herself. "You're too young for me," she said.

"As you wish," he replied, giving her a quizzical glance as if he'd been strictly clinical. Below the glass before her were hair lockets and charms for antique bracelets. "I have a sword," he said, "but unless you're any good at wielding it, it won't do you any good. You'll go waving it around and someone will knock it out of your hands." He spoke to the gold Formica counter.

"I want people to leave me alone," she replied. "I almost don't care what I use." She thought of her sister Eileen. Dead. Killed by a fucking louse of a husband, years ago, and she wouldn't end up that way. She walked toward the back aisles, imagining the smell of Eileen's red hair, peppermint and lavender. His store smelled somewhat like her, with a touch of medicinal saffron and sage.

Noah followed with quiet steps but when he reached to touch her from behind, startled, she wheeled and punched him in the face. "I'm sorry," she said, leaning over his body. "That was an accident." On impact her hand hurt again, like she'd cracked a bone or bothered an already present hairline fracture in her wrist, but his dazed look made clear that he barely tracked her movement, blood trickling from his nose, so she focused on his face, brought her own face closer. "Are you okay? I can do that when something is a sudden threat," she said, embarrassed. "But I didn't mean to hit you. It's when someone deceives me. Slithers in, if you understand."

"I understand," he said, his voice trembling.

She suddenly felt she'd pummeled a child. "When they're nice first, I just have problems fending them off," she explained. "Drawing boundaries. But I'm so sorry. You didn't deserve that. Let me help you up."

He sat without her help, shrugging. "I've got something for you," he said. "Sounds like you could use it. But you'll have to maintain it, feed it, take care of it. And it can be a little territorial. It's not an it, you see. It's a they. But it wouldn't harm a woman — do you want to see it?"

"Everything harms a woman," she said, a glassy look in her eyes, thinking that if her body were a glass tower, she would dream the world as stones.

"Not me," he said. "I help them. It's all I do — sometimes."

"What is it or they?" she asked, wanting to touch his delicate cheekbones.

"They're Madagascar tree boas," he whispered. "I'm not zoned to sell them, and they are one of a kind. They've been trained to be worn as a dress. You have to feed them bats. Birds. Can you handle that? If you don't want to kill these things, I know a place where you can buy them dead already. But no man will be able to touch you again." He looked at her for a long beat, then said, apropos of nothing, "I got them in Indiana."

She blinked, held out her hand, smiled, and said, "That's the best bizarre response I've ever heard after I punch a man out. Are you hallucinating, Noah?" He took her hand and she pulled him up, surprised to find herself looking up into the limpid lakes, a little breathless.

"I'll try not to touch you again," he said. "But you'll have to follow me to the back. You can't try the snake dress on out here. The snakes, they like to be right up against the skin. They can be formidable as a garment." He walked back, meandering, not waiting for her to follow — before he whipped around to say, like they were playmates, like they knew each other a long time, "Well? Are you coming or not, girl? Do you want to see the dress? It's heavy. That's your warning. The snakes are all female, by the way. They have thermo-receptive pits in between the labial scales. I think you'll find them very pretty. Green and grey."

She regarded his fine ass again and followed, murmuring, "At least he has an interesting pick up line."

"What?" he replied.

"Oh, nothing," she said. At her house, she had laundry and cleaning to come. It was Sunday, so she'd have to call her mother. When she arrived at the back, Noah shut the door behind them and the snakes came. She saw them immediately, three sleek creatures slithering near each other, bee-lining toward her on the ceiling pipes until they detached from the above plumbing fixtures, dropped to the floor, and wrapped first her ankles then her thighs, each approximately four feet long, heads away from her body, tasting the air, exploratory, as Noah looked into the corner where she saw a sloppy cot like an unmade bed and he said, "I'm terribly sorry I didn't clean up."

Mesmerized by the snakes, she replied, "It's not a date. Why do that?"

"I shouldn't have said that," he said. "I don't know why I did."

As she felt the snakes tighten, she asked, "Are they going to bite me?"

"No. They don't strike the woman. They're gentle with her. Ovoviviparous," he said. "And when they consider mating, they darken, heat up, as if to incubate some heat for reproduction."

"They're hanging on my legs," she muttered, like he couldn't see that. "I thought you said they made a dress." They had green and grayish green scales. She thought of putting in some green dreadlocks to match them. It had been a long time since she'd done something so daring.

"You have to show them the skin where the dress is supposed to go," he replied touching his hips and the sides of his chest, as if to demonstrate. "But not while I'm here. I'm not trying to be filthy. I'll give you some privacy...there's a mirror in the bathroom, so use that if you want to see how it looks. And you know what's the best part about this dress? You don't even have to be wearing it like a dress if they're in your house, the snakes. They were my grandmother's. But don't do any voluntary dating while you have them. You have to give them back before you do that. They sense things." On the far wall, there was a barred window with a torn teal curtain.

"Sense things?" she replied. "Like what?"

"Your fear. Your desire. You can't have either."

"No problem," she said. "I hate both. And how much are you going to charge me if this is something I might want to give back?"

"Nothing," he said. "I give the dress to those who need it. It's a few years I've been doing this now. You get protection. I get a break from feeding the snakes. They don't like me much. I'm male. I cheat them with my body like a stick. Or so they think." He smiled, his thin red lips closed in a bashful kind of grin. "I don't have anything, you know, any curves they like to hang onto." He went back out.

She removed her shirt. The snakes did not move. She took off her bra. One rose to encircle her hips, then her waist; a second climbed higher, settling around her breasts, tightening until fitted.

"Each knows its place," Noah yelled from the front. "Each takes that place, every time. You might be able to tell them apart before long, but I've never been able to."

She unbuttoned her denim skirt emblazoned with a silkscreen unicorn and removed it, her panties too. The last snake rose until it surrounded her thighs. Once united, the snakes seemed to communicate, tasting her with tiny tongues darting out and tickling like satin garment tags flitting all over her body. "Oh, you heavy things," she said. "I like you." Carrying her former garments in her left hand and her purse in her right, carefully, she walked out to Noah and said, "So, what do you think? Am I wearing it right?"

"Nice," he said. "It looks well. Don't feed them and then wear it. Give at least two days after that before an outing. They eat every few weeks, but right after feeding can regurgitate. They've just shed, but don't wear them during that process either. The eyes will go milky then. That's how you know."

"All right," she said.

"If they start hissing and striking, stop doing whatever you're doing — or get away from whomever they want to strike, all right?"

"Thanks," she said. "Do I get a little care packet with instructions? You've been at this a long time, huh?"

"Eight years," he said, handing her a brown paper grocery bag for her other clothes.

"Since you were a kid!" Nina said.

"I was not a kid!"

"Yes, you were."

"I was sixteen," he replied.

"Right. A real bachelor," she said, smiling. "An old man."

"Please don't make fun of me," he replied, and she felt instantly chagrined. He spoke in even tones as he said, "Keep a bowl of water around for humidity, like a large bowl they can't knock over. And if they hurt somebody, please tell the police snakes did it, but don't tell them where you got them." He stroked the body of the snake on her abdomen, like he would miss it, but this seemed a touch for a familiar. She noticed for the first time that his voice almost cracked, like his puberty remained. "These ladies tend to come back to me —" he went on, "but if they're implicated in something bad, the authorities will put them down. Don't let them get put down."

"Have they been implicated before?"

Noah shrugged. "You needed protection, didn't you? I'm just trying to help."

He grabbed her hand quickly, clutching and releasing, like in strange shake; a bell at the door tinkled as new customers entered and he helped an old couple seeking an armoire with French mirrors, refusing to look at her again.

"Thank you," she called.

"You're welcome," he shouted, overly loud, without looking in her direction. "Come back when you need to return them."

"So while I was wearing the dress, he freaked a bit," she told her friend June. "Like he thought they might strike him, but what an adorable guy. Weird, but cute. Not threatening."

"Maybe he thought you were uber hot wearing those snakes — and was afraid! Like they would strike him!" June said.

"*My* fear or *my* desire, he said," Nina replied. "Eight years he spent, watching the snakes make themselves comfortable on the fixtures near his grandmother's ceiling and then in that store. Sixteen when he started this."

"Surely he's not a virgin?"

"I'm sure he's had women," Nina replied. "As a teen. But there was a quality to him, gentle, strange. Maybe not too many."

"Wonder how many women he's given the snakes

to, or if he did have women, were the snakes watching? Women the snakes didn't wrap on. I think you should go back there and right now and de-virginize."

Nina smiled, though June could not see her. "He wouldn't be violent, at least," she said. "He didn't seem a drinker. Not married. Not disgustingly elitist, pretending to enjoy the lower class."

June had a mind for just one thing. "Do him! I like to see you into someone."

"Is it that rare?" Nina asked.

"Truth or lies?" June asked.

"Truth."

"Yes. Go back there and do that guy."

Nina smiled again. "No. I couldn't. He's just like — pure, or something. Kind. If I touch him, that will go away. Then he'll be just like any other guy."

"All right. Well, wear the dress tonight when you come out to Charlie Finn's."

At the pub, aside from being heavy, the dress caused a lot of looks, but the hissing and striking happened only once, with a leering drunk in a big tan trench who put his hand on her side to grope, a big man at least six feet tall. After that, she begged off and left June at the bar. "Honey, I didn't really want to be here anyway," she said, thinking that sometimes being alone was needed. Home, the snakes slithered clear of her body and traveled into and out of the bowl where she kept their water. She put on sweats and a t-shirt, thinking of Noah.

"I don't think you're a pervert because you like a young guy," June told her.

"It's not about age," Nina said. "It's that he's different. I can feel it."

The next day she paid him a visit. "So, I'm feeling pretty safe with the snakes in the house," she said.

"That's good," he replied, his face buried in sales books.

"So what do I do when I want to bring them back?" she asked.

He looked up, startled. "You want to bring them back already."

"They protected me at the bar last night," she said. "But I think, as a dress, they're pretty heavy."

"It's best to leave them at home, mostly," he said. "Unless you have a dangerous errand or something."

"Like the ATM at 2 a.m. off 3rd Street?" she asked.

"Yes, like that."

"Noah, why won't you look at me now?"

"I'm looking at you."

"No," she said. "You're looking down at your books. Did it bother you to give those snakes to me? Am I a freak to you now? A man hater?"

"You said I'm too young," he said.

"So you can't even look at me? Not that I'm not."

"I gave you the snakes because you wanted to be left alone," he said, observing the wall above her left shoulder. "Which means I need to leave you alone too." He squared his shoulders and stared her straight in the eye, saying, "I am a man, you know?"

"Did you think I doubted that?" she replied. They stared a moment. "Well, what if I have a question about the snakes and I can't come here?" she asked. "I haven't kept snakes for very long."

He ripped off a piece of the paper page he looked at, wrote a telephone number, and handed it over. "You can call," he said.

His avoidance struck her as extremely attractive.

She leaned closer. "You're cute," she said, kissing his gaunt cheek. "I like that." She sauntered out, waving his number in the air. "I'll call you," she said. "When you're needed."

"Your eye looks better," he said. "That's good."

That night there was an intruder at her window, Davey returning. She saw his spiked hair, the stitches in the place where she'd hit him, his face in the moonlight pushing through the hole where the window had been shoved open. "Get out! Get out of here!" she shouted.

"We're not done here," Davey replied, drunk again.

"Oh, yes, we are," she said. With only the hallway light and moonlight entering, she saw the snakes move in like long shadows. "I'm going to call the cops!" she told him, "You have to go!" But she needn't have worried about police; the snakes headed straight for the window. "Get out fast," she told him as the hissing commenced, when they got within a few feet. "Back out! My snakes — will kill you."

"What the fuck?" Davey said and then saw the serpentine bodies winding along the carpet, hissing louder.

"Get out of the window!" she repeated.

Wiping his eyes, stunned, he didn't move until the first snake to arrive struck him in the face, attempting to wrap its body around his neck. He had a knife in his hand, so went to stab the attached snake, but the other two had arrived and also began to strike. She walked out, hoping they'd follow her into another room, hearing Davey cursing and backing out, as fast as he could before running along the pavement near her window to exit her property.

Sure he was gone, she inspected the injured snake.

It bled. She called Noah, dimly registering it was two in the morning and he might have been asleep, but when he answered the phone, he seemed completely awake. "Hello?" she said. "Noah?"

"Yeah?"

"A snake got stabbed. What do I do?"

"Wrap it in a towel," he said. "Then leave it alone. I'm painting."

"Painting what? What if it bleeds to death? Is there, like, a snake hospital?" As she spoke, the other two snakes rose on her legs and curled on her thighs, scenting the air with their tongues. Waddling to the bathroom, two on her legs, carrying the third, Nina said, "She's hurt, Noah. I think she's really hurt."

"She'll be okay," he replied.

"You can't even see the injury," Nina said. The other two snakes started hissing, hissing and striking at nothing.

"I've got to go," he said. "I'm busy here."

"Holy fuck. Now the other two are going nuts," Nina said.

"You're scared," he replied. "That's all."

"I'm not scared," she said. "Except for the health of the snake."

"Then it's something else. Get off the phone."

The next day, she visited his shop. "How's the snake?" he asked.

"Seems okay."

"Those snakes heal really fast," he told her. "One survived a bullet." Now he looked again at the counter, absorbed, cleaning it. "Three days later, like nothing. No injury." He wore more jeans and a button up shirt.

She looked at his body. "Guess because Davey

came back, I needed the snakes," she said.

"Guess so," he replied.

"I like you, Noah," she said. "I didn't want to admit this."

He nodded.

"So do you like me or not? I mean, I'm not going to hang around here unless you like me. You talked to me before. Now you won't? It's me. I can't seem to keep a nice guy interested. Maybe I have nice guy repellent. I'm only ugly to nice guys…"

He looked up. "No. Not that! But you belong to the snakes now. So I can't be into you. Once I gave them to you, I had to stop looking at you because I do think you're pretty. And actually, I've thought about this problem only to realize there's no solution. Even if you give the snakes back, they're still here. I sleep back there. If they see you here, now that they've bonded with you, they'll protect you and continue to re-attach. If you experience desire, then I become a target. So the only time I could like you, even if I hardly ever experience desire, would be if I gave them to someone else, if they went somewhere else. But people who need them don't come around all the time. And what if you don't even really like me? If you aren't just curious about the guy who doesn't get laid, who owns the curio shop and the snakes. I could be just a freak show to you. A pity candidate." At Nina's hurt look, he said further, "But you've been through some hard stuff. Look, I don't want to upset the balance of your recovery. That's what the snakes give you. Recovery time. Man-free. I'm a guy. I have needs. You don't need me right now."

"Have you ever slept with a woman, Noah?" Nina asked, interrupting his somewhat manic talk.

"Yes," he said.

"Liar," she replied.

"And so what if I'm lying?" he asked. "Why are you asking me these things? Maybe I've had lots of women!"

"You're more nervous than I am," she replied. "But that's okay." She went behind the counter where he stood and pinned his body, stroking his face. "Noah," she said. "I'm older, but I want to sleep with you." She trailed her hand from his knee to his groin, kissing his cheek again and the side of his actual mouth. Gingerly, he put his hands on her waist.

"Here?"

"Here," she said. "Now."

A customer entered, said, "I want a rapier with a good sharp end. Do you have that?"

"Just a second," Noah said, looking up at the guy.

"Look, your girlfriend can wait, right? I'm on my lunch hour."

Noah's hands fell from her waist. "I can't, Nina," he said.

"Come and get the snakes," she replied. "First, find someone else to give them to. Then we could meet outside from the snakes. Or, if you can't find someone but you take them back here, you could come see me, for example, at my house, when we're alone."

"A fucking rapier, dimwit. Look, are you going to help me or not?"

"I don't—" he said. "I just can't de—"

"Come tonight," she said, patting his arm. "At seven. I won't even look at you."

Noah showed up with a grass carrier basket at seven. She let him in. All three snakes went to him as he opened the basket, petting them gently as they slithered in. "They know how to travel," he said. "Hey, your place is nice."

"The water bowl's been working while I kept them," she said. "It's more like a huge pie dish. Did you want it for your room?"

"Just let me take the snakes and go," he replied. but already the snakes had climbed back out from the basket and began to wrap his legs.

"What's the matter with them?" she asked. "Do they think you're their woman now? Don't they know you want to leave?"

"Stop looking at me, Nina," he said, as one struck and bit his leg. All three then hissed and kept hissing.

"I'm not afraid of you," she said. "I don't understand."

Another struck and bit him. "Fuck! Desire," he said. "You must desire me." The hissing grew horrible. He tried to catch them by their necks, to place each back into the basket like grappling with live electric wires. "Look into the corner, Nina," he said. "Go to another room."

"Of course I desire you!" she said. "But I don't want to go to another room!"

"If you don't go, they'll keep hurting me. They haven't struck at me before! No one desires me. I can hardly believe it, but get out of here! Help me! Please!"

"Many people desire you," Nina said, struggling to pull one snake away from his body and then another. "That's a horrible thing to say! You're attractive and kind and considerate. Your grandmother was cruel to make you take care of these things."

"Who do you think trained the snakes?" he asked, struck again. "She did. And she raised me."

"I need to unraise you," Nina replied.

"Fine," he said, twisting to evade the snakes. "But, somewhere else! Look at me like you hate me. Quickly!

They won't stop striking if you don't. I shouldn't have come."

Nina tried to find him less appealing, but the way he contorted to avoid snake strikes and tried to pull the animals from his body without hurting them — it made her like him more. And she was afraid for him, which created both fear and more desire. Yet, they would kill Noah. One then climbed and struck his neck, attempted to start wrapping. "Stop!" she told them, but they didn't listen.

He fell to his knees, shouting, "What are words to snakes? Get out of here, fast!"

She ran into the other room. She tied a lilac cashmere sweater over her head, shouting back, as if through a blanket, "Have they left you yet, Noah? Noah?"

"No," she heard him reply, weakly. "I'm lying flat and still. You do the same. Try to stop thinking."

She lay motionless and tried to think calm thoughts, those about fleece or rainbows, rabbits at the fair. "I still don't know how I'll get them into the basket with you here," he called. "Is there any way you can you leave the premises without passing me again? One's body is around my neck, loosely, but she's still trying to wrap."

Nina pictured him dying in her living room. She saw the knife Davey dropped a while back on the floor. She went to Noah. Looking down at all three snakes wrapping his body, one around his neck, one attempting his torso, she thought Noah looked rather beautiful, draped with snakes, prone, the soft kind of man she'd have liked a long time ago. He was again like a mute child, devastated with the surrounding horror. It was this person she wanted, this person she desired, she thought, the one who has known what I've known.

But as she felt this tenderness and care, felt it

strongly, they began striking him again, so she sat atop of him and tried to rip them loose, stabbing down the gray-green bodies, trying to cut them free.

They did not strike back. "They did nothing to harm me," she said, amazed, when she finally cleared the reptile bodies away. "They let me kill them."

"Their job was to protect," he said. "They would never have harmed you."

"I'm sorry I killed them," she replied. "Now, they won't heal, right?"

"If you didn't cut their heads off, they might," he answered. She got some bandages to treat his wounds. He looked at her in his delicate way, blinking his soft eyes that echoed his quiet demeanor.

She walked to the snakes and hid them from his view as she cut off each of their heads but brought the heads back to him in her hands, like bloody, aglyphous flowers.

He palmed her face. "You killed them," he said, as if this was too incredible to believe, stroking her cheeks, tracing the place where the bruise had lingered below her eye. "You killed my snakes for me."

"I did," she said, tossing their heads to the side, straddling him, kissing him. "I had to. They ruled your life. I only wanted you."

"But what will I do now?" he asked, lost, disoriented.

"Take care of your store," she said. "Be here with me." She put her hand down his pants. She stroked him there until what felt like a baby bird grew firmer, harder. She removed his clothes as you might undress an invalid.

Naked, he lay on her floor and crossed his arms over his chest, tucking his hands below his biceps. "I never slept with a woman," he said. "I lived with my grandmother. I am afraid of women."

She nodded. "Let me see them," she replied, preparing to wait as long as he needed her to, longer. "I want to see your gentle hands."

Words Like Love and Cacti

He said he couldn't stand the word love, it was a bane, a problem child on his radar, and so he asked me to express it a different way. "Can't you just say, 'I eat the flowers of succulents on your behalf?' Succulent is a good word. Close to love and passion."

I told him succulent was a good word for food. I told him it was a lot of words to be said for something expressed more eloquently, more simply in three — and wasn't he in favor of concision? He loved to say, after all, "Omit needless words!" But there were a lot of messages and calls about flowers later, which became our metaphor, so I researched cacti. Succulents don't all bloom. This was the challenge, his making things difficult.

Sometimes, were he in a particularly acerbic mood, I'd say things like, "I pluck the spines of every cacti genus then poke myself to please you." Vaguely, he thought this funny. He smiled, which saved my estimation, his smile like a Christmas tree. Lit up. Some days, he frowned. One day, frustrated, I said, "I climbed *Armatocereus* for you today. 40 feet high! I wore the garb of a shark swimmer and survived 4 inch spines. The flowers are almost white, but can be red — and appreciate this: There are even spines on the floral tubes, which I ate with relish! Took it all down my cavernous throat!"

He said, "That cactus sounds like a dinosaur. I appreciate the effort."

"I know," I said. "A big green dinosaur. Get close." I kissed his thin lips and stroked his tense shoulders.

His eyes were green, too. His heart was yellow. He wanted it pink if not red. We spoke about why he couldn't say love. I mean, he could — as in, "Love, Herbert" or "I love the Red Sox" — but not as in "I love you." It was the you following the I, paired with the loving. Or any "you" following any "I," pairing with loving. "I work alone," he said. "This is why we email."

"Sure," I said. "But what if you're not working? Come laze with me a while and be my cactus bloom." I was kind of going for the shepherd poem effect. My meter sucked.

He said, "It's tempting."

I talked about *Brasilopuntia, Browningia Calymmanthium,* and *Neobuxbaumia.* The last, I mentioned, were very rare. "Like you," I said, kissing his strident stem.

He bent more, later, much — but I said, "Don't bend too heavily. You'll break. No breaking on my watch."

He kindly replied that broken aloe healed burn wounds, but he wasn't sure if he was the burn or the salve.

"So breaking isn't bad?"

"Sometimes, no."

I kissed his spine, vertebrae by vertebrae, then said, "Okay, break more. Did you know that *Blossfeldia* is a single-species cactus genus, maxing out at 1/2 inch in diameter? The species, liliputana, comes from Lilliput in Gulliver's Travels, the tiny place. We are tiny. Grains of sand. Plants in sand. Small cacti. *Blossfeldia* have no tubercles, ribs, or spines, but are blessed with comparably large flowers, which exceed the diameter of the stems. That's how I feel about you. Large flowers, most days. No spines. You taste like aloe to my soul."

On a day I wasn't going to see him, my daughter Jane came home from school. She said, "Mommy! We got a rabbit in our class. SO cute! All quivery!" That was the only announcement. Then she cupped the tops of her hands toward each other and thrust her thumbs down until they met. She grinned. I got it. Hands heart. She then pointed to me before running to her room.

When he next arrived, I said, "I am tired of cacti and think we've grown beyond that. New solution. Do this, okay?" I showed him the words as silent signs. "You can use this on a sleeping person," I enthused. "To the deaf! Someone dead. A gravestone. An auntie! A stranger. Practice expressing it this way. It's easy. Or, maybe you can do this when we're not together, like toward your computer. I'll never know."

He smiled, brushed a loose piece of hair from my eyes. His eyes had pinked. They were wet.

"I'm done with cacti, you know," I said, but didn't wait for a response, instead kissed his every inch, toe to crown, crown to toe, warm and wary, climbing him carefully, his stem descending into me. I breathed my love into his growth, took him down hard and down fast and down plentiful.

He moaned softly. One word: "Woo."

"It's just a gesture," I said afterward, cupping my hands on my chest, thumbs touching, as if casually, then threw an arm over him where he laid breathing shallowly beside me, hands against his sides. "You don't have to say a word."

Man of Books

"I heard what you said
Marguerita heard Tom
And of course you're a bore
but in that you're not charmless"
- Velvet Underground

Some men you just can't hang onto, especially those that love books. Marguerita's mama had told her that.

Tom loved books. Because he loved books so much, Marguerita loved Tom. This bookishness presented no trouble for their relationship at first — because it was casual, because they had not slept together, because his knowledge of such topics was the kind of cornucopia awareness that made her tremble with how much she could learn, for she was unused to being schooled by anyone, and she was grateful. Still, the slow courtship occasionally bothered her in its lack of greater physical connection.

She had been a slut in the past. Old habits died slowly, if ever.

At first, she had listened to her mama in avoiding the smart ones. She sought instead the boys of summer who impressed her with their pectoral muscles and feats on waves, those who said, "Hey babe, let's go down to the shores," them or the rich boys who bought her fancy dates to satisfy her high dining urges, yet continually hoped for immediate sex. And too, there were the random boys she'd slept with without knowing, from any number of locations, almost right away and almost without thought, because the night was right, they'd said the right thing, or her loneliness felt irrefutably dominant, as if an invisible clamp on her arm forced her to direct it, as soon as possible, to their groins — though all of these boys were gone now.

But oh, the gratitude her rapid embraces fleetingly engendered, she remembered! Oh, the false fulfillment, which was satisfying for the entire twenty minutes it took to create — and often for a week or so afterward. But all desire for shallow pleasure left her now. Smart guys were the only ones she hadn't had, so she took a chance and combined her real interests with her body's interests when she found Tom, also known as Book Guy, because he did it for her.

Except, Book Guy, Tom, well, she wasn't sure he had a libido off the page.

He was cute. He was punctual, courteous, and handsome in the Ivy League way of being too clean behind his ears and messy in deportment. She found it thrilling that he could not only present a book for discussion, but also make several points about whatever book it was, and he smiled each time she pulled up in her wrecked red van to the corner shop, waved, and had even turned out her cafe chair before her arrival as if to say, "Here it is. Just waiting. And how's your family?" He drove a BMW. He was pale.

He always asked about family, some throwback to his East Coast childhood, she assumed. Sometimes she pictured him arriving on the scene of a raging house fire to say to the inhabitants, with ominous black smoke rising its heavy curtain into the twilight behind them, "So, how's your ma? Aunt Bette? Poodle?" before inquiring about *les pompiers*. He was calm, too, alternating this flat affect with nervous gestures, effusive and spare in an intellectual way. His wardrobe was tweed. And linen. Pressed cotton. His skin looked like vellum. Oh. How. Sexy.

Several times during their first meetings, she felt consumed with a girlish exuberance to touch him that led her to clutch his navy blue jacket sleeve as she made a point, brush a loose tangle of brown hair from his cool brow, or attempt to fix his eyebrows should they be curling strangely, for he always appeared slightly sloppy in grooming, though immaculate in composure. He spoke about desire, passion, literature, kissing, and submission. When he did, the conversation was sometimes desultory, sometimes elevated, and sometimes electric. Tom! She wanted to jump his bones. "A guy who likes books too much will never be able to handle a real heroine," her mother had said, warningly. "He only likes what's weak and ready to pillage with ink."

Marguerita blew this off. "He likes my mind, Mama," she said. "He's old-fashioned. It's cute."

As they met each week, she at first tried to mimic his mode of dress, remain conservative, wearing the sort of blouses of a schoolteacher on a date with another school-teacher, but later, as he continued to speak without touching her, without requesting other than their complicitly understood pattern of random, non-random meetings in public places, she upped the stakes by wearing slightly less — suits without blazers one month, black jeans and skimpy tops. The next month, she graduated to short skirts without nylons. Following that, she appeared in leather of the increasingly shrinking variety. If he noticed a change in her apparel, she saw it only in the sidelong glances he gave to her increasingly visible cleavage or the audible clearing of his throat as she sat beside him and in the way, sometimes, as they were about to leave each other, he seemed just about ready to jump up and walk her to her car.

"The point of the cultural dialectic," he went on recently, most of his longest monologues punctuated in her imagining with the sort of day-dreamt striptease where he shyly took his clothes off as he spoke, hiding behind screens between garments like a girl, "was that interpersonal relationships play only a small role re-garding the internal interpretations made by one person of the opposite sex regarding the other. A controlled response is what will happen based on such dynamics, not necessarily personal, especially in terms of fetishistic behavior and the like."

She laughed, imagining his neck-tie getting caught on his ankle when he tried to take it off, watching him hop, hop, hop, looking silly, though he wore none that day.

"You see?" he asked, seeming satisfied with his point, whereupon she nodded, feeling quite ready to force a different sort of reaction.

"That's nice, Tom," she said. "But what about the interpersonal role of relationships taking precedence over the generic nature of the fetish? Can it be performed with anyone for equal satisfaction? Dates, for example, Tom.

Would you, going on a date with me, present a different stimulus than a hypothetical date that could be imagined as more open-ended — or would I be just another cultural artifact for your interpretation that would lead you to question your own behavior, but not change it, based on the socio-economic or classist structures you know to exist, paired with your simultaneous mental dissection of my relative historical damage and value system? And would you wear a tie on this date?" She pictured a green tie with yellow stripes, the same one she'd imagined him kicking away in chagrin. "A really cute tie?"

"What?" he said. "Gleason R. wasn't talking about that sort of thing at all."

"Still," she said, stroking the tabletop with her fingertip, tracing the symbol for womanhood again and again: Circle. Line down. Cross the T. "What if he were?"

"If he were, it would be a different book we were discussing," Tom replied sanely.

"Ah," she said, enjoying the flush that began to creep into his cheek. "And what if I were to lean over right now, right now, and kiss you full on the mouth, with tongue, possibly some groping? Would that change anything about your perceived date dynamic, or would you then just come up for air and push me away before talking about women's sexual liberation movements in the modern age — or some text by Beauvoir or Lacan? Yes, you see, I have been listening to you."

It was at this moment that she saw a sudden ripple on his arm at the interstice between his jacket and his watch, an almost imperceptible movement of shadows like the ruffling of a deck of cards. His lips, too, appeared to ripple, creating the same visual phenomenon but in pink smooth tissue. "Wow. What the fuck is happening to you, Tom?" she asked. "You're rippling!"

"Nothing," he said. "Nothing's happening! I'm not rippling!"

She decided to ignore the ripple, focused on her point of sexual capture, "And if I said," she went on, "that I just want to take you home with me and fuck you, that I am a base animal and require no further mental stimulation until the act that provides the necessary satiation bridge, what would you say to that?"

"Ermm," he said.

"We don't speak now of hypothetical acts or fictionalized acts," she asserted, "such as those rendered by Cornet or Sade. We speak now of months, Tom, eight to be exact, of discussing books — and frankly, I feel beastly. I could use some satisfaction!"

Her book man shifted in his seat. He blinked again, said, "So you don't like what we do now?"

"Which is not to say that I don't feel tenderly towards you," she admitted, continuing in a soft voice almost a whisper, trailing off, and beginning again shortly thereafter with, "and I don't mean to suggest that the conversation hasn't helped me in many ways — or that I'm not grateful. It's just that — well, what are we doing here? If there is no attraction, why do we keep meeting? Tom, you can talk about books with people far smarter than me. Isn't there something else you want me for? Anything?"

She took this moment to apply, slowly, carefully, a cherry red lip gloss and watched as he watched her. She ran a pink tongue over her lips. She said, "Let's walk together, Tom. Somewhere away from here."

"Well, I-I can't," he said. "That is...I...well—"

"I understand you are afraid," she replied, as one might address a refugee frightened by mob-rule. "But, culturally, I am a small woman and I need you to walk me to my car. As you'll notice, it's not parked close tonight and you are the man and I am the weak female who requires escort." She waited a second before producing the *piece de resistance*, which she had been saving: "And I ask you, what would Montaigne have done?" She threw her hair back over her shoulder so that it might float upon her back while she walked and stated, "I'll tell you, Tom! He would have walked me to my car! Unless it is only possible for us to discuss things in the safe yellow light of the cafe. But you can leave here, can't you? *Get free?*" Below the table, she used a foot to trace his leg from his ankle to his knee before saying, "You can, Tom. And if I take you out from the café, you won't disappear like daylight, will you?"

Marguerita laughed, grabbing his hand and pulling, so he allowed her to lead him up out of his chair and into the evening scented with roses and jasmine from a nearby flower cart. She wanted to buy him a flower. A Middle Eastern woman in a wrinkled tuxedo manned the register as Marguerita purchased a dyed blue orchid and handed it to him saying, "Here is your sign or symbol, Tom," touching his sleeve lightly. "Your floral pussy or clitoris. A blue piece. From a woman. A modern stance. You like it?"

"It's nice," he said, but his cheeks were rippling again. Again, she smelled old paper. It was like in high school when she'd made love in the library stacks.

This turned her on. "It is also a romanticized gift," she stated, "regardless whether a man or a woman should buy it, not uncommon among those having such conversations as those pertaining to dating or love. Incidentally, I take this moment to remind you of *De Amore* by Andreas Capellanus, which was written in the 1180s on the subject of courtly love, where he said, 'Every action of a lover ends in the thought of his beloved.' Not that Capellanus didn't end his book with an extensive girl-bashing, disingenuous tirade, which I'll forego discussing in this moment — just consider the 'anus' hosted by the last part of his name, if not its translation to chaplain—but back to the flower... Hey, does something smell like books?"

Tom blushed. He sniffed the flower. "Thank you," he said. "Very sweet. Where's your car?"

"There," she replied, pointing. "Two blocks up." They walked into a darkened set of suburban blocks. She had in mind dragging him to an alley full of wisteria, an alley where she once read as a teen, one that was lit, here and there, with patches of diffuse amber light from the illuminated homes behind the fences, and as he ambled behind her, she walked briskly to let him watch her swinging hips' extra undulation due to her swivel walk and three inch heels that created a slow forties saunter that had driven many former men wild. With him behind her, giddy, she found it hard not to run.

Though progressing with a determined gait, Tom seemed less certain he wanted to follow her. "Are y-you sure you know where you're going?" he asked. "I d-don't see any cars here. No one is p-parked in this alley. W-where's your r-red van?"

"Listen, Tom," Marguerita said. "Do you think I'm pretty?"

"V-very pretty," he said. "You have p-perfect lips."

"So, how about you kiss me?"

Again, he blinked. "O-okay," he said.

"You know, you don't stutter when you talk about books," she replied. "Am I making you nervous?" She came closer and pushed him gently into the nearest wooden fence, only to notice more odd ripples of his skin. She put her hand below his shirt and felt them on his chest.

"I h-have to get back to the cafe," he said. "Soon. So, if you want to k-kiss me, d-do it quick."

Marguerita had engineered many seductions in her time, having been herself seduced in countless intervals, so she pressed her short frame against his tall slender body, making sure to rub her breasts against his chest as she put her hands upon his shoulders and stood on tip-toe to kiss him. Tom's lips were dry and flavored like mint, dollars, old notes. She pushed her tongue in his mouth, letting her hands move down his body, touching, finally touching the places she'd so often eroticized.

When he kissed her back and pulled her close, she felt intoxicated, but after a moment, he backed up and returned to the idea of gently trying to shrug her off. "I have to get b-back now," he said.

"No, you d-don't," she argued, adjusting her skirt in the front, adding, "You look good in my lipstick."

"Y-yes, I do," he said. "H-have to go. L-let us talk next week about D-derrida. D-did you want to suggest the text? Or perhaps, Angela C-carter? H-hell, even M-melville. But not F-freud. He b-bores me. On the b-boring list is as well is J-junot D-diaz."

"I like Junot," she said, dropping her gaze. "Let's get back to business."

"I thought you liked talking about reading," he said.

"I do," she replied. "But there's a time and place for everything. And about Junot, if you read his recent interview at *Narrativo*, which is a money grubbing terrible periodical that robs from the poor and aspiring writers to pay the rich already successful authors with their sub-missions practices, you would see he is much like you in how he thinks about reading and writing, but—" She quieted, her throat constricting briefly, at the sight of his mouth gaping in horror.

"I like *Narrativo*," he said, which did not compel her in any way except to make her want to embrace him, but she did not restrain him again, did not push her whole body against his as she examined his face, but instead used three fingertips from her right hand to slide up the back of his covered thigh. "But what I mean is," she said. "Who cares about *Narrativo*? P-please me, Tom. N-n-now."

As his eyes widened, she entertained an idea of him pressing her back against the nearby fence and fucking her in the nearby dark as she quietly quelled her response — desiring, too, the warm sensation of his palm against her lips to help her with her silence, so that she might taste his firm papery hand against her mouth as he thrust himself inside her.

Maybe she wanted him to tell her, finally, in a whisper, to shut the fuck up and be there with him, please, in that moment of carnal defilement — or to assert some complete control over her body, which was something she rarely ceded but so desperately wanted, and she thought how delicious it would be if he did her half-clothed in this way, wearing his same jacket with his pants down, his shirt tickling her abdomen. God, she loved Tom! A ticket from the police would be only mildly disturbing — possibly exciting. "Tom, I love you," she said. Her eyes sparkled. She smiled. She looked at him fondly.

But his skin — it rippled again, all over. He backed away. It was like she viewed him through the spinning blades of an area fan. "In the b-book a-bout love," he began.

"This is not a book, Tom," she said. "No books here."

"W-where the auth —"

"I don't care about the author," she challenged,

stepping forward to finally touch his pale skin like a lover — but when she unzipped his pants and put her hand inside them, she pulled her fingers out abruptly, for they were cut and bleeding, had been lacerated by sharp textures.

She stepped back, whitening. "Oh," she said.

"It's b-better we keep our exchange to b-books," he said. "B-better f-for you. Freer."

"Oh," she said again, her eyes so moist they almost spilled over. "But I don't think so. I would like to expand our relationship. Can't we do that? Tom?"

"I c-cant," he said as the rippling on his flesh became a tremor, this tremor overtaking his body until his skin assumed a vast retinue of breaks and fissures visible below his clothes before a wild flipping of wafer-thin pages began, flapping until his whole person seemed a book, revealing a man-sized series of coverless *oeuvres* towering in the shape of Tom, his human pages turned frantically as if thumbed by thousands of invisible hands desperate for the right passage. His expression was pained.

"T-this is all I c-can offer y-you," he said then, though his face flipped, too, and was distorted.

As she watched his fractured face, the only witness to its explosion, his whole body flew apart before her, fluttering to disburse into so many floating pages in the comfortable place where she had tried to read him, tried to love him, and had consumed so much literary content well before him — so briefly, foolishly, she reached out as if to catch his sheets to hold him together, but such unbound pages eluded her grasp and saddened her; he was a book left spineless, and soon, his sheets filled the street's whole expanse, engorged the alley with words and pages so beautiful that they shone like gold or the vellum of his skin until it was as if the alley itself had lit up brighter with the visceral flood of Tom.

"There goes Tom," she said. But the only page left of him for her, his clothes having collapsed where he'd stood, was the one that landed haphazardly and facedown in her hand, which she flipped to read and regard. It said: "I regret both being this way and that I cannot be much more. I regret you read me wrong, and I shouldn't have tried to teach you. What I'm trying to say, M, is that you are coarse. I don't mean that in a negative way. I loved you as I love all sentient beings and especially loved that you loved to read, but some kinds of love fall apart."

As she read this, she heard the Velvet Underground playing in her head. "Some kinds of love..."

She cried and closed her eyes but opened them again to review the last section of his note, which read, "Still, I'm so sorry. We could have been something, maybe, in another world. I guess what I'm lobbying for here is —" but he didn't finish his sentence, just signed off. At the bottom of that page was an ornamental font detail like the orchid she had bought him.

The real orchid, she then noticed, catching her breath as his pages continued to scatter, was at her feet, crushed accidentally by an earlier misstep of her black stiletto heels, which she had worn to impress him, which she now regretted wearing and felt cheapened by — for she would never see this man again outside of her retreating memory, she'd dressed like a slut tonight, he'd resultantly called her coarse, and all the other pages she tried to pick up to read him by were blank. She supposed he had turned into the mysterious, indecipherable man of books he'd always wanted to be: the one who said yes and no, and no, and no and no and no — so she couldn't touch him, which she wished she'd known sooner. But who could have known he would come closer and then fall apart? Even her romantic gift for him, that yonic flower blue as a banshee's wail, had been separated and soiled.

About the author

Heather Fowler is the author of the story collections *Suspended Heart* (Aqueous Books, 2010) and *This Time, While We're Awake* (Aqueous Books, forthcoming 2013). She received her M.A. in English and Creative Writing from Hollins University. Her work has been published online and in print in the US, England, Australia, and India, and appeared in such venues as *PANK, Night Train, storyglossia, Surreal South, JMWW, Prick of the Spindle, Short Story America,* and others, as well as having been nominated for both the story South Million Writers Award and Sundress Publications Best of the Net. Her poetry and fiction have been nominated for the Pushcart Prize. She is Poetry Editor at *Corium Magazine* and a Fiction Editor for the international refereed journal, *Journal of Post-Colonial Cultures & Societies*. Please visit her website at heatherfowlerwrites.com.

OTHER TITLES FROM PINK NARCISSUS PRESS

BLEEDING HEARTS: Book One of the Demimonde
An urban fantasy novel by Ash Krafton
Sophie Galen is an advice columnist who is saving the
world — one *damned* person at a time.
ISBN: 978-0-9829913-6-7

COURT OF DREAMS
A comic fantasy novel by Stuart Sharp
Join unlikely hero Thomas Greene on his journey through
the hidden world of the Court of Dreams.
ISBN: 978-0-9829913-2-9

ELF LOVE: An Anthology
Tales of lust, betrayal, murder and... elves.
ISBN: 978-0-9829913-0-5

FEASTING WITH PANTHERS
A literary fantasy by Lyle Blake Smythers
Warrior-poet Catalan and his band find themselves at the
center of a War Game between two mysterious sorcerers.
ISBN: 978-0-9829913-7-4

QUEER FISH
An eclectic anthology of gay speculative fiction.
Volume 1: 978-0-9829913-3-6
Volume 2: 978-0-9829913-9-8

RAPUNZEL'S DAUGHTERS and Other Tales
What happens after the "Happily Ever After"...?
ISBN: 978-0-9829913-1-2

WTF?! An Anthology
Stories that will leave the reader wondering "WTF?!"
ISBN: 978-0-9829913-4-3

www.ingramcontent.com/pod-product-compliance
Lightning Source LLC
Chambersburg PA
CBHW070340260626
47160CB00003B/1096